S0-BCM-865

Albert Camus THE PLAGUE (1947) It is as reasonable to represent one kind of imprisonment as another as to represent anything that exists by something that does not exist. DANIEL DE FOE.

I

The curious events which are the subject of this chronicle occurred in 1940, in Oran. There was a general feeling that they were out of place, out of the ordinary. At first glance, Oran is, in fact, an ordinary city and nothing more than a French prefecture on the Algerian coast. The city itself, we must admit, is ugly. Quiet in appearance, it takes some time to see what makes it different from so many other commercial cities, in all latitudes. How can we imagine, for example, a city without pigeons, trees, and gardens, where we do not encounter wing beating or rustling leaves, a neutral place to say the least? The change of seasons can only be seen in the sky. Spring is announced only by the quality of the air or by the baskets of flowers that small sellers bring back from the suburbs; it's a spring that we sell in the markets. During the summer, the sun burns overly dry houses and covers the walls with gray ash; you can no longer live in the shade of the closed shutters. In autumn, on the contrary, it is a deluge of mud. Sunny days only come in winter. A convenient way to get to know a city is to find out how you work in it, how you love it and how you die in it. In our small town, is it the effect of the climate, all of this is done together, with the same frantic and absent air. That is to say that we are bored and that we try to get into habits. Our fellow citizens work a lot, but always to enrich themselves. They are mainly interested in trade and they take care first, according to their expression, of doing business. Naturally, they also have a taste for simple joys, they like women, cinema, and sea bathing. But, very reasonably, they reserve these pleasures for Saturday evening and Sunday, trying, the other days of the week, to earn a lot of money. In the evening, when they leave their offices, they meet at a fixed time in cafes, they walk on the same boulevard or they sit on their balconies. The desires of the youngest are violent and brief, while the vices of the oldest do not go beyond associations of drug addicts, banquets of friendships and circles where we play big games on the luck of the cards. No doubt it will be said that this is not specific to our city and that, in short, all our contemporaries are like that. Without a doubt, nothing is more natural today than seeing people work from morning to night and then choose to waste time, cards, coffee, and chatting. But there are cities and countries where people have the suspicion of something else from time to time. In general, this does not change their lives. Only, there was suspicion and it's always won. Oran, on the contrary, is apparently a city without suspicion, that is to say a completely modern city. There is therefore no need to specify how we like each other at home. Men and women either devour each other quickly in what is called the act of love or engage in a long habit of two. Between these extremes, there is not often a middle ground. This is not original either. In Oran as elsewhere, for lack of time and reflection, we are forced to love each other without knowing it. What is more original in our city is the difficulty that one can find there to die. Difficulty, by the way, is not the right word and it would be more accurate to speak of discomfort. It's never nice to be sick, but there are cities and countries that support you with the disease, where you can, in a way, let go. A patient needs sweetness, he likes to lean on something, it's natural. But in Oran, the excesses of the climate, the importance of the business it deals with, the insignificance of the decor, the speed of twilight and the quality of the pleasures, all require good health. A patient is there alone. Think of the one who is going to die,

trapped behind hundreds of crackling walls of heat, while at the same minute, a whole population, on the phone or in cafes, talking about drafts, bills of lading and discounts. We will understand what can be uncomfortable in death, even modern, when it occurs in a dry place. These few indications perhaps give a sufficient idea of our city. Besides, nothing should be exaggerated. What should be emphasized is the mundane aspect of the city and of life. But we spend our days without difficulty as soon as we have habits. As long as our city promotes habits, we can say that everything is for the best. From this angle, no doubt, life is not very exciting. At least, we do not know the disorder in our country. And our frank, sympathetic and active population has always aroused reasonable esteem in travelers. This city without picturesque, without vegetation and without soul ends up looking restful, we finally fall asleep. But it is fair to add that it is grafted onto an unrivaled landscape, in the middle of a bare plateau, surrounded by bright hills, in front of a bay with a perfect design. We can only regret that it was built with its back to this bay and that, therefore, it is impossible to see the sea that we must always go looking for. Arrived there, we will admit without difficulty that nothing could make hope for our fellow citizens the incidents which occurred in the spring of that year and which were, we understood it then, like the first signs of the series of the serious events which are proposed to chronicle here. These facts will appear natural to some and, on the contrary, unlikely. But, after all, a columnist cannot take these contradictions into account. His task is only to say: "This has happened", when he knows that this has indeed happened, that this has interested the life of an entire people, and that there are therefore thousands of witnesses who will estimate in their hearts the truth of what he says. Besides, the narrator, who we will always know in time, would hardly have a title to assert in a while, would hardly have a title to assert in an enterprise of this kind if chance had not put it able to collect a certain number of depositions and if the force of things had not mixed him with everything he claims to relate. This is what authorizes him to do the work of a historian. Of course, a historian, even if he is an amateur, always has documents. The narrator of this story therefore has his own: his testimony first, that of the others then, since, by his role, he was led to collect the confidences of all the characters in this chronicle, and, lastly, the texts which ended up falling into his hands. He intends to draw from it when he sees fit and use it as he pleases. He still offers himself ... But it may be time to leave the comments and the language precautions to come to the story itself. The relationship of the first days requires some meticulousness. On the morning of April 16, Doctor Bernard Rieux left his office and ran into a dead rat in the middle of the landing. At the time, he dismissed the beast without paying attention and went down the stairs. But when he got to the street, the thought occurred to him that this rat was out of place and he retraced his steps to warn the janitor. Before the reaction of old Mr. Michel, he felt better what his discovery was unusual. The presence of this dead rat had seemed only bizarre to him while, for the concierge, it constituted a scandal. The latter's position was categorical: there were no rats in the house. No matter how much the doctor assured him that there was one on the first-floor landing, and probably dead, Mr. Michel's conviction remained intact. There were no rats in the house, so it had to be brought from outside. In short, it was a farce. The same evening, Bernard Rieux, standing in the corridor of the building, was looking for his keys before going up to his house, when he saw appearing, from the dark background of the corridor, a large rat with an uncertain gait and wet coat. The beast stopped, seemed to find a balance, took its run towards the doctor, stopped again, turned on itself with a little cry and finally fell while spilling blood from the half-open lips. The doctor looked at her for a moment and went upstairs. He wasn't thinking of the rat. This rejected blood brought him back to his concern. His wife, sick for a year, had to leave the next day for a mountain station. He found her lying in their room, as he had asked her to do. Thus, she prepared herself for the fatigue of displacement. She was smiling. - I feel very good, she said. The doctor looked at the face turned towards him in the light of the bedside lamp. For Rieux, at thirty years old

the truth. - Certainly, said the other. - I mean: can you pass a total sentence? - Total, no, it must be said. But I guess this condemnation would be groundless. Slowly, Rieux said that indeed such a conviction would be unfounded, but that in asking this question, he was only seeking to know whether or not Rambert's testimony could be without reservations. - I only admit unqualified testimony. I will therefore not support your information. - This is the language of Saint-Just, said the journalist, smiling. Rieux said without raising his tone that he knew nothing about it, but that it was the language of a man tired of the world in which he lived, yet having the taste of his fellows and determined to refuse, for his part, injustice and concessions. Rambert, neck in his shoulders, looked at the doctor. "I think I understand you," he said finally, getting up. The doctor accompanied him to the door: - Thank you for taking it this way. Rambert seemed impatient: - Yes, he said, I understand, forgive me for this inconvenience. The doctor shook his hand and told him that there was a curious report to be made on the quantity of dead rats that were found in the city at the moment. - Ah! exclaimed Rambert, that interests me. At five o'clock, as he was leaving for new visits, the doctor met a still young man on the stairs, with a heavy figure, a massive, hollow face, barred with thick eyebrows. He had sometimes met him among the Spanish dancers who lived on the top floor of his building. Jean Tarrou smoked a cigarette with diligence while contemplating the last convulsions of a rat who was bursting on a step, at his feet. He looked up at the doctor with calm eyes and a little support of his gray eyes, said hello and added that this appearance of rats was a curious thing. - Yes, said Rieux, but which ends up being annoying. - In a way, doctor, only in a way. We've never seen anything like it, that's all. But I find it interesting, yes, positively interesting. Tarrou ran his hand over his hair to throw it back, looked again at the rat, now motionless, then smiled at Rieux: - But, in short, doctor, it is mainly the business of the janitor. Precisely, the doctor found the janitor in front of the house, leaning against the wall near the entrance, an expression of weariness on his usually congested face. "Yes, I know," said old Michel to Rieux, who announced the new discovery to him. It's by two or three that we find them now. But it's the same in other houses. He seemed downcast and worried. He was rubbing his neck in a mechanical gesture. Rieux asked him how he was. The concierge couldn't say, of course, that it was wrong. Only he did not feel on his plate. In his opinion, it was morale that worked. These rats had kicked him, and everything would be much better when they were gone. But the next morning, April 18, the doctor who brought his mother back from the station found Mr. Michel with an even more hollow face: from the cellar to the attic, a dozen rats littered the stairs. The trash cans of the neighboring houses were full of them. The doctor's mother heard the news without being surprised. - These are things that happen. She was a little woman with silver hair, soft black eyes. - I'm happy to see you again, Bernard, she said. Rats can't do anything about it. Approved him; it was true that with her everything always seemed easy. Rieux however telephoned the communal deratization service, of which he knew the director. Had he heard of these rats that came in large numbers to die in the open air? Mercier, the director, had heard of it and, in his department, installed not far from the quays, we had discovered about fifty. However, he wondered if it was serious. Rieux couldn't decide, but he thought the rat extermination service should intervene. - Yes, said Mercier, with an order. If you think it's really worth it, I can try to get an order. "It's always worth it," said Rieux. Her cleaning lady had just told her that several hundred dead rats had been collected in the large factory where her husband worked. It was around this time, anyway, that our fellow citizens began to worry. Because, from the 18th, factories and warehouses in fact disgorged hundreds of corpses of rats. In some cases, we were forced to finish the animals, whose agony was too long. But, from the outer quarters to the center of the city, wherever Doctor Rieux came to pass, wherever our fellow citizens gathered, rats waited in heaps, in the trash, or in long lines, in the streams. The evening press took over the business from that day hadn't considered anything at all but started by meeting in council to deliberate. The order was given to the rat extermination service to collect the dead rats every morning at dawn. When the collection was finished, two service cars had to take the animals to the garbage incineration plant in order to burn them. But in the days that followed, the situation worsened. The number of rodents collected was increasing and the harvest was more abundant every morning. From the fourth day, the rats started to go out to die in groups. Reductions, basements, cellars, sewers, they went up in long lines staggering to waver in the light, turn on themselves and die near humans. At night, in the corridors or alleys, you could distinctly hear their little cries of agony. In the morning, in the suburbs, they were found spread out on the stream, a small flower of blood on the pointed muzzle, some swollen and putrid, others stiffened and whiskers still erect. In the city itself, we encountered them in small heaps, on the landings or in the courtyards. They also came to die alone in administrative halls, in school yards, on the terrace of cafes, sometimes. Our amazed fellow citizens discovered them in the busiest places in the city. Place d'Armes, the boulevards, the Promenade de Front-de-Mer, from time to time, were soiled. Cleaned at the dawn of its dead animals, the city gradually found them, more and more, during the day. On the sidewalks, it also happened that more than one nocturnal walker could feel the elastic mass of a still fresh corpse under their feet. You would have said that the very land where our houses were planted was purged of its load of humors, which it let rise to the surface of the boils and sanies which, until now, worked it internally. Let us only consider the amazement of our little town, so peaceful until then, and upset in a few days, like a healthy man whose thick blood would suddenly revolutionize! Things went so far that the Ransdoc agency (information, documentation, all information on any subject) announced, in its radio program of free information, six thousand two hundred and thirty-one rats collected and burned in the only day of the 25. This figure, which gave a clear meaning to the daily spectacle that the city had before its eyes, increased the distress. Up until then, we had only complained of a somewhat disgusting accident. We now realized that there was something threatening about this phenomenon, the extent of which could not yet be determined or detected. Only the old asthmatic Spaniard continued to rub his hands and repeated: "They are going out, they are going out", with senile joy. On April 28, however, Ransdoc announced a collection of about 8,000 rats and anxiety was at its height in the city. We demanded radical measures, we accused the authorities, and some who had houses by the sea were already talking about withdrawing. But the next day, the agency announced that the phenomenon had abruptly stopped and that the rat extermination service had collected only a negligible quantity of dead rats. The city breathed. However, it was the same day, at noon, that Doctor Rieux, stopping his car in front of his building, saw at the end of the street the janitor who was walking with difficulty, his head bent, arms and legs apart, in a puppet attitude. The old man held the arm of a priest whom the doctor recognized. It was Father Paneloux, a learned and militant Jesuit whom he had met sometimes and who was highly esteemed in our city, even among those who are indifferent to matters of religion. He waited for them. Old Michel had bright eyes and wheezing. He didn't feel very well and wanted to get some fresh air. But sharp pains in the neck, armpits and groins forced him to come back and ask for help from Father Paneloux. "They are lumps," he said. I had to try. Arm out of the door, the doctor ran his finger to the base of the neck that Michel held out to him; a kind of wooden knot had formed there. - Go to bed, take your temperature, I'll come see you this afternoon. The concierge left, Rieux asked Father Paneloux what he thought of this story of rats: - Oh! said the father, it must be an epidemic, and his eyes smiled behind the round glasses. After lunch, Rieux reread the telegram from the nursing home announcing the arrival of his wife, when the phone was heard. It was one of his former clients, a town hall employee, who called him. He had suffered for a long time from a narrowing of the aorta, and, as he was poor, Rieux had treated him for free. - Yes, he said, you remember me. But it's another. Come quickly, something happened to my neighbor. Her voice was fading. Rieux thought of the concierge and decided he would see him next. A few minutes later, he walked through the door of a low house on Faidherbe Street, in an outside neighborhood. In the middle of the cool, stinking staircase, he met the employee Joseph Grand, who was coming down to meet him. He was a man in his fifties, with a yellow mustache, long and hunched over, his narrow shoulders and skinny limbs. - It's better, he said arriving at Rieux, but I thought he was going there. He was blowing his nose. On the second and last floor, on the left door, Rieux read, drawn in red chalk: "Come in, I'm hanged." They entered. The rope hung from the suspension above an overturned chair, the table pushed into a corner. But it hung in the void. "I picked it up in time," said

Grand, who still seemed to be searching for words, even though he spoke the simplest language. I was just going out and I heard some noise. When I saw the inscription, how to explain it, I thought it was a joke. But he uttered a funny, and even sinister, groan, you could say. He scratched his head: - In my opinion, the operation must be painful. Naturally, I entered. They had pushed open a door and found themselves on the threshold of a bright, but poorly furnished room. A small, round man was lying on the copper bed. He breathed heavily and looked at them with congested eyes. The doctor stopped. In the intervals of breathing, he seemed to hear the little cries of rats. But nothing moved in the corners. Rieux went to the bed. The man did not fall from high enough, nor too suddenly, the vertebrae had held. Of course, a little asphyxiation. There should be an x-ray. The doctor injected camphor oil and said that everything would be fine within a few days. - Thank you, doctor, said the man in a muffled voice. Rieux asked Grand if he had warned the police station and the employee looked disconcerted: - No, he said, oh! no. I thought that the most urgent ... - Of course, cut Rieux, I will do so. But at that moment the patient fidgeted and stood up in bed, protesting that he was fine and that he was not worth it. - Calm down, said Rieux. This is no big deal, believe me, and I need to make my statement. - Oh! said the other. And he threw himself back to cry slowly. Grand, who had been fiddling with his mustache for a while, approached him. "Come on, Mister Cottard," he said. Try to understand. You could say that the doctor is responsible. If, for example, you wanted to start again ... But Cottard said, in the midst of his tears, that he would not start again, that it was only a moment of panic and that he only wanted us to leave him peace. Rieux was writing a prescription. - Okay, he said. Leave that, I'll be back in two or three days. But don't be silly. On the landing, he told Grand that he was obliged to make his statement, but that he would ask the commissioner not to investigate until two days later. - We have to watch him tonight. Does he have family? - I do not know her. But I can watch myself. He nodded. - Neither do he, notice him, I can't say that I know him. But we have to help each other. In the corridors of the house, Rieux looked mechanically towards the nooks and asked Grand if the rats had completely disappeared from his neighborhood. The employee did not know. He had indeed been told about this story, but he did not pay much attention to the noises in the neighborhood. - I have other concerns, he said. Rieux was already shaking his hand. He was in a hurry to see the janitor before writing to his wife. Evening newspaper criers announced that the invasion of rats had stopped. But Rieux found his patient half poured out of bed, one hand on his stomach and the other around his neck, vomiting with great tears a pinkish bile in a container of garbage. After long efforts, out of breath, the concierge went back to bed. The temperature was thirty-nine five, the glands of the neck and the limbs had swelled, two blackish spots widened on its side. He was now complaining of inner pain. - It burns, he said, this pig burns me. His sooty mouth made him chew the words and he turned to the doctor with protruding eyes where the headache brought tears. His wife looked anxiously at Rieux, who remained silent. - Doctor, she said, what is it? - It could be anything. But there is still nothing certain. Until tonight, diet and purifying. Let him drink a lot. Precisely, the concierge was devoured by thirst. When he got home, Rieux called his colleague Richard, one of the city's most important doctors. - No, said Richard, I haven't seen anything extraordinary. - No fever with local inflammations? - Ah! if, however, two cases with very inflamed lymph nodes. - Abnormally? - Uh, said Richard, normal, you know ... In the evening, in any case, the concierge was delirious and, at forty degrees, complained about the rats. Rieux attempted an abscess of fixation. Under the burning of the turpentine, the concierge shouted: "Ah! pigs! The nodes had grown larger, hard, and woody to the touch. The janitor's wife panicked: - Watch, said the doctor, and call me if necessary. The next day, April 30, an already warm breeze was blowing in a blue and humid sky. She brought a smell of flowers coming from the most distant suburbs. The morning noises in the streets seemed brighter, more joyful than usual. Throughout our little town, freed from the dull apprehension where she had lived during the week that day was that of renewal. Rieux himself, reassured by a letter from his wife, went down to the concierge lightly. And indeed, by morning, the fever had dropped to thirty-eight degrees. Weakened, the patient smiled in his bed. - It's better, isn't it, doctor? said his wife. - Let's wait again. But by noon the fever had suddenly risen to forty degrees, the patient was constantly delirious, and vomiting had resumed. The neck glands were painful to the touch and the janitor seemed to want to keep his head as far away from the body as possible. His wife was sitting at the foot of the bed, hands on the blanket, gently holding the patient's feet. She was looking at Rieux. - Look, said the boy, we need to isolate him and try exceptional treatment. I'm on the phone to the hospital and we'll take him by ambulance. Two hours later, in the ambulance, the doctor and the woman were bending over the patient. From his mouth, covered with fungus, scraps of words came out: "Rats!" " he said. Greenish, waxy lips, leaded eyelids, short, jerky breath, torn apart by the glands, pressed to the bottom of his berth as if he wanted to close it on him or as if something, came from the bottom of the earth, called him without respite, the concierge choked under an invisible weight. The woman was crying. - Is there no hope, doctor? "He is dead," said Rieux. The concierge's death, it can be said, marked the end of this period filled with disconcerting signs and the beginning of another, relatively more difficult, where the surprise of the early days gradually turned into panic. Our fellow citizens, they now realized, had never thought that our small town could be a place specially designated for rats to die there in the sun and that the janitors there perish from bizarre diseases. From this point of view, they were basically in error and their ideas were to be revised. If everything had stopped there, habits probably would have prevailed. But others among our fellow citizens, who were not always janitors or poor, had to follow the road on which Mr. Michel was the first to embark. It was from this moment that fear, and reflection with it, began. Before going into the details of these new events, however, the narrator believes it useful to give the opinion of another witness on the period just described. Jean Tarrou, whom we already met at the beginning of this story, had settled in Oran a few weeks earlier and had lived since then in a large hotel in the center. Apparently, he seemed comfortable enough to make a living from his income. But although the city was gradually getting used to him, no one could say where he came from or why he was there. We met him in all public places. Since early spring, we had seen him a lot on the beaches, swimming often and with obvious pleasure. Bonhomme, still smiling, he seemed to be the friend of all normal pleasures without being a slave to them. In fact, the only habit known to him was the frequent attendance of Spanish dancers and musicians, quite numerous in our city. His notebooks, in any case, also constitute a sort of chronicle of this difficult period. But it is a very particular chronicle which seems to obey a bias of insignificance. At first glance, it might seem that Tarrou was ingenious in looking at things and people through the big end of the spyglass. In general disarray, he set out, in short, to become the historian of what has no history. We can doubtless deplore this bias and suspect the dryness of the heart. But the fact remains that these notebooks can provide, for a chronicle of this period, a host of secondary details which, however, are important and whose quirkiness will even prevent this interesting character from being judged too quickly. The first notes taken by Jean Tarrou date from his arrival in Oran. They show, from the start, a curious satisfaction to be in a city as ugly by itself. There is a detailed description of the two bronze lions that adorn the town hall, benevolent considerations on the absence of trees, unsightly houses, and the absurd plan of the city. Tarrou still mixes dialogues heard on the trams and in the streets, without adding comments, except, a little later, for one of these conversations, concerning a man named Camps. Tarrou had attended the interview with two streetcar receivers: - You knew Camps well, said one. - Camps? A tall one with a black mustache? - That's it. He was at the switch. -Yes of course. - Well, he's dead. - Ah! and when then? - After the story of rats. - Here! And what did he get? - I don't know, fever. Besides, he was not strong. He had abscesses under his arm. He did not resist. - He looked like everyone else. - No, he had a weak chest and he played music at the Orphéon. Always blow into a piston, it wears out. - Ah! finished the second, when one is sick, one should not blow in a piston. After these few indications, Tarrou wondered why Camps entered the Orphéon against his most obvious interest and what were the deep reasons which had led him to risk his life for Sunday parades. Tarrou then seemed to have been favorably impressed by a scene which often took place on the balcony facing his window. Her bedroom looked out onto a small side street where cats slept in the shade of the walls. But every day after lunch, when the whole city was dozing in the heat, a little old man appeared on a balcony across the street. His white hair, well combed, straight and stern in his military-cut clothes, he called cats a "Twink, Twink", both distant and gentle. The cats raised their pale eyes from sleep, without disturbing themselves yet. The other ripped small pieces of paper over the street and the animals, attracted by the rain of white butterflies, advanced in the middle of the roadway, stretching out a hesitant paw towards the last pieces of paper. The little old man then spat on cats with force and precision. If one of the sputum hit its target, it would laugh. Finally, Tarrou seemed to have been definitively seduced by the commercial character of the city, the appearance, animation and even the pleasures seemed to be dictated by the necessities of trade. This singularity (this is the term used by the notebooks) was approved by Tarrou and one of his glowing remarks even ended with the exclamation: "Finally! These are the only places where the traveler's notes on this date seem to take on a personal character. It is difficult simply to appreciate its meaning and seriousness. Thus after having related that the discovery of a dead rat had pushed the cashier of the hotel to make an error in his note, Tarrou had added, in a writing less clear than usual: "Question : how to not waste your time? Answer: experience it in its full length. Means: spending days in the anteroom of a dentist, in an uncomfortable chair; live on your balcony on Sunday afternoon; listen to conferences in a language you do not understand, choose the longest and least convenient rail routes and travel upright naturally; queuing at the ticket offices and not taking their place, etc. »But immediately after these differences in language or thought, the notebooks begin a detailed description of the trams of our city, their form of gondola, their indecisive color, their usual filth, and end these considerations with a" it is remarkable "which explains nothing. In any case, here are the indications given by Tarrou on the history of rats: "Today, the little old man opposite is taken aback. There are no more cats. They have indeed disappeared, excited by the dead rats that we find in large numbers in the streets. In my opinion, there is no question of cats eating dead rats. I remember mine hated that. Still, they have to run into the cellars and the little old man is taken aback. It is less well combed, less vigorous. We feel him worried. After a while, he returned. But he had spat in the air once. But he had spat in the air once. "In the city, we stopped a tram today because we discovered a dead rat, who got there we don't know how. Two or three women came down. We threw the rat away. The tram left. "At the hotel, the night porter, who is a trustworthy man, told me that he was expecting misfortune with all these rats. "When the rats leave the ship ..." I replied that it was true for ships, but that it had never been checked for cities. However, his conviction is made. I asked him what misfortune, in his opinion, could be expected. He did not know, the misfortune being impossible to foresee. But he would not have been surprised if an earthquake did the trick. I recognized that it was possible, and he asked me if I was not worried. "The only thing that interests me," I told him, "is to find inner peace. "He understood me perfectly. "In the hotel restaurant, there is a whole interesting family. The father is a tall, thin man, dressed in black, with a hard collar. He has the middle of the bald head and two tufts of gray hair, right and left. Small round and hard eyes, a thin nose, a horizontal mouth, make him look like a well-behaved owl. He always arrives first at the restaurant door, disappears, lets his wife pass, petite like a black mouse, and then enters with a little boy and a little girl dressed on the heels dressed as learned dogs. When he arrives at his table, he waits for his wife to take a seat, sits down, and the two poodles can finally perch on their chairs. He says "you" to his wife and children, expresses polite nastiness at the first and definitive words to the heirs: "- Nicole, you are sovereignly unsympathetic! "And the little girl is ready to cry This is what it takes. "This morning the little boy was excited about the story of the rats. He wanted to say a word at the table: "We're not talking about rats at the table, Philippe. I forbid you in future to say this word. "Your father is right," said the black mouse. "The two poodles stuck their noses in their mash and the owl thanked with a nod that didn't say much. "Despite this fine example, we talk a lot in town about this story of rats. The newspaper got involved. The local chronicle, which usually is very varied, is now entirely occupied by a campaign against the municipality: "Have our city officials been aware of the danger that the rotten corpses of these rodents could present?" The hotel manager can't talk about anything else. But it's also that he's upset. Finding rats in the elevator of an honorable hotel seems inconceivable to him. To console him, I said to him, "But everyone is there." "Precisely," he replied, "we are now like everyone else." "He was the one who told me about the first cases of this surprising fever that we are starting to worry about. One of his chambermaids has it. "But surely it is not contagious," he said eagerly. "I told her I didn't care. "Ah! I see. Monsieur is like me, Monsieur is fatalistic. "I hadn't advanced anything like that, and I'm not a fatalist. I told him ... "It was then that Tarrou's notebooks began to speak in a little detail of this unknown fever that we were already worried about in the public. Noting that the little old man had finally found his cats with the disappearance of the rats, and was patiently correcting his shots, Tarrou added that we could already cite a dozen cases of this fever, most of which had been fatal. For documentary purposes, we can finally reproduce the portrait of Doctor Rieux by Tarrou. As far as the narrator can judge, he is fairly faithful: "Appears thirty-five years. Average height. Strong shoulders. Almost rectangular face. Dark, straight eyes, but protruding jaws. The strong nose is regular. Black hair cut very short. The mouth is arched with full lips and almost always tight. He looks a bit like a Sicilian peasant with his baked skin, his black hair and his clothes in hues always baked, his black hair and his clothes in hues always dark, but which suit him well. "He walks fast. He goes down the sidewalks without changing his pace, but two out of three goes back up on the opposite sidewalk by making a slight jump. He is distracted at the wheel of his car and often leaves his directional arrows raised, even after he has made his turn. Looks knowledgeable. Tarrou's figures were correct. Doctor Rieux knew something about it. With the body of the caretaker isolated, he had telephoned Richard to question him about these inguinal fevers. - I don't understand anything, said Richard. Two dead, one in forty-eight hours, the other in three days. I left the last one with all the appearances of convalescence one morning. - Notify me, if you have other cases, said Rieux. He called a few more doctors. The investigation thus carried out gave him twenty similar cases in a few days. Almost all had been fatal. He then asked Richard, president of the order of doctors of Oran, the isolation of the new patients. - But I can't help it, said Richard. Prefectural measures are needed. Besides, who tells you that there is a risk of contagion? - Nothing tells me, but the symptoms are worrying. Richard, however, felt that "he had no quality". All he could do was talk to the prefect. But while we were talking, the weather was spoiling. In the aftermath of the janitor's death, great mists covered the sky. Torrential and brief rains fell on the city; a stormy heat followed these sudden waves. The sea itself had lost its deep blue and, under the misty sky, it took shards of silver or iron, painful for the sight. The damp heat of this spring made us want the heat of summer. In the city, built as a snail on its plateau, barely open towards the sea, a dreary torpor reigned. In the middle of its long-plastered walls, among the streets with dusty windows, in the dirty yellow trams, you felt a little trapped in the sky. Alone, the old patient of Rieux triumphed over his asthma to rejoice in this time. - It's cooked, he said, it's good for the bronchi. It was cooking indeed, but no more and no less than a fever. The whole town had a fever, at least that was the impression that pursued Doctor Rieux, the morning he went to rue Faidherbe, to attend the investigation into Cottard's attempted suicide. But this impression seemed to him unreasonable. He attributed it to the nervousness and concerns he was beset with and admitted that there was an urgent need to get his ideas in order. When he arrived, the superintendent was not yet there. Grand was waiting on the landing and they decided to enter his house first, leaving the door open. City hall employee lived in two rooms, very summarily furnished. There was only a ray of white wood with two or three dictionaries, and a blackboard on which we could still read, half erased, the words "flowered alleys". According to Grand, Cottard had a good night's sleep. But he woke up in the morning, suffering from a headache and incapable of any reaction. Grand looked tired and nervous, walking up and down, opening, and closing on the table a large file filled with handwritten sheets. However, he told the doctor that he did not know Cottard well, but that he supposed he had a small credit. Cottard was a strange man. For a long time, their relations had been limited to a few greetings on the stairs. - I only had two conversations with him. A few days ago, I knocked over a box of chalk on the landing that I was taking home. There were red chalks and blue chalks. At that moment, Cottard went out on the landing and helped me pick them up. He asked me what these chalks of different colors were for. Grand then explained to him that he was trying to redo some Latin. Since high school, his knowledge had faded. - Yes, he said to the doctor, I was assured that it was useful for better understanding the meaning of French words. So, he wrote Latin words on his board. He copied with blue chalk the part of the words that changed according to declensions and conjugations, and, with red chalk, that which never changed. - I don't know if Cottard understood correctly, but he seemed interested and asked me for a red chalk. I was a little surprised but after all ... I couldn't guess, of course, that it would serve his purpose. Rieux asked what the subject of the second conversation was. But, accompanied by his secretary, the commissioner arrived who first wanted to hear Grand's statements. The doctor noticed that Grand, speaking of Cottard, always called him "the desperate." He even used the expression "fatal resolution" at one time. They discussed the motive for suicide and Grand was fussy about the choice of terms. We finally stopped on the words "intimate sorrows". The commissioner asked if there was anything in Cottard's attitude to predict what he called "his determination." "He knocked on my door yesterday," said Grand, to ask me for matches. I gave him my box. He apologized saying that between neighbors ... Then he assured me that he would return my box to me. I told her to keep it. The commissioner asked the employee if Cottard had seemed odd to him. - What seemed odd to me was that he seemed to want to start a conversation. But I was working. Grand turned to Rieux and added, looking embarrassed: - Personal work. The commissioner wanted to see the patient, however. But Rieux thought it best to prepare Cottard for this visit first. When he entered the room, the latter, dressed only in greyish flannel, was up in bed and turned to the door with an expression of anxiety. - It's the police, huh? - Yes, said Rieux, and don't get agitated. Two or three formalities and you will have peace. But Cottard replied that it was useless and that he did not like the police. Rieux was impatient. - I don't love it either. It's a question of answering their questions quickly and correctly, to end it once and for all. Cottard was silent and the doctor returned to the door. But the little man was already calling him and took his hands when he was near the bed: - We can't touch a sick person, a man who is hanged, can we, doctor? Rieux looked at him for a moment and finally assured him that there had never been any talk of anything like this and that as well, he was there to protect his patient. The latter seemed to relax and Rieux brought in the commissioner. Grand's testimony was read to Cottard and asked if he could clarify the reasons for his act. He replied only and without looking at the commissioner that "intimate grief was very good". The superintendent urged him to say if he wanted to start again. Cottard, animated, replied that he did not and that he only wanted to be left alone. - I will point out to you, said the commissioner in an irritated tone, that, for the moment, you are disturbing that of the others. But on a sign from Rieux, we stopped there. - You think, sighed the superintendent as he left, we have other cats to whip, since we talk about this fever ... He asked the doctor if it was serious and Rieux said he didn't know. - It's time, that's all, concludes the commissioner. It was time, no doubt. Everything was sticky as the day went on and Rieux felt his apprehension grow with each visit. The evening of that same day, in the faubourg, a neighbor of the old patient crowded on his groins and vomited in the midst of delirium. The nodes were much larger than those of the janitor. One of them started to fester and soon it opened like a bad fruit. When he got home, Rieux telephoned the departmental pharmaceutical depot. His professional notes only mention on this date: "Negative response". And already he was called elsewhere for similar cases. It was necessary to open the abscesses, it was obvious. Two scalpel blows and the glands poured out a mash mixed with blood. The patients were bleeding, quartered. But spots appeared on the stomach and legs, a ganglion stopped suppurating, then swelled up. Most of the time, the patient died, in a terrible smell. The press, so talkative in the rat affair, was silent. It's that rats die on the street and men die in their rooms. And the newspapers only cover the street. But the prefecture and the municipality were beginning to wonder. As long as each doctor was not aware of more than two or three cases, no one had thought of moving. But, in short, it is enough for someone to think about adding up. The addition was appalling. In just a few days, the number of fatal cases multiplied, and it became obvious to those concerned about this curious disease that it was a real epidemic. This is the moment that Castel, a colleague of Rieux, much older than him, chooses to come to see him. - Of course, he said, you know what it is, Rieux? - I'm waiting for the results of the analyzes. - I know that. And I don't need analyzes. I've been part of my career in China, and I've seen a few cases in Paris about 20 years ago. Only, we did not dare to give them a name, at the time. Public opinion is sacred: no panic, especially no panic. And then as a colleague said: "It is impossible, everyone knows that she disappeared from the West. Everyone knew it except the dead. Come on, Rieux, you know as well as moice that it is. Rieux was thinking. Through the window of his office, he looked at the shoulder of the stony cliff which closed in the distance on the bay. The sky, although blue, had a dull glow that softened as the afternoon wore on. - Yes, Castel, he said, it's hardly believable. But it seems to be the plague. Castel got up and went to the door. - You know what we will say, said the old doctor: "It has disappeared from temperate countries for years. "- What does it mean to disappear? replied Rieux, shrugging his shoulders. - Yes. And don't forget in Paris again, almost twenty years ago. - Well. Hopefully, it won't be any worse today than it was then. But it's really amazing. The word "plague" had just been spoken for the first time. At this point in the story that leaves Bernard Rieux behind his window, we will allow the narrator to justify the doctor's uncertainty and surprise, since, with nuances, his reaction was that of most of our fellow citizens. Plagues, indeed, are a common thing, but plagues are hard to believe when they fall on your head. There have been as many plagues in the world as there have been wars. And yet plagues and wars find people still so deprived. Dr. Rieux was unprepared, as were our fellow citizens, and that is how we must understand his hesitations. This is how we must also understand that he was divided between worry and confidence. When a war breaks out, people say, "It won't last, this is too silly. And no doubt a war is certainly too stupid, but that does not prevent it from lasting. Foolishness always insists, we would notice if we didn't always think of ourselves. Our fellow citizens in this regard were like everyone else, they thought of themselves, in other words they were humanists: they did not believe in the plagues. The scourge is not on a human scale, so we tell ourselves that the scourge is unreal, it's a bad dream that will pass. But it does not always pass and, from bad dreams to bad dreams, it is men who pass, and humanists in the first place, because they did not take their precautions. Our fellow citizens were no more guilty than others, they forgot to be modest, that's all, and they thought that everything was still possible for them, which supposed that the plagues were impossible. They continued to do business, they prepared trips and they had opinions. How would they have thought of the plague that suppresses the future, travel, and discussions? They thought they were free, and no one will ever be free as long as there are plagues. Even when Doctor Rieux recognized in front of his friend that a handful of dispersed patients had just died without warning of the plague, the danger remained unreal for him. Basically, when you're a doctor, you get an idea of the pain and you have a little more imagination. Looking out the window at his city, which had not changed, it was hardly if the doctor felt that slight disgust at the future be born in him that we call worry. He was trying to gather in his mind what he knew about this disease. Numbers floated in his memory and he said to himself that the thirty or so big plagues that history has known had caused nearly one hundred million deaths. But what is a hundred million dead? When you go to war, you hardly know what a dead man is. And since a dead man has weight only if he has been seen dead, a hundred million corpses sown throughout history are only a smoke in the imagination. The doctor remembered the plague of Constantinople which, according to Procope, had killed ten thousand victims in one day. Ten thousand dead make audiences to a big cinema five times. This is what should be done. We gather people at the exit of five cinemas, we drive them to a town square, and we make them die in heaps to see a little clear. At least, we could then put known faces on this anonymous crowding. But, of course, it's impossible to achieve, and who knows ten thousand faces? Besides, people like Procope did not know how to count, the thing is known. In Canton, seventy years ago, forty thousand rats died of the plague before the plague became interested in the inhabitants. But, in 1871, we couldn't afford to count rats. We were doing it roughly, with obvious chances of error. However, if a rat is thirty centimeters long, forty thousand rats placed end to end would do ... But the doctor was growing impatient. He let himself go and he shouldn't. Some cases do not make an epidemic and it is enough to take precautions. We had to stick to what we knew, stupor and prostration, red eyes, dirty mouth, headaches, buboes, terrible thirst, delirium, spots on the body, inner quartering, and at the end of it all... At the end of all that, a sentence went back to Doctor Rieux, a sentence which ended precisely in his manual the enumeration of the symptoms: "The pulse becomes threadlike and death occurs on occasion of an insignificant movement. "Yes, at the end of it all, we were hanging on a thread and three quarters of the people, that was the exact figure, were impatient enough to make this imperceptible movement that precipitated them. The doctor was still looking out the window. On one side of the glass, the cool spring sky, and on the other side the word that still echoed in the room: the plague. The word contained not only what science wanted to put in it, but a long series of extraordinary images that did not agree with this yellow and gray city, moderately animated at this hour, buzzing rather than noisy, happy in short , if it is possible that we can be both happy and dismal. And so peaceful and indifferent tranquility almost effortlessly denied the old images of the plague, Athens plagued and deserted by birds, Chinese cities filled with silent dying, the convicts of Marseilles piling dripping bodies in holes, building in Provence of the great wall which was to stop the furious wind of the plague, Jaffa and its hideous beggars, the damp and rotten beds glued to the clay of the Constantinople hospital, the sick drawn with hooks, the carnival of the masked doctors during the Black Plague, the couplings of the living in the cemeteries of Milan, the carts of the dead in terrified London, and the nights and days filled, everywhere and always, with the interminable cry of men. No, all that wasn't strong enough to kill the peace of that day. On the other side of the window, the tone of an invisible tram suddenly sounded and refuted cruelty and pain in a second. Only the sea, at the end of the dull checkerboard of the houses, testified to what is worrying and never rested in the world. And Doctor Rieux, who was looking at the gulf, thought of these pyres of which Lucretius speaks and which the Athenians struck by the disease raised in front of the sea. The dead were brought there during the night, but the place was lacking, and the living fought with blows torches to place those who had been dear to them, supporting bloody struggles rather than abandoning their corpses. One could imagine the glowing pyres in front of the still and dark water, the torch fights in the crackling night of sparks and thick poisonous vapors rising to the attentive sky. We could fear ... But this vertigo did not hold up to reason. It is true that the word "plague" had been spoken, it is true that at the very minute the scourge shook and threw one or two victims to the ground. But what, it could stop. What had to be done was to clearly recognize what should be recognized, finally cast out the shadows unnecessary and take appropriate action. Then the plague would stop because the plague could not be imagined or imagined falsely. If it stopped, and it was most likely, everything would be fine. Otherwise, you would know what it was and if there was no way to get around it. settle first and then defeat her. The doctor opened the window and the noise of the city suddenly swelled. From a nearby workshop rose the short, repeated hiss of a power saw.

Rieux shook himself. There was certainty, in everyday work. The rest was due to insignificant threads and movements, we couldn't stop there. The main thing was to do your job well. Doctor Rieux was there about his thoughts when Joseph Grand was announced to him. Employed at the town hall, and although his occupations were very diverse, he was used periodically in the statistics service, in civil status. He was thus brought to add up the deaths. And, naturally obliging, he had agreed to bring a copy of his results to Rieux himself. The doctor saw Grand enter with his neighbor Cottard. The employee held up a sheet of paper. "The numbers are going up, doctor," he announced. "Eleven dead in forty-eight hours." Rieux greeted Cottard and asked him how he felt. Grand explained that Cottard wanted to thank the doctor and apologize for the trouble he had caused him. But Rieux looked at the statistics sheet: - Come on, said Rieux, we may have to decide to call this disease by its name. So far, we have stomped on. But come with me, I have to go to the laboratory. "Yes, yes," said Grand, walking down the stairs behind the doctor. You have to call things by name. But what is this name? - I can't tell you, and besides that wouldn't be useful to you. - You see, the employee smiles. It is not so easy. They headed for the Place d'Armes. Cottard was still silent. The streets were starting to get crowded. The fleeting twilight of our country was already receding into darkness and the first stars appeared in the still clear horizon. A few seconds later, the lamps above the streets darkened the whole sky, lighting up, and the sound of conversations seemed to rise in a tone. - Forgive me, said Grand at the corner of Place d'Armes. But I have to take my tram. My evenings are sacred. As they say in my country: "We must never put off until tomorrow ..." Rieux had already noted this mania that Grand, born in Montélimar, had to invoke the phrases of his country and then add banal formulas which n 'were out of nowhere like "a dream time" or "a magical light". - Ah! said Cottard, that's right. You can't get him out of his house after dinner. Rieux asked Grand if he worked for the town hall. Grand replied that no, he worked for him. - Ah! Said Rieux to say something, and it's going on? - For years that I have been working there, obviously. Although in another sense, there is not much progress. - But, in short, what is it? said the doctor, stopping. Big mumbled, ensuring his round hat on his big ears. And Rieux understood very vaguely that it was something about the development of a personality. But the employee was already leaving them, and he was going up the Boulevard de la Marne, under the ficus trees, in a small hurried step. On the threshold of the laboratory, Cottard tells the doctor that he would like to see him for advice. Rieux, who fiddled in his pocket with the statistics sheet, invited him to come to his consultation, then, changing his mind, told him that he was going to his neighborhood the next day and that he would come and see him at the end of the afternoon. midday. When he left Cottard, the doctor realized that he was thinking of Grand. He imagined her in the midst of a plague, not one that probably wouldn't be serious, but one of the greatest plagues in history. "He's the kind of man who is spared in these cases. He remembered having read that the plague spared weak constitutions and above all destroyed vigorous complexions. And continuing to think about it, the doctor found the employee an air of little mystery. At first glance, indeed, Joseph Grand was nothing more than the little town hall employee he looked like. Long and thin, he floated in the middle of clothes he always chose too large, under the illusion that they would make more use of him. If he still kept most of his teeth on the lower gums, he had lost those of the upper jaw. Her smile, which raised her upper lip above all, gave her a shadowy mouth. If we add to this portrait a seminarian's approach, the art of razing the walls and sliding into doors, a scent of cellar and smoke, all the mines of insignificance, we will recognize that we could not imagine it other than in front of an office, applied to revise the prices of the city's shower-baths or to gather for a young editor the elements of a report concerning the new tax on the removal of household waste. Even for an unprejudiced mind, he seemed to have been brought into the world to exercise the discreet but indispensable functions of temporary municipal assistant at sixty-two and a half francs a day It was indeed the mention that he said to appear on the job sheets, after the word "qualification". When, twenty-two years ago, after graduating from a license which he could not exceed for lack of money, he had accepted this job, he had been made to hope, he said, for a rapid "tenure". It was only a question of giving evidence for some time of his competence in the delicate questions raised by the administration of our city. Thereafter, he could not fail, he was assured, to arrive at a position of editor which would allow him to live a large life. Admittedly, it was not ambition that made Joseph Grand act, he vouched for it with a melancholy smile. But the prospect of a material life ensured by honest means, and, consequently, the possibility of indulging in his favorite occupations without remorse. If he had accepted the offer, it was for honorable reasons and, so to speak, out of loyalty to an ideal. This temporary state of affairs had lasted for many years, life had increased in disproportionate proportions, and Grand's salary, despite some general increases, was still paltry. He had complained to Rieux about it, but no one seemed to be aware of it. This is where Grand's originality stands, or at least one of its signs. He could, in fact, have asserted, if not rights of which he was not sure, at least the assurances that had been given to him. First, however, the office manager who hired him had been dead for a long time, and the employee, moreover, did not remember the exact terms of the promise made to him. Last but not least, Joseph Grand could not find his words. It is this peculiarity that best painted our fellow citizen, as Rieux noted. It was indeed she who always prevented him from writing the letter of complaint that he meditated, or from taking the step that the circumstances required. According to him, he felt particularly prevented from using the word "right" on which he was not firm, or that of "promises" which would have implied that he claimed his due and would therefore have taken on a character boldness, hardly compatible with the modesty of the functions he occupied. On the other hand, he refused to use the terms "benevolence", "solicit", "gratitude", which he believed did not reconcile with his personal dignity. Thus, for lack of finding the right word, our fellow citizen continued to exercise his obscure functions until quite an advanced age. Besides, and always according to what he said to Doctor Rieux, he noticed from the usage that his material life was assured, in any case, since it was enough for him, after all, to adapt his needs to his needs. resources. He thus recognized the correctness of one of the favorite words of the mayor, big industrialist of our city, who asserted with force that finally (and he insisted on this word which carried all the weight of reasoning), finally therefore, we never had seen no one starve. In any case, the almost ascetic life that Joseph Grand led had finally freed him from all concerns of this kind. He kept looking for his words. In a certain sense, we can say that his life was exemplary. He was one of those men, rare in our city as elsewhere, who still have the courage of their good feelings. The little that he confided in him testified indeed to kindnesses and attachments that we dare not confess these days. He was not ashamed to admit that he loved his nephews and his sister, the only relative he had looked after and that he went to visit every two years in France. He recognized that the memory of his parents, who died when he was still young, made him sad. He did not refuse to admit that he loved above all a certain bell from his neighborhood which sounded softly around five in the evening. But to evoke such simple emotions, however, a single word cost him a thousand pains. In the end, this difficulty had caused him the greatest concern. "Ah! doctor, he said, I would like to learn to express myself. He told Rieux about it every time he met him. The doctor that evening, watching the employee leave, suddenly understood what Grand had meant: he was probably writing a book or something. Up to the laboratory where he finally went, that reassured Rieux. He knew that impression was stupid, but he couldn't believe that the plague could really take hold in a city where you could find modest civil servants who cultivated honorable fads. Exactly, he did not imagine the place of these manias in the middle of the plague and he therefore judged that, practically, the plague was without future among our fellow citizens. The next day, thanks to an insistence deemed inappropriate, Rieux obtained the summons to the prefecture of a health commission. - It is true that the population is worried, recognized Richard. And then the gossip exaggerates everything. The prefect said to me, "Let's be quick if you want, but in silence. He is moreover convinced that this is a false alarm. Bernard Rieux took Castel in his car to reach the prefecture. - Do you know, said the latter, that the department has no serum? - I know. I called the depot. The director was overwhelmed. You have to bring it from Paris. - I hope it won't be long. - I already wired, replied Rieux. The prefect was pleasant, but nervous. - Let's start, gentlemen, he said. Should I summarize the situation? Richard thought it was useless. The doctors knew the situation. The question was only what action should be taken. - The question, said the old Castel brutally, is whether it is the plague or not. Two or three doctors exclaimed. The others seemed to hesitate. As for the prefect, he jumped and turned mechanically towards the door, as if to verify that she had indeed prevented this enormity from spreading in the corridors. Richard declared that in his opinion, we should not give in to panic: it was a fever with inguinal complications, that was all that could be said, the hypotheses, in science as in life , being always dangerous. The old Castel, who was quietly chewing on his yellow mustache, looked up at Rieux with clear eyes. Then he turned a sympathetic glance to the audience and remarked that he knew very well that it was the plague, but that, of course, to recognize it officially would require ruthless action. He knew that it was, basically, what made his colleagues back off and, therefore, he was willing to admit for their tranquility that it was not the plague. The prefect was agitated and declared that, in any case, it was not a good way of reasoning. - The important thing, said Castel, is not that this way of reasoning is good, but that it makes you think. As Rieux was silent, he was asked his opinion: - It is a typhoid fever but accompanied by buboes and vomiting. I made the bubo incision. I was thus able to provoke analyzes where the laboratory believes it recognizes the stocky bacillus of the plague. To be complete, it must be said, however, that certain specific modifications of the microbe do not coincide with the conventional description. Richard pointed out that this allowed for hesitation and that we should at least wait for the statistical result of the series of analyzes, started a few days ago. - When a microbe, says Rieux, after a short silence, is able in four days to quadruple the size of the spleen, to give the mesenteric nodes the size of an orange and the consistency of porridge, it does not allow precisely no hesitation. The foci of infection are increasing. At the rate where the disease is spreading, if it is not stopped, it risks killing half the city before two months. Therefore, it doesn't matter if you call it plague or growing fever. It's only important that you keep him from killing half the city. Richard believed that nothing should be pushed to the black and that the contagion of elsewhere was not proven since the parents of his patients were still unharmed. "But others are dead," said Rieux. And, of course, the contagion is never absolute, without which we would obtain infinite mathematical growth and lightning depopulation. It's not about pushing anything black. It's about taking precautions. Richard, however, thought of summing up the situation by recalling that to stop this disease, if it did not stop by itself, it was necessary to apply the serious prophylaxis measures provided for by law; that, to do this, it had to be officially recognized that it was the plague; that the certainty was not absolute in this respect and that consequently, it required reflection. - The question, insisted Rieux, is not whether the measures provided for by law are serious but whether they are necessary to prevent half of the city from being killed. The rest is a matter of administration and, precisely, our institutions have provided a prefect to settle these questions. - No doubt, said the prefect, but I need you to officially recognize that this is an epidemic of plague. "If we don't recognize it," said Rieux, "it still risks killing half the city." Richard intervened with some nervousness. - The truth is that our colleague believes in the plague. His description of the syndrome proves it. Rieux replied that he had not described a syndrome, he had described what he had seen. And what he had seen were buboes, spots, delusional fevers, fatal in forty-eight hours. Did Mr. Could Richard take responsibility for saying that the epidemic would end without stringent prophylaxis? Richard hesitated and looked at Rieux: - Honestly, tell me your thoughts, are you sure it is the plague? - You are posing the problem badly. It's not a question of vocabulary, it's a question of time. - Your thought, said the prefect, would be that, even if it were not a question of plague, the prophylactic measures indicated in times of plague should nevertheless be applied. - If it is absolutely necessary that I have a thought, it is indeed this. The doctors consulted and Richard ended up saying: - So we have to take responsibility for acting as if the disease were a plague. The formula was warmly approved: - Is that also your opinion, my dear colleague? asked Richard. - The formula doesn't matter to me, said Rieux. Let's just say that we shouldn't act like half the city is not going to be killed, because then it will be. In the midst of the general annoyance, Rieux left. A few moments later, in the suburb which smelled of fried food and urine, a woman screaming to death, bloody groins, turned to him. The day after the conference, the fever jumped again. It even appeared in the newspapers, but in a benign form since they only made a few allusions to it. The day after, in any case, Rieux could read small white posters that the prefecture had quickly posted in the most discreet corners of the city. It was difficult to draw proof from this poster that the authorities were looking at the situation in the face. The measures were not draconian, and much seemed to have been sacrificed to the desire not to worry public opinion. The whole of the decree announced, in fact, that some cases of pernicious fever, which one could not yet say if it was contagious, had appeared in the commune of Oran. These cases weren't characterized enough to be really worrying, and there was no doubt that the population could keep its cool. Nevertheless, and in a spirit of prudence which could be understood by everyone, the prefect took some preventive measures. Understood and applied as it should be these measures were designed to put an end to any threat of an epidemic. Consequently, the prefect did not doubt for a moment that his constituents brought the most devoted collaborations to his personal effort. The poster then announced general measures, including scientific control by injecting toxic gases into the sewers and close monitoring of the water supply. She recommended to the inhabitants the most extreme cleanliness and finally invited the carriers of fleas to come to the municipal dispensaries. On the other hand, the families were obliged to declare the cases diagnosed by the doctor and to consent to the isolation of their patients in the special rooms of the hospital. These rooms were also equipped to care for the sick in the shortest possible time and with the greatest chance of recovery. A few additional articles subjected the patient's room and the transport vehicle to compulsory disinfection. For the rest, we confined ourselves to recommending to relatives that they submit to health surveillance. Dr. Rieux suddenly turned away from the poster and went back to his office. Joseph Grand, who was waiting for him, raised his arms again when he saw him. - Yes, said Rieux, I know, the numbers are going up. The day before, a dozen patients had died in the city. The doctor told Grand that he might see him in the evening, since he was going to visit Cottard. "You are right," said Grand. You will do him good because I find him changed. - And how is that? - He became polite. - Wasn't it before? Grand hesitated. He could not say that Cottard was rude, the expression would not have been right. He was a quiet, withdrawn man who looked a bit like a boar. His room, a modest restaurant, and fairly mysterious outings, was Cottard's whole life. Officially, he was a representative in wines and liqueurs. From time to time, he was visited by two or three men who must have been his clients. Sometimes in the evening he went to the cinema opposite the house. The employee even noticed that Cottard seemed to prefer gangster movies. On all occasions, the representative remained lonely and suspicious. All that, according to Grand, had changed: - I don't know how to say, but I have the impression, you see, that he is trying to reconcile people, that he wants to put everyone with him . He talks to me often; he offers to go out with him, and I don't always know how to refuse. Besides, he interests me, and, in short, I saved his life. Since his suicide attempt, Cottard has had no further visits. In the streets, at suppliers, he sought all sympathies. We had never been so gentle talking to grocers, so much interest in listening to a tobacco seller. - This tobacconist, remarked Grand, is a real viper. I told Cottard, but he said I was wrong and that she had good things that you had to know how to find. Two or three times finally, Cottard had taken Grand Two or three times finally, Cottard had taken Grand to restaurants and the city's luxurious cafes. He had started dating them indeed. - We are good there, he said, and then we are in good company. Grand had noticed the staff's special attentions to the representative and he understood the reason by observing the excessive tips that he left. Cottard seemed very sensitive to the kindnesses with which he was paid back. One day when the butler had escorted him and helped him put on his overcoat, Cottard had said to Grand: "He's a good boy, he can testify. - Witness what? Cottard had hesitated. - Well, that I'm not a bad man. Besides, he had mood swings. One day when the grocer had been less pleasant, he had returned home in a state of disproportionate fury: - He passes with the others, this scoundrel, he repeated. - What others? - All the others. Grand had even witnessed a curious scene with the tobacco merchant. In the middle of a lively conversation, she talked about a recent arrest that had made noise in Algiers. He was a young shop assistant who had killed an Arab on a beach. - If we put all this scum in prison, said the merchant, honest people could breathe. But she must have stopped in front of the sudden agitation of Cottard who threw himself out of the store, without a word of apology. Tall and the merchant, arms dangling, watched him flee. Subsequently, Grand was to report to Rieux other changes in Cottard's character. The latter had always been of very liberal opinions. His favorite phrase: "The big ones always eat the little ones" proved it well. But for some time now, he had been buying only the well-meaning newspaper from Oran, and it was hard to believe that he was ostentatious about reading it in public places. Likewise, a few days after getting up, he had asked Grand, who was going to the post office, to send a hundred-franc money order which he sent every month to a distant sister. But when Grand left: "Send him two hundred francs," asked Cottard, "it will be a pleasant surprise for her." She thinks I never think of her. But the truth is that I like it a lot. Finally, he had had a curious conversation with Grand. The latter had been obliged to answer Cottard's questions, intrigued by the little work that Grand did every evening. - Well, said Cottard, you're making a book. - If you want, but it's more complicated than that! - Ah! cried Cottard, I would like to do like you. Grand had seemed surprised and Cottard had stammered that being an artist had to fix many things. - Why? asked Grand. - Well, because one artist has more rights than another, everyone knows that. We pass him more things. - Come on, said Rieux to Grand, the morning of the posters, the story of rats turned his head like many others, that's all. Or he is afraid of fever. Grand replied: - I don't think so, doctor, and if you ask me ... The deratization car passed under their window with a loud exhaust noise. Rieux was silent until it was possible to be heard and absently asked the employee's opinion. The other looked at him seriously: - He's a man, he says, who has something to blame himself for. The doctor shrugged. As the commissioner said, there were other cats to whip. In the afternoon, Rieux had a conference with Castel. The sera weren't arriving. - Besides, asked Rieux, would they be useful? This bacillus is weird. - Oh! said Castel, I don't agree with you. These animals always have an air of originality. But, basically, it's the same thing. - You suppose so at least. In fact, we know nothing about it. - Obviously, I suppose so. But everyone is there. Throughout the day, the doctor felt the little dizziness growing in him every time he thought of the plague. Finally, he recognized that he was afraid. He entered cafes full of people twice. He too, like Cottard, felt a need for human warmth. Rieux thought it was stupid, but it helped him remember that he had promised the representative a visit. In the evening, the doctor found Cottard at the table in his dining room. When he entered, there was a sprawling detective story on the table. But the evening was already late, and certainly it must have been difficult to read in the emerging darkness. Rather, Cottard had to sit a minute ago and think in the dark. Rieux asked him how he was. Cottard, when he sat down, grumbled that he was fine and that he would be even better if he could be sure no one was looking after him. Rieux pointed out that you couldn't always be alone. - Oh! it's not that. I'm talking about the people who are trying to get you in trouble. Rieux was silent. - It is not my case, notice it well. But I was reading this novel. There's an unfortunate man who's stopped all of a sudden, we took care of him and he didn't know. We talked about him in the offices, we wrote his name on cards. Do you think that's fair? You find that we have the right to do that to a man? "It depends," said Rieux. In a sense, you never have the right, indeed. But all of this is secondary. Do not stay locked up for too long. You have to go out. Cottard seemed to get upset, said that he was only doing that, and that, if necessary, the whole neighborhood could testify for him. Outside the neighborhood itself, there was no shortage of relationships. - Do you know Mr. Rigaud, the architect? He is my friend. The shadow thickened in the room. The rue du Faubourg came alive and a dull, relieved exclamation greeted, outside, the moment when the lamps lit. Rieux went to the balcony and Cottard followed him. From all the surrounding neighborhoods, as every evening in our city, a light breeze carried murmurs, smells of grilled meat, the joyful and fragrant buzz of freedom which gradually swelled the street, invaded by a noisy youth. At night, the loud cries of invisible boats, the rumor rising from the sea and the passing crowd, this hour that Rieux knew well and loved in the past seemed to him oppressive today because of all he knew. - Can we turn on? he said to Cottard. When the light came back on, the little man looked at him with blinking eyes: - Tell me, doctor, if I got sick, would you take me on duty in the hospital? - Why not? Cottard then asked if it happened that someone who was in a clinic or a hospital was arrested. Rieux replied that it had been seen, but that everything depended on the patient's condition. - Me, said Cottard, I trust you. Then he asked the doctor if he would take him into town in his car. In the center of the city, the streets were already less populated and the lights scarcer. Children were still playing outside the doors. When Cottard asked, the doctor stopped his car in front of a group of these children. They were playing hopscotch and yelling. But one of them, with stuck black hair, the perfect parting, and a dirty face, stared at Rieux with clear and intimidating eyes. The doctor looked away. Cottard, standing on the sidewalk, shook his hand. The representative spoke in a hoarse and difficult voice. Two or three times he looked behind him. - People talk about an epidemic. Is that true, doctor? - People always talk, it's natural, said Rieux. - You are right. And then when we have a dozen dead, it will be the end of the world. This is not what we need. The engine was already snoring. Rieux had his hand on his gear lever. But he looked again at the child who had not stopped staring at him with his grave and calm air. And suddenly, without transition, the child smiles at him with all his teeth. - So, what do we need? asked the doctor, smiling at the child. Cottard suddenly grabbed the door and, before fleeing, shouted in a voice full of tears and rage: - An earthquake. A real! There was no earthquake and the next day was spent, for Rieux, only in long races around the city, in talks with the families of the sick and in discussions with the sick themselves. Never had Rieux found his job so heavy. Until then, the sick made it easier for him, they gave themselves to him. For the first time, the doctor felt them reluctant, taking refuge in the depths of their illness with a sort of suspicious astonishment. It was a struggle he was not used to yet. And around ten o'clock in the evening, his car stopped in front of the house of the old asthmatic whom he was last visiting, Rieux was having trouble tearing himself away from his seat. He was lingering to look at the dark street and the stars that appeared and disappeared in the dark sky. The old asthmatic was up in bed. He seemed to be breathing better and counted the chickpeas he passed from one pot to the other. He greeted the doctor with a happy expression. - So, doctor, is it cholera? - Where did you get this? - In the newspaper, and the radio said that too. - No, it's not cholera. - In any case, said the old man very excited, they are going strong, eh, big heads! - Don't believe it, said the doctor. He had examined the old man and now he was sitting in the middle of this miserable dining room. Yes, he was afraid. He knew that in the suburb even a dozen patients would wait for him the next morning, bent over their buboes. Only in two or three cases had the buboes' incision improved. But for the most part it would be the hospital and he knew what the hospital meant for the poor. "I don't want it to be used for their experiments," said the wife of one of the patients. He wouldn't serve their experiences; he would die and that was it. The measures adopted were insufficient, that was very clear. As for the "specially equipped" rooms, he knew them: two pavilions hastily moved from their other patients, their sealed windows, surrounded by a cordon. If the epidemic did not stop by itself, it would not be defeated by the measures that the administration had imagined. However, in the evening, official press releases remained optimistic. The next day, the Ransdoc agency announced that the prefectural measures had been received with serenity and that already about thirty patients had declared themselves. Castel had telephoned Rieux: - How many beds do the pavilions offer? - Eighty. - There are certainly more than thirty patients in the city? - There are those who are afraid and the others, the most numerous, those who have not had time. - Burials are not watched. - No. I phoned Richard that full measures, not sentences, were needed and that there was a real barrier or nothing at all to eradicate the epidemic. - So what? - He replied that he had no power. In my opinion, it will go up. In three days, in fact, the two pavilions were filled. Richard understood that we were going to decommission a school and plan for an auxiliary hospital. Rieux waited for the vaccines and opened the buboes. Castel returned to his old books and made long stations at the library. "The rats died from the plague or something very similar to it," he concluded. They put tens of thousands of fleas in circulation that will transmit the infection in a geometric proportion, if you don't stop it in time. Rieux was silent. At that time, time seemed to be fixed. The sun was pumping the puddles of the last showers. Beautiful blue skies overflowing with a yellow light, purring planes in the rising heat, everything in the season invited serenity. In four days, however, the fever made four surprising leaps: sixteen dead, twenty-four, twenty-eight and thirty-two. On the fourth day, it was announced that the auxiliary hospital would be opened in a kindergarten. Our fellow citizens who, until then, had continued to mask their anxiety under jokes, seemed in the streets more dejected and quieter. Rieux decided to telephone the prefect: - The measures are insufficient. - I have the figures, said the prefect, they are indeed worrying. - They are more than worrying, they are clear. - I will ask the General Government for orders. Rieux hung up on Castel: - Orders! And it would take imagination. - And the serums? - They will arrive in the week. The prefecture, through Richard, asked Rieux for a report to be sent to the capital of the colony to solicit orders. Rieux put in a clinical description and some figures. The same day, around 40 people were killed. The prefect took it upon himself, as he said, to make the prescribed measures worse the next day. Mandatory reporting and isolation were maintained. The sick people's homes had to be closed and disinfected, relatives subjected to a security quarantine, burials organized by the city under the conditions that we will see. A day later, the sera arrived by plane. They could suffice for the cases being treated. They were insufficient if the epidemic were to spread. They replied to Rieux's telegram that the security stock had been exhausted and that new manufacturing had started. Meanwhile, and from all the surrounding suburbs, spring was coming to the markets. Thousands of roses were fading in the merchants' baskets along the sidewalks, and their sweet smell was floating all over the city. Apparently, nothing had changed. The trams were always full during rush hour, empty and dirty during the day. Tarrou watched the little old man and the little old man spat on cats. Grand came home every night for his mysterious work. Cottard was going around in circles and Mr. Othon, the examining magistrate, still ran his menagerie. The old asthmatic poured out his peas and we sometimes met journalist Rambert, looking calm and interested. In the evening, the same crowd filled the streets and the queues lengthened in front of the cinemas. Besides, the epidemic seemed to be receding and, for a few days, there were only a dozen dead. Then suddenly it shot up. The day the death toll reached 30 again, Bernard Rieux looked at the official dispatch that the prefect had handed him, saying: "They were afraid. The dispatch said, "Declare the plague. Close the city. II From this moment, it can be said that the plague was everyone's business. Until then, despite the surprise and concern that these singular events had brought them, each of our fellow citizens had continued his occupations, as he could, in his ordinary place. And no doubt, this had to continue. But once the doors are closed, they realized that they were all, and the narrator himself, caught in the same bag and that it was necessary to arrange it. Thus, for example, a feeling as individual as that of separation from a loved one suddenly became, from the first weeks, that of an entire people, and, with fear, suffering principal of this long time of exile. One of the most remarkable consequences of the closing of the doors was, in fact, the sudden separation into which were placed beings who were not prepared for it. Mothers and children, spouses, lovers who thought they were doing a temporary separation a few days earlier, who had kissed on the platform of our station with two or three recommendations, certain to meet again a few days or weeks later late, sinking into stupid human confidence, barely distracted by this departure from their usual preoccupations, they were suddenly removed without recourse, prevented from joining or communicating. Because the closure was made a few hours before the prefectural decision was published and, of course, it was impossible to consider particular cases. We can say that this brutal invasion of the disease had the first effect of forcing our fellow citizens to act as if they had no individual feelings. In the early hours of the day when the decree entered into force, the prefecture was assaulted by a crowd of applicants who, on the phone or with officials, exposed equally interesting situations and, at the same time, also impossible to examine. In truth, it took several days for us to realize that we were in an uncompromising situation, and that the words "compromise", "favor", "exception" no longer made sense. Even the slight satisfaction of writing was denied to us. On the one hand, in fact, the city was no longer connected to the rest of the country by the usual means of communication, and, on the other hand, a new decree prohibited the exchange of all correspondence, to prevent letters from being able to become the vehicles of infection. At the start, a privileged few were able to touch each other, at the gates of the city, with sentries from the guard posts, who agreed to send messages outside. It was still in the early days of the epidemic, at a time when the guards found it natural to give in to compassionate movements. But after a while, when the same guards were fully convinced of the seriousness of the situation, they refused to take on responsibilities whose extent they could not foresee. Long distance telephone calls, authorized at the outset, caused such congestion in public booths and on lines, that they were completely suspended for a few days, then severely limited to what were called urgent cases, such as death, birth. and marriage. The telegrams then remained our only resource. Beings that were linked by intelligence, heart, and flesh, were reduced to looking for the signs of this ancient communion in the capitals of a ten-word dispatch. And since, in fact, the formulas that can be used in a telegram are quickly exhausted, long shared lives or painful passions quickly summed up in a periodic exchange of ready-made formulas like: "Go well. Think of you. Tenderness. Some of us, however, stubbornly wrote and relentlessly imagined combinations to match the outdoors that always ended up being illusory. Even if some of the means that we had imagined succeeded, we knew nothing about it, receiving no answer. For weeks, we were reduced to constantly repeating the same letter, copying the same calls, so that after a while, the words that first came out bleeding from our hearts were emptied of their meaning. We then copied them mechanically, trying to give signs of our difficult life by means of these dead sentences. And finally, to this sterile and stubborn monologue, to this arid conversation with a wall, the conventional call of the telegram seemed preferable to us. After a few days, when it became clear that no one would be able to get out of our city, we had the idea of asking whether the return of those who had left before the epidemic could be authorized. After a few days of reflection, the prefecture replied in the affirmative. But she added that the returnees could not, in any case, leave the city and that, if they were free to come, they would not be able to leave. Here again, a few families, moreover rare, took the situation lightly, and putting before all prudence the desire they were to see their parents again, invited the latter to take advantage of the occasion. But, very quickly, those who were prisoners of the plague understood the danger to which they exposed their loved ones and resigned themselves to suffering this separation. At the height of the disease, there was only one case where human feelings were stronger than the fear of a tortured death. It was not, as you might expect, two lovers that love threw towards each other, over suffering. It was only old doctor Castel and his wife, who had been married for many years. Mrs. Castel, a few days before the epidemic, went in a nearby town. It was not even one of these households that offered the world an example of exemplary happiness and the narrator is able to say that, in all probability, these spouses, until now, were not certain of be satisfied with their union. But this brutal and prolonged separation had put them in a position to ensure that they could not live far apart from each other, and that with this suddenly exposed truth, the plague was little. It was an exception. In the majority of cases, the separation, it was obvious, should only end with the epidemic. And for all of us, the feeling that made our life and that, however, we thought we knew well (the Oranese, as we have already said, have simple passions), took on a new face. Husbands and lovers who had the greatest confidence in their partner found themselves jealous. Men who thought they were light in love found consistency. Sons, who had lived near their mother barely looking at her, put all their worry and regret in a fold of her face that haunted their memories. This brutal separation, without burrs, without foreseeable future, left us disconcerted, unable to react against the memory of this presence, still so close and already so distant, which now occupied our days. In fact, we suffered twice - first from our suffering and then from that which we imagined to the absent, son, wife, or lover. In other circumstances, moreover, our fellow citizens would have found a way out of a more external and active life. But, at the same time, the plague left them idle, reduced to turning in circles in their dreary city and delivered, day after day, to the disappointing games of the memory. Because, in their aimless walks, they were always led to cross the same paths, and, most of the time, in such a small city, these paths were precisely those that in another era they had traveled with the absent . So, the first thing the plague brought to our fellow citizens was exile. And the narrator is convinced that he can write here, on behalf of all, what he himself experienced then, since he experienced it at the same time as many of our fellow citizens. Yes, it was the feeling of exile that this hollow that we constantly carried in us, this precise emotion, the unreasonable desire to go back or on the contrary to press the march of time, these burning arrows of memory. If, sometimes, we let ourselves go to the imagination and we liked to wait for the doorbell to return or a familiar step on the stairs, if, at these times, we agreed to forget that the trains were immobilized, if we then managed to stay home at a time when, normally, a traveler brought by the evening express could be returned to our neighborhood, of course, these games could not last. There always came a time when we clearly saw that the trains were not arriving. We knew then that our separation was destined to last and that we had to try to work out over time. From then on, in short, we reintegrated our condition as prisoners, we were reduced to our past, and if even some of us were tempted to live in the future, they quickly renounced it, at least as far as he was concerned. was possible for them, by experiencing the wounds that ultimately the imagination inflicts on those who trust it. In particular, all of our fellow citizens quickly deprived themselves, even in public, of the habit they might have had of calculating the duration of their separation. Why? It is that when the most pessimistic had fixed it for example at six months, when they had exhausted in advance all the bitterness of these coming months, hoisted with great difficulty their courage at the level of this test, tense their last strength to remain without faltering at the height of this suffering stretched over such a long series of days, so, sometimes, a meeting friend, a notice given by a newspaper, a fleeting suspicion or a sudden clairvoyance, gave them the idea that after all, there was no reason why the disease should not last more than six months, and perhaps a year, or more. At that time, the collapse of their courage, will and patience was so abrupt that it seemed to them that they could never climb out of this hole again. They therefore forced themselves never to think about the end of their deliverance, to no longer look to the future and to always keep their eyes down, so to speak. But, naturally, this prudence, this way of cunning with pain, of closing their guard to refuse the fight were badly rewarded. Same As long as they avoided this collapse which they did not want at any cost, they actually deprived themselves of those moments, which were quite frequent, when they could forget the plague in the images of their upcoming meeting. And thus, stranded halfway between these abysses and summits, they floated rather than lived, abandoned to days without direction and to sterile memories, wandering shadows that could only have gained strength by agreeing to take root in the land of their pain. They thus experienced the deep suffering of all prisoners and all exiles, which is to live with a memory that is useless. This very past they were constantly thinking about only tasted regret. They would have liked, in fact, to be able to add to it all that they regretted not having done when they could still do it with the one or that they were waiting for - just as in all circumstances, even relatively happy, of their life as prisoners, they mixed the absent, and what they were then could not satisfy them. Impatient of their present, enemies of their past and deprived of a future, we looked like those who human justice or hatred keep behind bars. Finally, the only way to escape this unbearable vacation was to make the trains run again in imagination and fill the hours with the repeated chimes of a stubbornly silent bell. But if it was exile, in most cases it was exile at home. And although the narrator only knew the exile of everyone, he must not forget those, like the journalist Rambert or others, for whom, on the contrary, the sorrows of separation were amplified by the fact that , travelers surprised by the plague and retained in the city, they found themselves far away both from the being they could not reach and from the country which was theirs. In general exile, they were the most exiled, because if time aroused in them, as in all, the anguish which is their own, they were also attached to space and constantly collided with the walls which separated their a stinky refuge from their lost homeland. They were probably the ones we saw wandering at all hours of the day in the dusty city, silently calling evenings that they were the only ones to know, and the mornings of their country. They then fed their sickness with imponderable signs and disconcerting messages such as a flight of swallows, a dew of sunset, or those bizarre rays that the sun sometimes leaves in the deserted streets. This outside world which can always save everything, they closed their eyes on him, stubborn that they were to caress their too real dreams and to pursue with all their strength the images of a land where a certain light, two or three hills , the favorite tree and the faces of women made up an irreplaceable climate for them. To finally speak more expressly of the lovers, who are the most interesting and whose narrator is perhaps better placed to speak, they found themselves still tormented by other anxieties among which must be pointed out remorse. This situation, in fact, allowed them to view their feelings with a kind of feverish objectivity. And it was rare that, on these occasions, their own failings were not clearly apparent to them. They found the first opportunity in the difficulty they had in precisely imagining the actions of the absent. They then deplored the ignorance where they were of his schedule; they accused themselves of the lightness with which they had neglected to inform themselves of it and pretended to believe that, for a being who loves, the timetable of the loved one is not the source of all joys. It was easy for them, from that moment, to go back in their love and to examine its imperfections. In ordinary times, we all knew, consciously or not, that there is no love that cannot be surpassed, and yet we accept, with more or less tranquility, that ours remains mediocre. But the memory is more demanding. And, very consistently, this misfortune which came to us from the outside, and which struck an entire city, did not only bring us unjust suffering which we could have been indignant about. It also caused us to make ourselves suffer and thus made us consent to the pain. This was one of the ways the disease had to distract and confuse the issue. Thus, everyone had to accept to live day by day, and alone in front of the sky. This general abandonment which could in the long run soak the characters started, however, by rendering them futile. For some of our fellow citizens, for example, they were then subjected to another slavery which put them in the service of the sun and the rain. It seemed, when they saw them, that they were receiving for the first time, and directly, the impression of the weather. They looked happy on the simple visit of a golden light, while the rainy days put a thick veil on their faces and their thoughts. They escaped a few weeks earlier this unreasonable weakness and enslavement because they were not alone in front of the world and, to a certain extent, the being who lived with them placed themselves before their universe. From that moment, on the contrary, they were apparently delivered to the whims of heaven, that is to say, they suffered and hope for no reason. In these extremes of solitude, finally, nobody could hope for the help of the neighbor and each one remained alone with his concern. If one of us, by any chance, tried to confide in or say something about his feelings, the response he received, whatever it was, hurt him most of the time. He then realized that he and his interlocutor were not talking about the same thing. He, in fact, spoke from the bottom of long days of rumination and suffering and the image he wanted to communicate had long cooked in the fire of expectation and passion. The other, on the contrary, imagined a conventional emotion, the pain that one sells on the markets, a melancholy of series. Benevolent or hostile, the answer always fell wrong, it had to be given up. Or at least, for those to whom the silence was unbearable, and since the others could not find the true language of the heart, they were resigned to adopt the language of the markets and to speak, them also, on the conventional mode, that of simple relationship and news item, some sort of daily chronicle. There again, the most real pains took the habit of being translated into the banal formulas of conversation. It was only at this price that prisoners of the plague could obtain the compassion of their concierge or the interest of their listeners. However, and most importantly, as painful as these anxieties were, however heavy to bear even this empty heart, it could well be said that these exiles, in the first period of the plague, were privileged. At the very moment, in fact, when the population began to panic, their thought was entirely turned towards the being they expected. In general distress, the selfishness of love preserved them, and, if they thought of the plague, it was only to the extent that it gave their separation the risks of being eternal. They thus brought to the very heart of the epidemic a salutary distraction that one was tempted to take for composure. Their despair saved them from panic, their misfortune was good. For example, if one of them died of the disease, it was almost always without him being able to take care. Taken from this long inner conversation which he supported with a shadow; he was then thrown without transition to the thickest silence on earth. He had had time for nothing. While our fellow citizens were trying to come to terms with this sudden exile, the plague put guards at the gates and hijacked the ships that were heading for Oran. Since the closure, not a vehicle had entered the city. From that day on, it felt like the cars were going around in circles. The port also presented a singular aspect, for those who looked at it from the top of the boulevards. The usual entertainment that made it one of the first ports on the coast had suddenly died out. Some ships kept in quarantine can still be seen. But, on the quays, large unarmed cranes, the wagons overturned on their sides, solitary piles of drums or bags, testified that the trade, too, had died of the plague. Despite these unusual shows, our fellow citizens apparently had trouble understanding what was happening to them. There were common feelings like separation or fear, but personal concerns also continued to come to the fore. No one had yet really accepted the disease. Most were especially sensitive to what was bothering their habits or affecting their interests. They were annoyed or irritated and these are not feelings that can be opposed to the plague. Their first reaction, for example, was to incriminate the administration. The prefect's response in the presence of critics whose press echoed ("Could we not consider a relaxation of the measures envisaged?") Was quite unexpected. So far, neither the newspapers nor Ransdoc have received official statistics on the disease. The prefect communicated them, day after day, to the agency, asking it to make a weekly announcement. Again, however, public reaction was not immediate. Indeed, the announcement that the third week of the plague had counted three hundred and two deaths did not speak to the imagination. On the one hand, perhaps not all of them were dead from the plague. And, on the other hand, no one in town knew how many people a week died in ordinary times. The city had two hundred thousand inhabitants. It was not known whether this proportion of deaths was normal. These are even the kinds of details that we never care about, despite the obvious interest they present. The public lacked, in a way, points of comparison. It was only in the long run, seeing the increase in deaths, that the public became aware of the truth. The fifth week in fact gave three hundred and twenty-one deaths and the sixth, three hundred and forty-five. The increases, at least, spoke volumes. But they were not strong enough for our fellow citizens to keep in the midst of their anxiety the impression that it was an accident, no doubt unfortunate, but after all temporary. They continued to circulate in the streets and sit at the cafe terrace. On the whole, they were not cowardly, exchanged more jokes than lamentations, and pretended to accept cheerfully obvious inconveniences. Appearances were saved. Towards the end of the month, however, and roughly during the prayer week discussed below, more serious changes changed the appearance of our city. First, the prefect took measures regarding vehicle traffic and supplies. Supply was limited and petrol rationed. Electricity savings were even prescribed. Only the essential products reached Oran by road and by air. This is how we saw the traffic gradually decrease until it became almost zero, luxury stores close overnight, others line their windows with negative signs, while lines of buyers parked in front their doors. Oran thus took on a singular aspect. The number of pedestrians became more numerous and even, during off-peak hours, many people reduced to inaction by the closing of shops or certain offices filled the streets and cafes. For the moment, they were not yet unemployed, but on leave. Oran gave then, around three o'clock in the afternoon for example, and under a beautiful sky, the deceptive impression of a city in celebration whose circulation would have been stopped and the stores closed to allow the development of an event public, and whose inhabitants would have invaded the streets to participate in the festivities. Naturally, the cinemas took advantage of this general holiday and did big business. But the circuits that the films completed in the department were interrupted. After two weeks, the establishments were forced to exchange their programs, and after a while the cinemas ended up screening the same film. Their revenues, however, did not decrease. Finally, cafes, thanks to the considerable stocks accumulated in a city where the wine and alcohol trade holds the first place, could also supply their customers. In fact, we drank a lot. After a cafe billboard that "Wine Probe Kills the Microbe," public opinion that alcohol is a preservative against infectious disease has gained momentum in public opinion. Every night, around two o'clock, a fairly considerable number of drunkards expelled from cafes filled the streets and spread themselves in optimistic words. But all of these changes, in a sense, were so extraordinary and had taken place so quickly that it was not easy to think of them as normal and lasting. The result is that we continue to put our personal feelings first. Coming out of the hospital, two days after the doors closed, Dr. Rieux met Cottard who looked up at him with satisfaction. Rieux congratulated him on his looks. - Yes, it's going very well, said the little man. Tell me, doctor, this damn plague, huh! it's starting to get serious. The doctor recognized him. And the other noted with a kind of playfulness: - There is no reason why it should stop now. Everything will be turned upside down. They walked together for a while. Cottard said that a large grocer in his neighborhood had stored food for high prices and that cans were found under his bed when he was picked up to take him to the hospital. "He died there. The plague doesn't pay. Cottard was so full of stories, true or false, about the epidemic. It was said, for example, that in the center, one morning, a man with the signs of the plague, and in the delirium of the disease, had rushed outside, thrown on the first woman met and hugged her shouting that he had the plague. - Well! remarked Cottard, in a kind tone that did not go with his assertion, we will all go crazy, that's for sure. Likewise, by the afternoon of the same day, Joseph Grand had ended up making personal confidences to Doctor Rieux. He had seen the photograph of Madame Rieux on the desk and looked at the doctor. Rieux replied that his wife was being treated outside the city. "In a way," said Grand, "this is a chance. "The doctor replied that it was probably a chance and that it was only to be hoped that his wife would recover. - Ah! said Grand, I understand. And for the first time since Rieux knew him, he began to speak in abundance. Although he was still searching for his words, he almost always managed to find them as if, for a long time, he had thought about what he was saying. He married very young with a poor girl from his neighborhood. It was even to get married that he interrupted his studies and took a job. Neither Jeanne nor he ever left their neighborhood. He was going to see her at her house, and Jeanne's parents laughed a little about this pretending to be silent and clumsy. The father was a railroad worker. When he was at rest, we always saw him sitting in a corner, near the window, thoughtful, watching the movement of the street, his huge hands flat on his thighs. The mother was still at home, Jeanne was helping her. She was so tiny that Grand couldn't see her crossing a street without being anxious. The vehicles seemed excessive to him. One day, in front of a Christmas shop, Jeanne, who was looking at the window in wonder, turned over to him saying: "How beautiful! He had clasped her wrist. This is how the marriage was decided. The rest of the story, according to Grand, was very simple. It's the same for everyone: we get married, we still love a little, we work. We work as long as we forget to love. Jeanne also worked since the promises of the office manager had not been kept. Here it took a little imagination to understand what Grand meant. Fatigue helped, he let himself go, he kept silent more and more and he did not support his young wife in the idea that she was loved. A working man, poverty, the slowly closed future, the silence of the evenings around the table, there is no place for passion in such a universe. Probably, Jeanne had suffered. She had stayed however: sometimes we suffer a long time without knowing it. The years had passed. Later, she was gone. Of course, she hadn't left alone. "I liked you, but now I'm tired ... I'm not happy to leave, but you don't have to be happy to start again. That's basically what she wrote to him. Joseph Grand in turn had suffered. He could have started again, as Rieux pointed out to him. But lo and behold, he didn't have faith. Simply, he was always thinking of her. What he wanted was to write him a letter to justify himself. "But it's difficult," he said. I've been thinking about it for a long time. As long as we loved each other, we understood each other without words. But we don't always love each other. At one point, I should have found the words that would have kept her, but I couldn't. Grand was blowing his nose in a sort of checkered towel. Then he wiped his mustaches. Rieux looked at him. - Excuse me, doctor, said the old man, but how can I put it? ... I trust you. With you, I can speak. So, it gives me emotion. Obviously, Grand was a thousand leagues from the plague. In the evening, Rieux telegraphed to his wife that the city was closed, that he was fine, that she had to continue looking after herself and that he was thinking of her. Three weeks after the doors closed, Rieux found a young man waiting for him outside the hospital. "I suppose," said the latter, "that you recognize me." Rieux thought he knew him, but he hesitated. - I came before these events, said the other, to ask you about the living conditions of the Arabs. My name is Raymond Rambert. - Ah! yes, said Rieux. Well, you now have a great story. The other looked nervous. He says it was not that and that he came to ask Doctor Rieux for help. - I apologize, he added, but I don't know anyone in this city and the correspondent of my newspaper has the misfortune of being a fool. Rieux offered to walk him to a clinic in the center because he had some orders to give. They went down the alleys of the Negro quarter. Evening was approaching, but the city, once so noisy at that time, seemed curiously lonely. A few bugler rings in the still golden sky only testified that the military seemed to be doing their job. Meanwhile, along the steep streets, between the blue, ocher, and purple walls of the houses between the blue, ocher and purple walls of the Moorish houses, Rambert spoke, very agitated. He had left his wife in Paris. Truth be told, it wasn't his wife, but it was the same thing. He had wired her when the city closed. He had initially thought it was a temporary event and had only sought to correspond with it. His colleagues in Oran had told him they could do nothing, the post office had sent him back, a secretary of the prefecture had laughed in his face. He had finished, after waiting two hours in a queue, by accepting a telegram in which he had written: "Everything is fine. See you soon. But in the morning, when he got up, it suddenly occurred to him that after all, he didn't know how long it could last. He had decided to leave. As he was recommended (in his profession, we have facilities), he had been able to touch the director of the prefectural cabinet and had told him that he had nothing to do with Oran, that it was not his business to stay there, that he was there by accident and that it was right that he should be allowed to go, even if, once outside, we had to subject him to quarantine. The director had told him that he understood very well, but that we could not make an exception, that he was going to see, but that the situation was serious and that nothing could be decided. "But, after all," said Rambert, "I'm a stranger to this city." - No doubt, but after all, let's hope the epidemic won't last. Finally, he had tried to console Rambert by pointing out to him that he could find in Oran the matter of an interesting report and that there was no event, all things considered, which did not have its good side . Rambert shrugged. We got to the center of town: - It's stupid, doctor, you understand. I was not born to report. But maybe I was born to live with a woman. Isn't that in order? Rieux says that in any case it seemed reasonable. On the downtown boulevards, it was not the ordinary crowd. Some passers-by hurried towards distant residences. None of them smiled. Rieux thought it was the result of Ransdoc announcement that was made that day. At the end of twenty-four hours, our fellow citizens began to hope again. But the same day, the figures were still too fresh in the memories. - It's that, said Rambert without warning, she and I met recently, and we get along well. Rieux said nothing. "But I bore you," replied Rambert. I just wanted to ask you if you can't give me a certificate that says I don't have this hell of a disease. I think it might help me. Rieux nodded, he received a little boy who threw himself into his legs and gently put him back on his feet. They left and arrived at the Place d'Armes. The branches of ficus and palm trees hung motionless, gray with dust, around a statue of the Republic, powdery and dirty. They stopped under the monument. Rieux knocked on the floor, one after the other, his feet covered with a whitish coating. He looked at Rambert. The felt a little behind, the shirt collar unbuttoned under the tie, unshaven, the journalist looked stubborn and sulky. - Be sure that I understand you, said Rieux at last, but your reasoning is not good. I cannot give you this certificate because in fact I do not know if you have this disease or not and because even then I cannot certify that between the second you leave my office and the one where you enter the prefecture, you will not be infected. And then even ... - And then even? said Rambert. - And then, even if I gave you this certificate, it would be of no use to you. - Why? - Because there are thousands of men in this town in your case and we cannot, however, let them out. - But what if they don't have the plague themselves? - This is not a sufficient reason. This story is stupid, I know, but it concerns us all. You have to take it as it is. - But I'm not from here! - From now on, alas! you'll be here like everyone else. The other was animated: - It's a question of humanity, I swear it. Maybe you don't realize what separation means like this for two people who get along well. Rieux did not reply immediately. Then he said he thought he was aware of it. With all his might, he wanted Rambert to find his wife and all those who loved each other to be reunited, but there were decrees and laws, there was the plague, his role was to do what he had to. - No, said Rambert bitterly, you can't understand. You speak the language of reason; you are in the abstract. The doctor looked up at the Republic and said he did not know if he spoke the language of reason, but he spoke the language of evidence and it was not necessarily the same thing. The journalist adjusted his tie: - So, does that mean I have to do it differently? But he went on with a sort of challenge, I will leave this town. The doctor says he still understands it, but it doesn't concern him. "Yes, that concerns you," said Rambert with a sudden burst. I came to you because I was told that you had a big part in the decisions made. I thought then that, for at least one case, you could undo what you had helped to do. But you don't care. You haven't thought of anyone. You disregarded those who were separated. Rieux recognized that, in a sense, this was true, he had not wanted to take it into account. - Ah! I see, said Rambert, you are going to speak of public service. But the public good is made for everyone's happiness. - Come on, said the doctor who seemed to come out of a distraction, there is that and there is something else. We must not judge. But you are wrong to get angry. If you can get away from this, I'll be very happy. Simply, there are things that my function prohibits me. The other shook his head impatiently. - Yes, I'm wrong to get angry. And I took you enough time like this. Rieux asked him to keep him informed of his proceedings and not to hold a grudge against him. Surely there was a plan on which they could meet. Rambert suddenly seemed puzzled: - I believe him, he said, after a silence, yes, I believe him in spite of myself and in spite of everything you told me. He hesitated: "But I cannot approve of you." He lowered his felt tip to the forehead and took a quick step. Rieux saw him enter the hotel where Jean Tarrou lived. After a while, the doctor shook his head. The journalist was right in his impatience for happiness. But was he right when he accused him? "You live in abstraction. "Was it really an abstraction that those days spent in his hospital where the plague worked double duty, bringing to five hundred the average number of victims per week? Yes, there was a bit of abstraction and unreality in misfortune. But when abstraction starts killing you, you have to deal with abstraction. And Rieux only knew that it was not the easiest. It was not easy, for example, to run this auxiliary hospital (there were now three) under his care. He had arranged in a room, overlooking the consultation room, a reception room. The excavated soil formed a lake of cresylated water in the center of which was an island of bricks. The patient was transported to his island, stripped quickly and his clothes fell into the water. Washed, dried, covered with the rough shirt of the hospital, it passed into the hands of Rieux, then it was transported to one of the rooms. We had to use the yards of a school which now contained a total of five hundred beds, almost all of which were occupied. After the morning reception which he directed himself, the vaccinated patients, the incised buboes, Rieux still checked the statistics, and returned to his consultations in the afternoon. Finally, in the evening, he made his visits and returned late at night. The previous night, her mother had noticed, while handing her a telegram from young Rieux, that the doctor's hands were shaking. - Yes, he said, but by persevering, I will be less nervous. He was vigorous and resistant. In fact, he wasn't tired yet. But his visits, for example, became unbearable to him. Diagnosing epidemic fever was like having the patient removed quickly. Then began the abstraction and the difficulty indeed because the family of the patient knew that they would not see any more the latter that cured or dead "Pity, doctor! Said Mrs. Loret, the mother of the maid who worked at the Hôtel de Tarrou. What did it mean? Of course, he felt sorry. But that didn't move anyone. You had to phone. Soon the ambulance bell rang. The neighbors, at first, opened their windows and looked. Later, they closed them hastily. Then began the struggles, the tears, the persuasion, the abstraction in short. In these apartments overheated by fever and anxiety, scenes of madness unfolded. But the patient was taken away. Rieux could leave. The first few times, he confined himself to phoning and running to other patients, without waiting for the ambulance. But the parents then closed their doors, preferring the tête-à-tête with the plague to a separation from which they now knew the outcome. Cries, injunctions, police interventions, and later, of the armed force, the patient was taken by storm. For the first few weeks, Rieux was forced to stay until the ambulance arrived. Then, when each doctor was accompanied on his rounds by a volunteer inspector, Rieux was able to run from patient to patient. But in the beginning, every evening was like that evening when, entering Mrs Loret's house, in a small apartment decorated with fans and artificial flowers, he was received by the mother who said to him with a badly drawn smile: - I hope this is not the fever everyone is talking about. And he, pulling up his sheet and shirt, silently contemplated the red spots on his stomach and thighs, the swelling of the glands. The mother looked between her daughter's legs and shouted, unable to control herself. Every night mothers screamed like this, with an abstract air, in front of bellies offered with all their mortal signs, every evening arms clung to those of Rieux, useless words, promises and tears rushed, all Evenings of ambulance patches triggered crises as vain as any pain. And at the end of this long series of evenings, always similar, Rieux could hope for nothing other than a long series of similar scenes, indefinitely renewed. Yes, the plague, like abstraction, was monotonous. Only one thing maybe changed, and it was Rieux himself. He felt it that evening, at the foot of the monument to the Republic, only aware of the difficult indifference that was beginning to fill it, still looking at the hotel door where Rambert had disappeared. After these exhausting weeks, after all these twilights in which the city poured into the streets to turn around in circles, Rieux understood that he no longer had to defend himself against pity. We tire of pity when pity is useless. And in the feeling of this heart slowly closing in on itself, the doctor found the only relief from these overwhelming days. He knew that his task would be facilitated. That's why he was delighted. When his mother, receiving him at two o'clock in the morning, was distressed by the empty gaze he placed on her, she deplored precisely the only softening that Rieux could then receive. To fight against abstraction, you have to look a little like it. But how could it be sensitive to Rambert? Abstraction for Rambert was all that stood in the way of his happiness. And the truth is, Rieux knew the reporter was right, in a sense. But he also knew that sometimes abstraction is stronger than happiness and that it is only then necessary to take it into account. This was what was to happen to Rambert, and the doctor was able to learn it in detail by confidences that Rambert later gave him. He was thus able to follow, and on a new level, this kind of dreary struggle between the happiness of each man and the abstractions of the plague, which constituted the whole life of our city during this long period. But where some saw abstraction, others saw the truth. The end of the first month of plague was overshadowed by a marked upsurge of the epidemic and a vehement preaching from Father Paneloux, the Jesuit who had assisted old Michel at the start of his illness. Father Paneloux had already distinguished himself by frequent collaborations in the bulletin of the Geographical Society of Oran, where his epigraphic reconstructions were authoritative. But he had gained a wider audience than a specialist by lecturing on modern individualism. He had made himself the warm defender of a demanding Christianity, also distant from modern libertinism and obscurantism of past centuries. On this occasion, he did not bargain for harsh truths to his audience. Hence his reputation. However, towards the end of this month, the ecclesiastical authorities of our city decided to fight against the plague by their own means, by organizing a week of collective prayers. These demonstrations of public piety were to end on Sunday with a solemn mass placed under the invocation of Saint Roch, the plague-stricken saint. On this occasion, Father Paneloux was asked to speak. For the past fortnight, he had wrested himself from his work on Saint Augustine and the African Church which had given him a special place in his order. Of a fiery and passionate nature, he had resolutely accepted the mission with which he was charged. Long before this preaching, there was talk of it in town and it marked, in its own way, an important date in the history of this period. The week was attended by a large audience. It is not that ordinary people of Oran are usually particularly pious. On Sunday morning, for example, sea bathing is a serious competition for mass. Nor was it that a sudden conversion would have enlightened them. But, on the one hand, the closed city and the prohibited port, the baths were no longer possible, and, on the other hand, they were in a very particular state of mind where, without having admitted to the bottom of themselves the surprising events that struck them, they obviously felt that something had changed. Many, however, still hoped that the epidemic would end and that they would be spared with their families. As a result, they still didn't feel obliged to anything. The plague was for them only an unpleasant visitor who had to leave one day since she had come. Frightened, but not desperate, the moment had not yet arrived when the plague would appear to them as the very form of their life and when they would forget the existence that, until it, they had been able to lead. In short, they were waiting. With regard to religion, like many other problems, the plague had given them a peculiar turn of mind, as far from indifference as from passion and which could be defined fairly well by the word "objectivity". Most of those who followed the week of prayers would have made, for example, the statement that one of the faithful had to make before Doctor Rieux: "In any case, it cannot hurt. Tarrou himself, after having noted in his notebooks that the Chinese, in such cases, will play the tambourine in front of the genius of the plague, remarked that it was absolutely impossible to know if, in reality, the tambourine was more effective than prophylactic measures. He added only that, to settle the question, it was necessary to be informed about the existence of a genius of the plague and that our ignorance on this point sterilized all opinions that we could have. The cathedral of our city, in any case, was almost filled by the faithful throughout the week. During the first days, many inhabitants still stayed in the palm and pomegranate gardens which stretch out in front of the porch, to listen to the tide of invocations and prayers which ebbed even in the streets. Little by little, the example helped, the same listeners decided to enter and mix a shy voice with the audience's responses. And on Sunday, a considerable crowd invades the nave, overflowing as far as the forecourt and the last stairs. Since the day before, the sky had darkened, the rain was pouring down. Those standing outside had opened their umbrellas. An odor of incense and wet cloths floated in the cathedral when Father Paneloux climbed into the pulpit. He was of medium height, but stocky. When he leaned on the edge of the pulpit, clasping the wood between his big hands, we saw only a thick, black shape surmounted by the two spots of his cheeks, rubicunds under the steel glasses. He had a strong, passionate voice, which carried far, and when he attacked the audience with a single vehement and hammered sentence: "My brothers, you are in misfortune, my brothers, you have deserved it", a eddy walked through the audience to the square. Logically, what followed did not seem to connect with this pathetic exordia. It was the continuation of the speech which only made it clear to our fellow citizens that, by a skillful oratorical process, the father had given in one go, as one strikes a blow, the theme of his entire preaching. Paneloux, immediately after this sentence, in fact, quoted the text of the Exodus relating to the plague in Egypt and said: "The first time that this plague appears in history, it is to strike the enemies of God. Pharaoh opposes eternal purposes and the plague makes him fall to his knees. From the beginning of all history, the scourge of God has placed the proud and the blind at its feet. Meditate on it and fall to your knees. The rain redoubled outside and this last sentence, pronounced in the middle of an absolute silence, made even deeper by the crackling of the downpour on the stained glass windows, sounded with such an accent that some listeners, after a second of hesitation, slipped from their chairs onto the prie-Dieu. Others believed that it was necessary to follow their example so that, step by step, without another noise than the creak of near, without another noise than the crunch of a few chairs, the whole audience was soon on their knees. Paneloux then straightened up, took a deep breath and resumed in an increasingly accentuated tone: "If, today, the plague is watching you, it is that the time to think has come. The righteous cannot fear this, but the wicked are right to tremble. In the huge barn of the universe, the relentless plague will beat human wheat until the straw is separated from the grain. There will be more straw than grain, more called than chosen, and this misfortune was not wanted by God. For too long this world has made do with evil, for too long it has relied on divine mercy. It was enough to repent, everything was allowed. And to repent, everyone felt strong. When the time comes, we would certainly experience it. Until then, the easiest thing was to let go, divine mercy would do the rest. Well, it couldn't last. God who for so long bent over the men of this city his face of pity, tired of waiting, disappointed in his eternal hope, has just looked away. Deprived of the light of God, here we are for a long time in the darkness of the plague! Someone in the room snorted, like an impatient horse. After a short pause, the father continued, in a lower tone: "We read in the Golden Legend that in the days of King Humbert, in Lombardy, Italy was ravaged by a plague so violent that hardly the living were they enough to bury the dead and this plague raged especially in Rome and Pavia. And a good angel appeared visibly, who gave orders to the bad angel who wore a hunting spear and he ordered him to strike the houses; and as many times as a house was beaten, as many died as they left. "Paneloux stretched out his two short arms here in the direction of the square, as if he were showing something behind the moving curtain of the rain:" My brothers, he said forcefully, it is the same deadly hunt that runs today in our streets. See it, this angel of the plague, beautiful like Lucifer and brilliant like the evil itself, raised above your roofs, the right hand carrying the red spear at the level of its head, the left hand indicating the one of your houses. At the moment, perhaps, his finger stretches out towards your door, the spike echoes on the wood; just now, the plague enters your home, sits in your room, and waits for your return. She is there, patient, and attentive, assured as the very order of the world. This hand she will hold out to you, no earthly power and not even, know it well, vain human science can't make you avoid it. And beaten in the bloody area of pain, you will be thrown back with the straw. "Here the father took on the image even more magnificently pathetic of the plague. He spoke of the huge piece of wood spinning above the city, striking at random and rising bloodied, finally scattering blood and human pain "for sowing that would prepare the harvests of the truth". At the end of his long period, Father Paneloux stopped, his hair on his forehead, his body agitated by a tremor that his hands communicated to the pulpit and resumed, more quietly, but in an accusing tone: "Yes, the time to think. You thought it would be enough for you to visit God on Sunday to be free from your days. You thought that a few genuflections would pay enough for your criminal recklessness. But God is not lukewarm. These spaced relationships were not enough for his devouring tenderness. He wanted to see you longer, it's his way of loving you and, frankly, it's the only way to love. This is why, tired of waiting for your coming, he let the scourge visit you as he has visited all the cities of sin since men have a history. You now know what sin is, as Cain and his sons knew, those before the flood, those of Sodom and Gomorrah, Pharaoh and Job and also all the accursed. And like all of them have done, it's a new way of looking at people and things since the day this city closed its walls around you and the scourge. You know now, and finally, that you have to get to the point. Now a damp wind was sweeping under the nave and the candle flames curled sizzling. A thick smell of wax, coughs, and a sneeze went up to Father Paneloux who, returning to his presentation with a subtlety which was much appreciated, resumed in a calm voice: "Many of you, I know, wonder precisely where I'm coming from. I want to bring you to the truth and teach you how to rejoice, despite everything I have said. The time is no longer when advice, a fraternal hand were the means to push you towards good. Today, the truth is an order. And the way to salvation is a red spear that shows you and pushes you there. It is here, my brothers, that the divine mercy finally manifests, which has put good and evil in everything, anger and pity, pestilence, and salvation. This very plague which bruises you, it lifts you up and shows you the way. "Long ago, Christians in Abyssinia saw the plague as an effective means of divine origin to gain eternity. Those who were not wounded wrapped themselves in the sheets of the plague victims in order to die certainly. No doubt this fury of salvation is not recommendable. It marks an unfortunate rush, very close to pride. One should not be in a hurry than God and everything that claims to accelerate the unchanging order, which He established once and for all, leads to heresy. But, at least, this example has its lesson. To our more discerning minds, it only highlights that exquisite glow of eternity that lies at the bottom of all suffering. This light illuminates the twilight paths that lead to deliverance. It manifests the divine will which, without failure, transforms evil into good. Even today, through this journey of death, anguish, and clamor, it guides us towards essential silence and towards the principle of all life. This, my brothers, is the immense consolation that I wanted to bring to you so that it is not only words that chastise you to take away from here, but also a verb that soothes. We felt that Paneloux had finished. Outside, the rain had stopped. A sky mixed with water and sun poured a younger light on the square. From the street rose noises of voices, vehicle slides, all the language of a city waking up. The listeners discreetly gathered their belongings in a muffled stir. The father spoke again however and said that after having shown the divine Origin of the plague and the punitive character of this plague, he was finished and that he would not call for his conclusion to an eloquence which would be inappropriate, touching such a tragic subject. It seemed to him that everything should be clear to everyone. He only recalled that on the occasion of the Great Plague in Marseille, the columnist Mathieu Marais complained of being plunged into hell, to live thus without help and without hope. Well! Mathieu Marais was blind! Never more than today, on the contrary, did Father Paneloux feel the divine help and the Christian hope which were offered to all. He hoped against all hope that, despite the horror of these days and the cries of the dying, our fellow citizens would address to heaven the only word that was Christian and that was love. God would do the rest. This sermon had an effect on our fellow citizens, it is difficult to say. Mr. Othon, the examining magistrate, declared to Doctor Rieux that he had found Father Paneloux's statement "absolutely irrefutable". But not everyone had such a categorical opinion. Simply, the sermon made more sensitive to some the vague idea that they had been sentenced to an unimaginable imprisonment for an unknown crime. And while some continued their small life and adapted to confinement, for others, on the contrary, their only idea was therefore to escape from this prison. People had first agreed to be cut off from the outside as they would have accepted any temporary annoyance that would disturb only a few of their habits. But, suddenly aware of a sort of sequestration, under the cover of the sky where summer was beginning to sizzle, they confusedly felt that this seclusion threatened their whole life and, when evening came, the energy that they regained with freshness sometimes threw them into desperate acts. First of all, and whether or not by coincidence, it was from this Sunday that there was in our town a kind of fear general enough and deep enough that we could suspect that our fellow citizens were really starting to realize their situation. From this point of view, the climate in which we lived in our city was slightly modified. But, in truth, was the change in the climate or in the hearts, that is the question. A few days after the preaching, Rieux, who was commenting on this event with Grand, on his way to the outskirts, struck a man waddling in front of them in the night, without trying to move forward. At the same time, the lampposts of our city, which were lit more and more later, suddenly shone. The high lamp behind the walkers suddenly lit up the man who was laughing quietly, eyes closed. On his whitish face, distended by a mute hilarity, the sweat flowed in large drops. They passed. - He's crazy, said Grand. Rieux, who had just taken his arm to train him, felt that the employee was shaking with irritation. - There will soon be only crazy people in our walls, said Rieux. Fatigue helping, he felt his throat dry. - Let's drink something. In the little cafe they entered, which was lit by a single lamp above the counter, people were talking in low voices, for no apparent reason, in thick, reddish air. At the counter, Grand, to the doctor's surprise, ordered an alcohol which he drank in one gulp and which he declared to be strong. Then he wanted to go out. Outside, it seemed to Rieux that the night was full of groans. Somewhere in the dark sky, above the lampposts, a dull whistle reminded him of the invisible plague which tirelessly stirred the hot air. - Fortunately, fortunately, said Grand. Rieux wondered what he meant. - Fortunately, said the other, I have my job. - Yes, said Rieux, it's an advantage. And determined not to listen to the hiss, he asked Grand if he was happy with the job. - Well, I think I'm on the right track. - You still have some for a long time? Great seemed to come alive, the heat of the alcohol passed through his voice. - I do not know. But the question is not there, doctor, it is not the question, no. In the dark, Rieux guessed that he was waving his arms. He seemed to be preparing something which came abruptly, with volubility: - What I want, you see, doctor, is that the day the manuscript arrives at the publisher, the latter gets up after reading it and said to his collaborators: "Gentlemen, hats off! This sudden statement surprised Rieux. It seemed to him that his companion was making the gesture of discovering himself, bringing his hand to his head, and bringing his arm horizontally. Up there, the bizarre whistle seemed to pick up with more force. - Yes, said Grand, it has to be perfect. Although little aware of the uses of literature, Rieux nevertheless had the impression that things should not happen as simply and that, for example, publishers, in their offices, should be bareheaded. But, in fact, you never knew, and Rieux preferred to be silent. Despite himself, he listened to the mysterious rumors of the plague. We were approaching the Grand district and as it was a little elevated, a light breeze refreshed them which at the same time cleaned the city of all its noises. Grand, however, continued to speak, and Rieux did not understand everything the good man said. He only understood that the work in question already had many pages, but that the pain the author took to bring it to perfection was very painful for him. "Evenings, whole weeks on a word... and sometimes a simple conjunction. Here Grand stopped and took the doctor by a button on his coat. The words stumbled out of his badly stocked mouth. - Please understand, doctor. It's pretty easy to choose between but and and. It's already more difficult to choose between and then. The difficulty increases with then and then. But surely, the hardest part is knowing whether to put on or not. - Yes, said Rieux, I understand. And he set out again. The other looked confused, came up to him again. "Excuse me," he mumbled. I don't know what I like tonight! Rieux tapped him lightly on the shoulder and told him that he wanted to help him and that his story interested him very much. Grand seemed a little reassured and, arriving in front of the house, after hesitating, offered the doctor to come up for a moment. Rieux accepted. In the dining room, Grand invited him to sit at a table full of papers covered with erasures in microscopic writing. - Yes, that's it, said Grand to the doctor who was questioning him. But do you want to drink something? I have some wine. Rieux refused. He was looking at the sheets of paper. - Don't look, said Grand. This is my first sentence. It gives me trouble, a lot of trouble. He too was contemplating all these leaves and his hand seemed invincibly attracted to one of them which he raised transparently before the light bulb without a lampshade. The leaf was trembling in his hand. Rieux noticed that the employee's forehead was moist. "Sit down," he said, "and read it to me. The other looked at him and smiled with a kind of gratitude. - Yes, he said I think I want to. He waited a bit, still looking at the sheet, then sat down. Rieux listened at the same time to a sort of confused buzz which, in the city, seemed to respond to the whistles of the scourge. He had, at this precise moment, an extraordinarily acute perception of this city which lay at his feet, of the closed world which it formed and the terrible howls which it stifled in the night. Grand's voice rose in a low voice: "On a beautiful morning in May, an elegant amazon was crossing the flowery paths of Bois-de Boulogne on a superb chestnut mare. Silence returned and with it the indistinct rumor of the suffering city. Grand had put the sheet down and was still contemplating it. After a moment, he looked up: - What do you think? Rieux replied that this beginning made him curious to know the rest. But the other said with animation that this point of view was not the right one. He clapped his papers with the back of his hand. - This is only an approximation. When I have managed to render the picture that I have in my imagination perfectly, when my sentence looks like this trotting walk, one-two-three, one-two-three, then the rest will be easier and above all the illusion will be such, from the start, that it will be possible to say: "Low hat! But, for that, he still had work to do. He would never consent to deliver this sentence as is to a printer. Because, despite the contentment that she sometimes gave him, he realized that she did not quite stick to reality yet and that, to a certain extent, she kept an ease of tone that related her from afar, but who looked like it all the same, in a cliché. That was, at least, the meaning of what he said when we heard men running under the windows. Rieux stood up. - You will see what I do with it, said Grand, and turned to the window, he added: "When it is all over." But the hurried footsteps resumed. Rieux was already coming down and two men passed him when he was in the street. Apparently, they were going towards the gates of the city. Some of our fellow citizens in fact, losing their heads between the heat and the plague, had already allowed themselves to go to violence and had tried to deceive the vigilance of the dams to flee out of the city. Others, like Rambert, also tried to escape this atmosphere of emerging panic, but with more stubbornness and skill, if not more success. Rambert had initially continued his official proceedings. According to what he said, he had always thought that stubbornness triumphed over everything and, from a certain point of view, it was his job to be resourceful. He had therefore visited a large number of officials and people whose competence was not usually discussed. In this case, however, this competence was of no use to them. They were, most of the time, men who had precise and well-classified ideas on everything related to banking, or export, or citrus fruits, or even the wine trade; who had indisputable knowledge in litigation or insurance issues, not to mention solid degrees and obvious good will. And even the most striking thing about all of them was the goodwill. But in matters of plague, their knowledge was almost zero. Before each of them, however, and whenever possible, Rambert had pleaded his case. The gist of his argument was always to say that he was a stranger to our city and that, therefore, his case needed special consideration. In general, the journalist's interlocutors readily accepted this point. But they ordinarily represented to him that this was also the case for a number of people and that, therefore, his business was not as special as he imagined. To which Rambert could answer that it did not change anything at the bottom of his argument, he was told that this changed something about the administrative difficulties which opposed any favorable measure which might create what was called, with an expression of great repugnance, a precedent.

According to the classification that Rambert proposed to Doctor Rieux, this kind of reasoners constituted the category of formalists. Beside them, one could still find the well-spoken, who assured the plaintiff that none of this could last and who, lavish good advice when asked for decisions, consoled Rambert by deciding that he was only a temporary boredom. There were also the important ones, who asked their visitor to leave a note summarizing his case and who informed him that they would rule on this case; the futile, who offered him accommodation vouchers or addresses for economic pensions; the methodics, who had a card filled out and then classified it; the overwhelmed, who raised their arms, and the unwelcome, who looked away; Finally, there were the traditional ones, by far the most numerous, who indicated to Rambert another office or a new step to take. The journalist was thus exhausted in visits and he had taken a fair idea of what could be a town hall or a prefecture, by dint of waiting on a moleskin bench in front of large posters inviting to subscribe to treasury bonds, exempt from taxes, or to enlist in the colonial army, by dint of entering offices where faces were as easily predicted as the zipper filing cabinet and the shelves of files. The advantage, as Rambert said to Rieux, with a hint of bitterness, is that all of this obscured the real situation. The progress of the plague practically escaped him. Not to mention that the days passed thus faster and, in the situation in which the whole city was, it could be said that each day passed brought each man closer, provided he did not die, to the end of his ordeals. Rieux had to admit that this was true, but that it was a bit too general. At one point, Rambert conceived hope. He had received a blank information bulletin from the prefecture, which he was asked to fill out exactly. The newsletter was concerned about his identity, marital status, resources, past and present, and what was called his resume. He had the impression that it was an investigation intended to identify the cases of people likely to be returned to their habitual residence. Some confused information, collected in an office, confirmed this impression. But, after a few specific steps, he managed to find the service that had sent the bulletin and he was then told that this information had been collected "for the case". - For what? asked Rambert. He was told that it was in case he fell ill and died of the plague, so that he could, on the one hand, warn his family and, on the other hand, know whether to charge the costs of city budget hospital or if one could expect reimbursement from loved ones. Obviously, this proved that he was not entirely separated from the one who was waiting for him, society taking care of them. But that was no consolation. What was more remarkable, and Rambert remarked accordingly, was the way in which, at the height of a disaster, an office could continue its service and take initiatives from another time, often without the knowledge of higher authorities, for the only reason that it was made for this service. The period that followed was for Rambert both the easiest and the most difficult. It was a period of numbness. He had seen all the offices, made all the steps, the exits on that side were blocked for the moment. He then wandered from coffee to coffee. He would sit in the morning on a terrace in front of a glass of lukewarm beer, read a newspaper with the hope of finding some signs of an imminent end to the disease, look in the face at passers-by in the street, turned away in disgust from their expression of sadness and after having read, for the hundredth time, the signs of the stores which faced him, the advertisement of the great aperitifs that already no longer served, he got up and walked randomly in the streets city lights. From solitary walks in cafes and from cafes to restaurants, he thus reached evening. Rieux caught sight of him, one evening precisely, at the door of a cafe where the journalist hesitated to enter. He seemed to make up his mind and went to sit at the back of the room. It was that hour when in the cafes, in higher order, the delay in giving light was delayed as much as possible. The twilight invaded the room like gray water, the pink of the setting sky was reflected in the windowpanes, and the marble of the tables glistened weakly in the beginning darkness. In the middle of the deserted room, Rambert looked like a lost shadow and Rieux thought it was time for his abandonment. But it was also the time when all the prisoners in this city felt theirs and something had to be done to hasten their release. Rieux turned away. Rambert also spent long moments in the station. Access to the platforms was prohibited. But the waiting rooms that were reached from the outside remained open, and sometimes beggars settled there on hot days because they were shady and cool. Rambert came to read old timetables, signs forbidding spitting and the rules of the train police. Then he would sit in a corner. The room was dark. An old cast-iron stove had been cooling for months, in the middle of the decals in eight of old watering. On the wall, some posters pleaded for a happy and free life in Bandol or Cannes. Rambert was touching here this kind of awful freedom that we find at the bottom of destitution. The images that were most difficult for him to bear at the time, at least according to what he said to Rieux, were those of Paris. A landscape of old stones and waters, the pigeons of the Palais-Royal, the Gare du Nord, the deserted districts of the Pantheon, and some other places in a city that he did not know he had loved so much pursued Rambert and I prevented them from doing anything specific. Rieux only thought that he identified these images with those of his love. And the day Rambert told him that he liked waking up at four in the morning and thinking about his city, the doctor had no trouble translating from the depths of his own experience that he liked to imagine then the woman whom 'he had left. It was the hour, in fact, when he could seize her. At four o'clock in the morning, we usually do nothing and sleep, even if the night was a night of betrayal. Yes, we sleep at this hour, and this is reassuring since the great desire of a worried heart is to have endlessly the being he loves or to be able to immerse this being, when the time of absence has come , in a dreamless sleep that cannot end until the day of the meeting. Shortly after the preaching, the heat began. We were arriving at the end of June. In the aftermath of the late rains that had preached on Sunday, summer suddenly burst into the sky and over the houses. A great, hot wind rose first, which blew for a day and dried out the walls. The sun set. Continuous waves of heat and light flooded the city all day long. Apart from the arcaded streets and the apartments, it seemed that there was not a point in the city which was not placed in the most blinding reverberation. The sun was chasing our fellow citizens on every street corner and, if they stopped, it would hit them. As these first heats coincided with a skyrocketing increase in the number of victims, which amounted to nearly seven hundred a week, a kind of dejection took possession of the city. Among the suburbs, between the flat streets and the houses with terraces, the animation decreased and, in this district where people still lived on their doorstep, all the doors were closed and the shutters closed, without one being able to know if it was the plague or the sun that we heard protecting ourselves from. From a few houses, however, came groans. Previously, when this happened, we often saw curious people standing in the street, listening. But, after these long alerts, it seemed that everyone's heart had hardened, and everyone was walking or living alongside complaints as if they had been the natural language of men. The brawls at the gates, during which the gendarmes had to use their weapons, created a deaf agitation. There were surely wounded, but there was talk of dead in the city where everything was exaggerated by the effect of heat and fear. It is true, in any case, that the discontent did not cease growing, that our authorities had feared the worst and seriously considered the measures to be taken in the event that this population, maintained under the scourge, would have revolted. The newspapers published decrees which renewed the ban on going out and threatened prison terms with offenders. Patrols roamed the city. Often, in the deserted and overheated streets, we saw advancing, first announced by the sound of hooves on the paving stones, guards on horseback who passed between rows of closed windows. The patrol gone; a heavy suspicious silence fell on the threatened city. From time to time, shots were fired from special teams tasked, by a recent order, with killing dogs and cats that might have communicated fleas. These dry detonations contributed to put in the city an atmosphere of alert. In the warmth and the silence, and for the terrified hearts of our fellow citizens, everything took on greater importance. The colors of the sky and the smells of the earth which make the passage of the seasons were, for the first time, sensitive to all. Everyone understood with dread that the heat would help the epidemic, and at the same time, everyone saw that summer was coming. The cry of the swifts in the evening sky grew fainter over the city. He was no longer able to measure up to these June twilights which are rolling back the horizon in our country. The flowers on the markets no longer came in buds, they were already bursting, and, after the morning sale, their petals littered the dusty sidewalks. It was clearly seen that spring had died out, that it had lavished itself in thousands of flowers bursting everywhere and that it was now going to doze off, to crash slowly under the double weighing of the plague and heat. For all of our fellow citizens, this summer sky, these streets that turned pale with the tones of dust and boredom, had the same threatening meaning as the hundreds of dead whose city grew daily. The incessant sunshine, these hours of sleep and vacation, no longer invited as before to the feasts of water and flesh. They sounded hollow on the contrary in the closed and silent city. They had lost the copper shine of happy seasons. The sun of the plague extinguished all the colors and made flee all joy. This was one of the great revolutions of the disease. All of our fellow citizens usually welcomed summer with joy. The city then opened towards the sea and poured its youth on the beaches. That summer, on the contrary, the near sea was prohibited, and the body was no longer entitled to its joys. What to do in these conditions? Tarrou is still the most faithful image of our life then. He followed, of course, the progress of the plague in general, noting precisely that a turning point in the epidemic had been marked by the radio when it no longer announced hundreds of deaths per week, but eighty, one hundred seven and a hundred and twenty deaths a day. "The newspapers and the authorities are playing with the plague at the very end. They imagine they are taking points away from him because one hundred and thirty is less than nine hundred and ten. He also evoked the pathetic or spectacular aspects of the epidemic, like this woman who, in a deserted district, with closed shutters, had suddenly opened a window, above him, and uttered two loud cries before folding down the shutters on the thick shadow of the room. But he also noted that the mint lozenges had disappeared from pharmacies because many people sucked them to guard against possible contagion. He also continued to observe his favorite characters. We learned that the little old cat was also living in tragedy. One morning, indeed, gunfire had broken out and, as Tarrou wrote, a few spits of lead had killed most of the cats and terrorized the others, who had left the street. The same day, the little old man had gone out on the balcony at the usual time, had marked a certain surprise, had bent over, had scrutinized the end of the street, and had resigned himself to waiting. His hand was hitting the balcony grill. He had waited again, crumbled a bit of paper, returned, gone out again, then, after a while, he had suddenly disappeared, angrily closing his patio doors behind him. In the following days, the same scene was repeated, but one could read on the features of the little old man an increasingly manifest sadness and dismay. After a week, Tarrou waited in vain for the daily apparition and the windows remained stubbornly closed in understandable grief. "In plague, no spitting on cats" was the conclusion of the notebooks. On the other hand, when Tarrou came home in the evening, he was always sure to meet in the hall the dark figure of the night porter who wandered up and down. The latter kept reminding everyone that he had foreseen what was happening. To Tarrou, who admitted to having heard him predict a misfortune, but who reminded him of his idea of an earthquake, the old guard replied: "Ah! if it was an earthquake! A good shake and we no longer talk about it ... We count the dead, the living, and voila. But this crap from sickness! Even those who don't have it in their hearts. The director was no less overwhelmed. At first, the travelers, prevented from leaving the city, had been kept at the hotel by the closure of the city. But little by little, the epidemic continuing, many preferred to stay with friends. And the same reasons that had filled all the rooms in the hotel had kept them empty since then, since there were no new travelers arriving in our city. Tarrou remained one of the rare tenants and the manager never missed an opportunity to point out to him that, without his desire to be pleasant to his last customers, he would have closed his establishment long ago. He often asked Tarrou to assess the likely duration of the epidemic "They say, remarked Tarrou, that the cold thwarts these kinds of illnesses. The director panicked, "But it's never really cold here, sir. Anyway, that would take us several more months. He was sure, moreover, that travelers would stay away from the city for a long time. This plague was the ruin of tourism. In the restaurant, after a short absence, we saw Mr. Othon, the owl man, reappear, but only followed by the two learned dogs. Information obtained, the woman had looked after and buried her own mother and continues at this moment her quarantine. - I don't like it, said the director to Tarrou. Quarantine or not, she is suspect, and so are they. Tarrou pointed out to him that, from this point of view, everyone was suspect. But the other was categorical and had very clear views on the question: - No, sir, neither you nor I are suspect. They are. But Mr. Othon did not change for so little and, this time, the plague was at his expense. In the same way, he entered the dining room, sat before his children, and always spoke distinguished and hostile words to them. Alone, the little boy had changed his appearance. Dressed hostile. Alone, the little boy had changed his appearance. Dressed in black like his sister, a little more packed in on himself, he seemed the little shadow of his father. The night watchman, who did not like Mr. Othon, had said to Tarrou: - Ah! that one, he'll die fully clothed. Like that, no need for a toilet. It will go straight. The sermon of Paneloux was also reported, but with the following comment: "I understand this sympathetic ardor. At the beginning of the plagues and when they are finished, we always do a little rhetoric. In the first case, the habit is not yet lost and, in the second, it has already returned. It is in times of misfortune that you get used to the truth, that is to say, to silence. Let's wait. "Tarrou finally noted that he had had a long conversation with Doctor Rieux which he only recalled that it had had good results, pointed out in this connection the light brown color of the eyes of Mrs. Rieux mother, stated strangely about him that 'a look where so much kindness was read would always be stronger than the plague, and finally devoted fairly long passages to the old asthmatic cared for by Rieux. He had gone to see him, with the doctor, after their interview. The old man had greeted Tarrou with sneers and rubbing his hands. He was in bed, leaning against his pillow, above his two pots of peas: "Ah! yet another, he said when he saw Tarrou. The world is upside down, more doctors than sick people. It's going fast, huh? The priest is right, it is well deserved. The next day, Tarrou returned without warning. If we believe his notebooks, the old asthmatic, a mercer by trade, had judged at fifty that he had done enough. He had gone to bed and hadn't risen since. His asthma was, however, reconciled with standing. A small income had brought him to the seventy-five years that he was carrying cheerfully. He couldn't bear the sight of a watch and, in fact, there was not one in his whole house. "A watch," he said, "is expensive and stupid. He assessed the time, and especially the mealtime, which was the only one that mattered to him, with his two pots, one of which was full of peas when he woke up. He filled the other, pea by pea, with the same applied and regular movement. He thus found his bearings in a day measured at the pot. "All fifteen pots," he said, "I need my snack." It's very simple. According to his wife, moreover, he had given signs of his vocation at a very young age. Nothing, in fact, had ever interested him, neither his work, nor his friends, nor the cafe, nor the music, neither the women, nor the walks. He had never left his city, except one day when, forced to go to Algiers for family matters, he stopped at the station closest to Oran, unable to push the adventure further. He had returned home by the first train. To Tarrou, who had seemed to be astonished at the cloistered life he led, he had roughly explained that according to religion, the first half of a man's life was an ascent and the other half a descent, that in the descent the days of the man no longer belonged to him, that they could be taken away from him at any time, that he could therefore do nothing with it and that the best precisely was to n ' do nothing. The contradiction, moreover, did not frighten him, because he had said shortly after to Tarrou that surely God did not exist, since, otherwise, the priests would be useless. But, to a few reflections which followed, Tarrou understood that this philosophy held closely to the mood given to him by frequent quests in his parish. But what finished the portrait of the old man is a wish that seems deep and that he made several times in front of his interlocutor: he hoped to die very old. "Is he a saint? Wondered Tarrou. And he replied, "Yes, if holiness is a collection of habits. "But, at the same time, Tarrou undertook the rather meticulous description of a day in the stenched city and thus gave a fair idea of the occupations and the life of our fellow citizens during this summer:" No one laughs but drunkards, said Tarrou , and they laugh too much. "Then he began his description:" In the early morning, light breaths roam the still deserted city. At this hour, which is between the dead of the night and the agonies of the day, it seems that the plague suspends its effort for an instant and catches its breath. All the shops are closed. But in some places, the sign "Closed due to plague" attests that they will not open later with the others. Newspaper vendors still asleep do not shout the news, but, leaning against the corner of the streets, offer their merchandise to the streetlamps in a gesture of sleepwalkers. Earlier, awakened by the first trams, they will spread throughout the city, stretching out at arm's length the leaves where the word "Plague" bursts out. "Will there be an autumn of plague? Professor B... answers: No." "One hundred and twenty-four dead, this is the result of the ninety-fourth day of plague." "Despite the paper crisis which is becoming more and more acute and which has forced certain periodicals to decrease the number of their pages, another newspaper was created: the Courier of the Epidemic, which gives itself the task of "Inform our fellow citizens, in the interests of scrupulous objectivity, of the progress or setbacks of the disease; to provide them with the most authoritative testimony on the future of the epidemic; to lend the support of its columns to all those, known or unknown, who are ready to fight against the scourge; to support the morale of the population, to transmit the directives of the authorities and, in a word, to group all the good wills to fight effectively against the evil which strikes us ". In reality, this newspaper very quickly confined itself to publishing announcements of new products, infallible for preventing the plague. "Around six in the morning, all these newspapers start to sell in the queues that settle at the doors of the stores, more than an hour before their opening, then in the trams arriving, crowded, from the suburbs. Trams have become the only means of transport and they are barely moving forward, their steps and their guardrails crammed full. Oddly enough, however, all occupants, as far as possible, turn their backs to avoid mutual contagion. At the stops, the tram dumps a load of men and women, eager to leave and be alone. Frequently erupting scenes are caused by bad humor alone, which becomes chronic. "After the passage of the first trams, the city wakes up little by little, the first breweries open their doors on counters loaded with signs:" No more coffee "," Bring your sugar ", etc. Then the shops open, the streets come alive. At the same time, the light rises, and the heat gradually sinks the July sky. This is the time when those who do nothing risk themselves on the boulevards. Most seem to have taken on the task of warding off the plague with the display of their luxury. Around 11 a.m. every day, on the main arteries, a parade of young men and women where you can experience this passion for living that grows in the midst of great misfortunes. If the epidemic spreads, so will the moral. We will see the Milanese saturnalia at the edge of the graves. "At noon, the restaurants fill up in the blink of an eye. Very quickly, small groups that could not find space formed at their door. The sky begins to lose its light due to excess heat. In the shade of the big blinds, the food candidates wait their turn, at the edge of the crisp street. If restaurants are overrun, it's because they greatly simplify the food problem. But they leave the anxiety of contagion intact. Guests waste long minutes patiently wiping their silverware. Not long ago, some restaurants were saying, "Here, the cutlery is scalded." But little by little, they gave up all advertising since the customers were forced to come. The client, moreover, spends readily. The fine wines or supposed such, the most expensive supplements, it is the beginning of a frantic race. It is also said that scenes of panic erupted in a restaurant because a discomforting customer had turned pale, got up, faltered, and quickly got out. "Around two o'clock the city gradually empties, and this is the moment when silence, dust, sun and plague meet on the street. All along the big gray houses the heat flows constantly. These are long prisoner hours that end in fiery evenings crumbling over the populous and chattering city during the first days of the heat, from time to time, and without anyone knowing why, the evenings were deserted. But now the first freshness brings relaxation, if not hope. They all take to the streets, giddy to talk, quarrel or lust after each other and under the red July sky the city, loaded with couples and clamors, drifts towards the breathless night. In vain, every evening on the boulevards, an inspired old man, wearing felt and lavallière, crosses the crowd, repeating without ceasing: "God is great, come to him", all rush on the contrary towards something they do not know well or which seems to them more urgent than God. In the beginning, when they believed it was a disease like any other, religion was in its place. But when they saw that it was serious, they remembered the enjoyment. All the anguish which is painted in the daytime on the faces is then resolved, in the fiery and dusty twilight, in a sort of haggard excitement, an awkward freedom which infects a whole people. "And I too am like them. But what! death is nothing for men like me. It's an event that proves them right. It was Tarrou who asked Rieux for the interview he talks about in his notebooks. The evening when Rieux was waiting for him, the doctor rightly looked at his mother, sitting quietly in the corner of the dining room, on a chair. She spent her days there when the care of the household no longer occupied her. Hands on her knees, she waited. Rieux wasn't even sure if it was him, she was waiting for. But, however, something changed in his mother's face when he appeared. Everything that a hard-working life had put into silence seemed to come alive then. Then she fell into silence. That evening, she was looking out the window, in the now deserted street. Night lighting was cut by two-thirds. And, from time to time, a very weak lamp put some reflections in the shadows of the city. - Are we going to keep the lighting down for the whole plague? said Mrs. Rieux. - Probably. - As long as it doesn't last until winter. It would be sad, then. - Yes, said Rieux. He saw his mother's gaze on his forehead. He knew that the worry and overwork of the past few days had left his face. - Didn't it work today? said Mrs. Rieux. - Oh! as usual. As usual! That is to say, the new serum sent by Paris seemed to be less effective than the first and the statistics were mounting. We still did not have the opportunity to inoculate the preventive serums elsewhere than in families already affected. Industrial quantities would have been necessary to generalize its use. Most buboes refused to pierce, as if the season for their hardening had come, and they tortured the sick. Since the day before, there had been two cases of a new form of the epidemic in the city. The plague then became pulmonary. The same day, during a meeting, the exhausted doctors, in front of a disoriented prefect, had asked for and obtained new measures to avoid the contagion that was spreading from mouth to mouth, in plague. As usual, we still didn't know anything. He looked at his mother. The beautiful brown look brought back years of tenderness. - Are you afraid, mother? - At my age, we no longer fear much. - The days are very long and I'm never there again. - I don't mind waiting for you if I know you have to come. And when you're not around, I think about what you're doing. Do you have any news? Do you have any news? - Yes, all is well if I believe the last telegram. But I know she says that to calm me down. The doorbell rings. The doctor smiled at his mother and went to open it. In the half-light of the landing, Tarrou looked like a big bear dressed in gray. Rieux made the visitor sit down in front of his desk. He himself stood behind his chair. They were separated by the only light in the room on the desk. - I know, said Tarrou without preamble, that I can speak straight with you. Rieux silently approved. - In a fortnight or a month, you will be of no use here, you are overwhelmed by events. - It's true, said Rieux. - The organization of the health service is poor. You are short of people and time. Rieux still recognized that it was the truth. - I learned that the prefecture is planning a kind of civil service to force able-bodied men to participate in the general rescue. - You are well informed. But the discontent is already great, and the prefect hesitates. - Why not ask for volunteers? - We did, but the results were meager. - We did it officially, a little without believing it. What they lack is imagination. They are never on the scale of plagues. And the remedies they imagine are barely up to a common cold. If we let them, they will perish and we with them. - It is likely, said Rieux. I must say that they also thought of the prisoners, however, for what I will call the big jobs. - I would prefer that they were free men. - Me too. But why, in short? - I hate death sentences. Rieux looked at Tarrou: - So? he says. - So, I have an organizational plan for voluntary health facilities. Let me take care of it and leave the administration aside. Besides, she is overwhelmed. I have friends everywhere and they will make the first nucleus. And of course, I will participate. - Of course, said Rieux, you can imagine that I accept with joy. We need help, especially in this business. I take care of getting the idea accepted at the prefecture. Besides, they have no choice. But ... Rieux is thinking. - But this work can be deadly, you know that. And in any case, I must warn you. Have you thought it through? Tarrou looked at him with gray eyes. - What do you think of Paneloux's preaching, doctor? The question was asked naturally and Rieux answered it naturally. - I have lived too much in hospitals to like the idea of collective punishment. But, you know, Christians sometimes speak like this, without ever actually thinking it. They are better than they appear. - You think, however, like Paneloux, that the plague has its beneficence, that it opens your eyes, that it forces you to think! The doctor shook his head impatiently. - Like all the diseases of this world. But what is true of the evils of this world is also true of the plague. This can be used to grow a few. However, when you see the misery and the pain it brings, you have to be crazy, blind, or cowardly to resign yourself to the plague. Rieux had barely raised his voice. But Tarrou waved as if to calm him down. He was smiling. "Yes," said Rieux, shrugging his shoulders. But you didn't answer me. Have you thought about it? Tarrou moved a little into his chair and put his head in the light. - Do you believe in God, doctor? The question was still asked naturally. But this time, Rieux hesitated. - No, but what does that mean? I'm in the night, and I try to see clearly. It's been a long time since I stopped finding this original. - Isn't that what separates you from Paneloux? - I do not believe. Paneloux is a man of studies. He has not seen enough die and that is why he speaks for the truth. But the least country priest who administers his parishioners and who has heard the breath of a dying man thinks like me. He would cure misery before wanting to demonstrate its excellence. Rieux stood up, his face now in the shadows. "Let's leave that," he said, "since you don't want to answer. Tarrou smiles without moving from his chair. - Can I answer with a question? In turn the doctor smiled: "You like mystery," he said. Let's go. - Here, said Tarrou. Why do you show yourself so much devotion since you don't believe in God? Your answer may help me answer myself. Without going out of the shadows, the doctor said that he had already answered, that if he believed in an almighty God, he would stop healing men, leaving him this care. But that nobody in the world, no, not even Paneloux who believed to believe in it, believed in a God of this kind, since nobody abandoned himself completely and that in that at least, he, Rieux, believed to be on the way to the truth, by fighting against creation as it was. - Ah! Said Tarrou, so what is your idea of your job? "Roughly," replied the doctor, returning to the light. Tarrou hissed softly and the doctor looked at him. - Yes, he said, you tell yourself that it takes pride. But I only have the pride I need, believe me. I don't know what awaits me or what will come after all this. At the moment there are sick people and they must be cured. Then they will think and so will I. But the most urgent thing is to cure them. I defend them as best I can, that's all. - Against whom? Rieux turned to the window. He could see the sea in the distance, a more obscure condensation of the horizon. He only experienced his fatigue and at the same time struggled against a sudden and unreasonable desire to indulge a little more in this singular man, but whom he felt brotherly. - I don't know, Tarrou, I swear I don't know. When I got into this job, I did it abstractly, in a way, because I needed it, because it was a situation like the others, one of those that young people are offering themselves. Maybe also because it was particularly difficult for a worker's son like me. And then we had to see him die. Do you know that there are people who refuse to die? Have you ever heard a woman shout, "Never! At the time of dying. I do. And then I realized that I couldn't get used to it. I was young and my disgust thought I was addressing the very order of the world. Since then I have become more modest. Simply put, I'm still not used to seeing death. I don't know anything more. But after all, ... Rieux was silent and sat down again. He felt dry mouth. - After all? said Tarrou gently. - After all..., said the doctor, and he hesitated again, looking at Tarrou attentively, it is something that a man like you can understand, can it not, but since the order of the world is regulated by death, perhaps it is better for God that one does not believe in him and that we fight with all our strength against death, without looking up at the sky where he is silent. - Yes, approved Tarrou, I can understand. But your victories will always be temporary, that's all. Rieux seemed to darken. - Always, I know it. This is no reason to stop fighting. - No, that's not a reason. But then I imagine what this plague must be for you. - Yes, said Rieux. An endless defeat. Tarrou stared at the doctor for a moment, then got up and walked heavily towards the door. And Rieux followed him. He was already joining him when Tarrou, who seemed to be looking at his feet, said to him: "Who taught you all that, doctor?" The answer came immediately: - Misery. Rieux opened the door of his office and, in the corridor, told Tarrou that he was coming down too, going to see one of his patients in the suburbs. Tarrou offered to accompany him and the doctor agreed. At the end of the corridor, they met Mrs Rieux to whom the doctor introduced Tarrou. - A friend, he said. - Oh! said Mrs. Rieux, I am very glad to know you. When she left, Tarrou turned around again. On the landing, the doctor tried in vain to make the timer work. The stairs remained plunged into the night. The doctor wondered if this was the effect of a new saving measure. But we couldn't know. For some time now, in homes and in the city, everything has been going haywire. Maybe it was just that the janitors, and our fellow citizens in general, were no longer taking care of anything. But the doctor did not have time to wonder further, for Tarrou's voice echoed behind him: - One more word, doctor, even if you seem ridiculous: you are absolutely right. Rieux shrugged for himself in the dark. - I don't know, really. But you, what do you know? - Oh! said the other without being moved, I have little to learn. The doctor stopped and Tarrou's foot behind him slipped on a step. Tarrou caught up by taking Rieux's shoulder. - Do you think you know everything about life? asked the latter. The answer came in the dark, carried by the same quiet voice: - Yes. When they came out onto the street, they realized it was quite late, maybe eleven o'clock. The city was mute, populated only by brushing. Far away, the tone of an ambulance rang. They got into the car and Rieux started the engine. "You will have to come to the hospital tomorrow for the preventive vaccine," he said. But, to finish and before entering this story, tell yourself that you have a one in three chance of leaving it. - These assessments do not make sense, doctor, you know as well as I do. A hundred years ago, an epidemic of plague killed all the inhabitants of a city of Persia, except precisely the washer of the deads who had never ceased to exercise his profession. - He kept his third chance, that's all, said Rieux in a suddenly muffled voice. But it is true that we still have everything to learn about this. They were now entering the suburbs. Lighthouses lit up the deserted streets. They stopped. In front of the car, Rieux asked Tarrou if he wanted to enter and the other said yes. A reflection of the sky lit up their faces. Rieux suddenly laughed in friendship: - Come on, Tarrou, he said, what makes you take care of this? - I do not know. My moral maybe. - And which one? - Comprehension. Tarrou turned to the house and Rieux no longer saw his face until they were with the old asthmatic. The next day, Tarrou set to work and assembled a first team which was to be followed by many others. The narrator's intention, however, is not to give these health facilities more importance than they once had. In its place, it is true that many of our fellow citizens would yield today to the temptation to exaggerate its role. But the narrator is rather tempted to believe that by giving too much importance to beautiful actions, we ultimately pay an indirect and powerful homage to evil. Because we let suppose then that these beautiful actions are so expensive only because they are rare, and that wickedness and indifference are much more frequent drivers in the actions of men. This is an idea that the narrator does not share. The evil in the world almost always comes from ignorance, and goodwill can do as much damage as wickedness if it is not enlightened. Men are often good than bad, and in truth that is not the question. But they ignore more or less, and this is called virtue or vice, the most vice desperate being that of ignorance which believes to know everything, and which then authorizes itself to kill. The murderer's soul is blind and there is no real kindness or beautiful love without all the clairvoyance possible. This is why our health facilities which were carried out thanks to Tarrou must be judged with objective satisfaction. This is why the narrator will not make himself the eloquent cantor of the will and a heroism to which he attaches only a reasonable importance. But he will continue to be the historian of the torn and demanding hearts that the plague then made to all our fellow citizens. Those who devoted themselves to health facilities did not have so much merit to do so, in fact, because they knew that it was the only thing to do and it was not to decide that which would have been incredible. These formations helped our fellow citizens to enter further into the plague and persuaded them in part that, since the disease was there, it was necessary to do what it was necessary to fight against it. Because the plague thus became the duty of some, it really appeared for what it was, that is to say everyone's business. This is good. But you don't praise a teacher for teaching that two and two make four. We may congratulate him on having chosen this beautiful profession. So let's say it was commendable that Tarrou and others had chosen to demonstrate that two and two made four rather than the opposite, but also say that this goodwill was common to them with the teacher, with all those who have the same heart than the teacher and who, for the honor of man, are more numerous than we think, it is at least the conviction of the narrator. He sees very clearly the objection that could be made to him, which is that these men were risking their lives. But there is always an hour in history when anyone who dares to say that two and two make four is punished with death. The teacher knows this well. And the question is not what reward or punishment awaits this reasoning. The question is whether two and two, yes or no, make four. For those of our fellow citizens who were risking their lives then, they had to decide whether or not they were in the plague and whether or not it was necessary to fight against it. Lots of new moralists in our town were going then, saying that nothing was for nothing and that it was necessary to kneel. And Tarrou, and Rieux, and their friends could answer this or that, but the conclusion was always what they knew: you had to fight this or that way and not kneel down. The whole point was to prevent as many men as possible from dying and to experience final separation. There was only one way to fight the plague. This truth was not admirable, it was only consistent. This is why it was natural for the old Castel to put all his confidence and energy into making serums on the spot, using makeshift equipment. Rieux and he hoped that a serum made with the cultures of the same microbe that infested the city would have more direct effectiveness than sera from outside, since the microbe differed slightly from the bacillus of the plague as it was classically defined. . Castel hoped to have his first serum soon enough. This is also why it was natural for Grand, who was not a hero, to now provide a sort of secretariat for health units. Part of the teams trained by Tarrou were dedicated to preventive assistance work in overcrowded areas. We tried to introduce the necessary hygiene, we counted the attics and cellars that the disinfection had not visited. Another part of the teams assisted the doctors in the home visits, ensured the transport of plague victims, and even, subsequently, in the absence of specialized personnel, drove the cars of the sick and the dead. All of this required logging and statistical work that Grand had agreed to do. From this point of view, and more than Rieux or Tarrou, the narrator believes that Grand was the real representative of this tranquil virtue that animated health facilities. He had said yes without hesitation, with the goodwill that was his. He had only asked to be helpful in small jobs. He was too old for the rest. From 6 p.m. to 8 p.m. he could give his time. And as Rieux thanked him warmly, he was surprised: "It is not the most difficult. There's the plague, you have to defend yourself, that's clear. Ah! if everything was so simple! And he came back to his sentence. Sometimes, in the evening, when the card work was finished, Rieux spoke with Grand. They had ended up mingling Tarrou with their conversation and Grand confided with an increasingly evident pleasure in his two companions. The latter followed with interest the patient work that Grand continued in the middle of the plague. They too, finally, found there a kind of relaxation. "How is the Amazon?" Tarrou often asked. And Grand invariably replied: "She trots, she trots", with a difficult smile. One evening, Grand said that he had definitely abandoned the adjective "elegant" for his Amazon and that he now called her "slim". "It's more concrete," he added. Another time, he read to his two listeners the first sentence thus modified: "On a beautiful May morning, a slender Amazon, mounted on a superb chestnut mare, crossed the flowery paths of the Bois de Boulogne. - You see, said Grand, you can see it better and I preferred: "On a May morning", because "May" lengthened the trotting a little. He then showed great concern with the "superb" goal. He said that didn't speak for him, and he was looking for the term that would suddenly photograph the sumptuous mare he imagined. "Fat" was wrong, it was concrete, but a bit derogatory. "Gleaming" had tried it for a moment, but the rhythm did not lend itself to it. One evening he announced triumphantly that he had found: "A black chestnut mare. The black discreetly indicated elegance, still according to him. - It is not possible, said Rieux. - And why? - Chestnut does not indicate the race, but the color. - What color? - Well, a color that is not black, anyway! Great seemed very affected. - Thank you, he said, you are there, fortunately. But you see how difficult it is. - What would you think of "sumptuous"? said Tarrou. Grand looked at him. He thought: - Yes, he said, yes! And a smile came to him little by little. Sometime later, he admitted that the word "flowering" embarrassed him. As he had never known anything but Oran and Montelimar, he sometimes asked his friends for directions on how the alleys of the Bois were flowered. Strictly speaking, they had never given the impression of being in Rieux or Tarrou, but the conviction of the employee shaken them. He was surprised at their uncertainty. "There are only artists who can watch. But the doctor found him once in great excitement. He had replaced "flowered" with "full of flowers". He was rubbing his hands. "Finally, we see them, we feel them. Hats off, gentlemen! He read the sentence triumphantly: "On a beautiful May morning, a slender Amazon riding a sumptuous chestnut mare crossed the paths full of flowers in the Bois de Boulogne. But, read aloud, the three genitives who ended the sentence resounded annoyingly and Grand stuttered a little. He sat down, looking overwhelmed. Then he asked the doctor for permission to leave. He needed to think a little. It was around this time, it was later learned, that he gave the office signs of distraction which were deemed regrettable at a time when the town hall was faced, with a reduced staff, with overwhelming obligations. His service suffered and the office manager severely criticized him, reminding him that he was paid to do a job that, precisely, he did not do. "It seems," said the head of the office, "that you do voluntary service in health facilities, outside of your work. It's none of my business. But what concerns me is your work. And the first way to make yourself useful in these terrible circumstances is to do your job well. Or else, the rest is useless. "He is right," said Grand to Rieux. "Yes, he is right," agreed the doctor. - But I'm distracted, and I don't know how to get out of the end of my sentence. He had thought of deleting "de Boulogne", believing that everyone would understand. But then the sentence seemed to relate to "flowers" which, in fact, related to "aisles". He had also considered the possibility of writing: "The alleys of the Woods full of flowers. But the "Wood" situation between a noun and a qualifier that he arbitrarily separated was a thorn in the flesh. Some evenings, it is true that he looked even more tired than Rieux. Yes, he was tired by this research which absorbed him entirely, but he still continued to make the additions and the statistics that the additions and the statistics needed by the health facilities needed. Patiently, every evening, he would clear up the cards, accompany them with curves and he would slowly strive to present the states as precise as possible. Quite often, he would join Rieux in one of the hospitals and ask him for a table in some office or infirmary. He settled there with his papers, exactly as he settled at his table in the town hall, and in the air thickened by disinfectants and by the disease itself, he waved his leaves to dry the ink. He was honestly trying to stop thinking about his Amazon and do only the right thing. Yes, if it is true that men are keen to offer themselves examples and models that they call heroes, and if there is absolutely one in this story, the narrator rightly proposes this insignificant hero and erased who had for him only a little kindness at heart and an apparently ridiculous ideal. This will give truth its due, the addition of two and two its total of four, and heroism the secondary place which must be hers, just after, and never before, the generous requirement of happiness. It will also give this column its character, which must be that of a relationship made with good feelings, that is to say feelings that are neither ostensibly bad nor uplifting in the ugly way of a show. At least that was the opinion of Dr. Rieux when he read the newspapers or listened to the radio calls and encouragement that the outside world was sending to the city. At the same time as the aid sent by air and by road, every evening, on the airwaves or in the press, pitying or admiring comments fell on the now lonely city. And every time the tone of epic or award speech impatient the doctor. Certainly, he knew that this concern was not feigned. But it could only be expressed in the conventional language by which men try to express what binds them to humanity. And that language couldn't apply to Grand's little daily efforts, for example, unable to account for what Grand meant in the midst of the plague. At midnight, sometimes, in the great silence of the then deserted city, when he got back to his bed for too short a sleep, the doctor turned the button on his post. And the far reaches of the world, across thousands of kilometers, unknown and fraternal voices awkwardly tried to say their solidarity and said it, in fact, but at the same time demonstrated the terrible helplessness in which every man finds himself to truly share a pain he cannot see: "Oran! Oran! "In vain, the call crossed the seas, in vain Rieux was on alert, soon the eloquence rose and showed even better the essential separation which made two strangers of Grand and the speaker. "Oran! yes, Oran! But no, thought the doctor, love or die together, there is no other resource. They are too far. And precisely what remains to be traced before arriving at the top of the plague, while the scourge united all its forces to throw them on the city and take hold of them definitively, it is the long desperate and monotonous efforts that the last individuals, like Rambert, did to regain their happiness and to remove from the plague that part of themselves that they defended against all attack. This was their way of refusing the enslavement that threatened them, and although this refusal, apparently, was not as effective as the other, the narrator's opinion is that it had its meaning and that 'He also testified, in his vanity and his very contradictions, for what there was then to trust in each of us. Rambert struggled to keep the plague from covering him. Having acquired proof that he could not leave the city by legal means, he was determined, he had told Rieux, to use the others. The reporter started with the waiters. A waiter is always aware of everything. But the first people he interviewed were mostly aware of the very serious penalties that punished these types of businesses. In one case, he was even taken for a provocateur. He had to meet Cottard at Rieux's house to advance a little. He and Rieux had spoken to him again that day of the fruitless steps the journalist had taken in the administration. A few days later, Cottard met Rambert in the street, and greeted him with the roundness that he now put in all his reports: - Still nothing? he had said. - No nothing. - You can't count on the desks. They are not made to understand. - It is true. But I'm looking for something else. It's difficult. - Ah! said Cottard, I see. He knew a sector and to Rambert, who was surprised, he explained that, for a long time, he had frequented all the cafes in Oran, that there were friends and that he was informed about the existence of a organization that handled these kinds of operations. The truth was that Cottard, whose expenses now exceeded revenues, had become involved in smuggling of rationed goods. He was thus selling cigarettes and bad alcohol, the prices of which were constantly rising, and which were earning him a small fortune. - Are you sure? asked Rambert. - Yes, since I was offered it. - And you didn't take advantage of it? - Don't be suspicious, said Cottard with a good-natured look, I didn't take advantage of it because I don't want to leave. I have my reasons. He added after a silence: - You do not ask me what are my reasons? "I suppose," said Rambert, "that it doesn't concern me. - In a sense, that doesn't concern you, indeed. But in another ... Well, the only obvious thing is that I feel much better here since we have the plague with us. The other listened to his speech- How to join this organization? - Ah! said Cottard, it's not easy, come with me. It was four o'clock in the afternoon. Under heavy skies, the city cooked slowly. All the stores had their blinds lowered. The roads were deserted. Cottard and Rambert took arcaded streets and walked a long time without speaking. It was one of those hours when the plague became invisible. This silence, this death of colors and movements, could be those of summer as well as those of the plague. It was unknown whether the air was heavy with threats or with dust and burns. You had to observe and think to join the plague. Because it was only betrayed by negative signs. Cottard, who had affinities with her, pointed out for example to Rambert the absence of dogs which, normally, should have been on the side, panting, at the threshold of the corridors, in search of an impossible freshness. They took the Boulevard des Palmiers, crossed the river. They took the Boulevard des Palmiers, crossed the Place d'Armes and went down towards the Marine district. To the left, a cafe painted in green was sheltered under an oblique blind of large yellow canvas. On entering, Cottard and Rambert wiped their foreheads. They took their places on folding garden chairs, in front of green sheet metal tables. The room was absolutely deserted. Flies sizzled in the air. In a yellow cage placed on the wobbly counter, a parrot, all feathers dropped, was collapsed on its perch. Old paintings, depicting military scenes, hung on the wall, covered in filth and spider webs in thick filaments. On all the sheet metal tables, and in front of Rambert himself, chicken droppings were drying, the origin of which he could hardly explain until, from a dark corner, after a bit of commotion, a magnificent rooster hopped out. The heat at this moment seemed to rise again. Cottard took off his jacket and knocked on the sheet. A little man, lost in a long blue apron, came out from the bottom, saluted Cottard as far as he could see him, advanced with a vigorous kick away from the rooster and asked, amid the chuckles of the bird, what 'It was necessary to serve these gentlemen. Cottard wanted white wine and asked about a certain Garcia. According to the dwarf, it had already been a few days since he had been seen in the cafe. - Do you think he will come tonight? - Hey! said the other, I'm not in his shirt. But do you know his time? - Yes, but it is not very important. I only have a friend to introduce her to. The boy was wiping his sweaty hands against the front of his apron. - Ah! Mister also does business. - Yes, said Cottard. The dwarf snorted: - So come back tonight. I'm going to send the kid to him. As he left, Rambert asked what business it was. - Contraband, of course. They pass goods at the gates of the city. They sell at a high price. - Good, said Rambert. Do they have accomplices? - Exactly. In the evening, the blind was raised, the parrot jabbered in its cage and the metal tables were surrounded by men in shirtsleeves. One of them, the straw hat behind, a white shirt open on a burnt earthen chest, stood up at Cottard's entrance. A regular, tanned face, black and small eye, white teeth, two or three rings on his fingers, he looked about thirty years old. - Hi, he said, we drink at the counter. They took three rounds in silence. - Shall we go out? Garcia said. They went down to the harbor and Garcia asked what he wanted. Cottard told him that it was not exactly for business that he wanted to present Rambert to him, but only for what he called "an outing." Garcia walked straight ahead, smoking. He asked questions, saying "He" when speaking of Rambert, without seeming to notice his presence. - To do what? he said. - He has his wife in France. - Ah! And after a while: - What is his job? - Journalist. - It's a profession where we talk a lot. Rambert was silent. - He's a friend, said Cottard. They walked in silence. They had arrived at the platforms, whose access was prohibited by large gates. But they went to a small refreshment bar where fried sardines were sold, the smell of which came to them. - Anyway, Garcia concludes, it's not about me, it's about Raoul. And I have to find it. It won't be easy. - Ah! asked Cottard animatedly, is he hiding? Garcia did not answer. Near the refreshment stand, he stopped and turned to Rambert for the first time. - The day after tomorrow, at eleven o'clock, at the corner of the customs barracks, at the top of the city. He pretended to leave but turned to the two men. "There will be fees," he said. It was a finding. "Of course," agreed Rambert. A little later, the journalist thanked Cottard: - Oh! no, said the other cheerfully. It is my pleasure to be of service to you. And then, you are a journalist, you will reward me one day or another. Two days later, Rambert and Cottard climbed the large streets without shade that lead to the top of our city. Part of the customs barracks had been turned into an infirmary and people stood outside the front door, hoping for an unauthorized visit, or looking for information that, by the hour, would be out of date. In any case, this gathering allowed many comings and goings and one could suppose that this consideration was not foreign to the way in which the meeting of Garcia and Rambert had been fixed. - It's curious, said Cottard, this obstinacy to leave. In short, what is happening is very interesting. "Not for me," replied Rambert. - Oh! of course, we risk something. But, after all, there was so much risk, before the plague, of crossing a busy intersection. At this point, Rieux's car stopped at their height. At this point, Rieux's car stopped at their height. Tarrou was driving and Rieux seemed to be half asleep. He woke up to make the introductions. - We know each other, said Tarrou, we live in the same hotel. He offered to Rambert to drive him into town. - No, we have an appointment here. Rieux looked at Rambert: "Yes," said the latter. - Ah! asked Cottard, the doctor knows? - Here is the examining magistrate, warns Tarrou, looking at Cottard. He changed his figure. Mr. Othon was walking down the street and striding toward them with a vigorous but measured step. He took off his hat as he passed the small group. - Hello, judge! said Tarrou. The judge said hello to the occupants of the car, and, looking at Cottard and Rambert who had stayed behind, nodded gravely. Tarrou introduced the annuitant and the reporter. The judge looked up to the sky for a second and sighed, saying it was a very sad time. - I am told, Mr. Tarrou, that you are responsible for the application of prophylactic measures. I cannot approve of you too much. Do you think, doctor, that the disease will spread? Rieux said that it was to be hoped not and the judge repeated that it was always to be hoped, the designs of Providence are impenetrable. Tarrou asked him if events had brought him more work. - On the contrary, the cases which we call under ordinary law are decreasing. I only have to deal with serious breaches of the new provisions. There has never been more respect for the old laws. - It is, said Tarrou, that in comparison they seem good, necessarily. The judge left the dreamy air he had taken, gazing as if suspended in the sky. And he examined Tarrou coldly. - What does it do? he says. It's not the law that counts, it's the conviction. We can't help it. - This one, said Cottard when the judge was gone, is enemy number one. The car started. A little later, Rambert and Cottard saw Garcia arrive. He walked over to them without making any sign and said hello, "We must wait." Around them, the crowd, dominated by women, waited in total silence. Almost all of them carried baskets of which they had the vain hope that they could pass them on to their sick parents and the idea even crazier that these could use their provisions. The door was guarded by armed sentries and, from time to time, a strange cry crossed the courtyard that separated the barracks from the door. In the audience, worried faces turned to the hospital wing. The three men watched this spectacle when a clear and serious "hello" on their back made them turn around. Despite the heat, Raoul was dressed very well. Tall and strong, he wore a dark double-breasted suit and a felt-tip felt. His face was quite pale. With brown eyes and a tight mouth, Raoul spoke quickly and precisely: - Let's go down to the city, he said. Garcia, you can leave us. Garcia lit a cigarette and let them go. They walked quickly, matching their look to that of Raoul who was placed in their midst. - Garcia explained to me, he said. It can be done. Anyway, it will cost you ten thousand francs. Rambert replied that he accepted. - Lunch with me tomorrow at the Spanish restaurant in the Navy. Rambert said it was understood and Raoul shook his hand, smiling for the first time. After he left, Cottard apologized. He was not free the next day and besides Rambert no longer needed him. When the journalist entered the Spanish restaurant the next day, all heads turned in his path. This shady cellar, located below a small yellow street and parched by the sun, was only a small yellow street and parched by the sun, was frequented only by men, mostly Spanish. But as soon as Raoul, seated at a back table, made a sign to the journalist and Rambert went to him, curiosity disappeared from the faces which returned to their plates. Raoul had at his table a tall, skinny, unshaven fellow with disproportionately broad shoulders, a horse face and thinning hair. His long thin arms, covered with black hair, came out of a shirt with rolled up sleeves. He nodded three times when Rambert was introduced to him. His name had not been pronounced and Raoul only spoke of him by saying "our friend". - Our friend believes he can help you. He's going to ... Raoul stopped because the waitress was intervening for Rambert's order– He will put you in touch with two of our friends who will let you know about the guards who have acquired us. It will not all be over then. The guards have to judge for themselves when the time is right. The easiest way would be for you to stay for a few nights with one of them, who lives near the doors. But first, our friend must give you the necessary contacts. When everything is settled, he will pay the costs. The friend nodded his horse head once more without ceasing to grind up the tomato and pepper salad he was eating. Then he spoke with a slight Spanish accent. He proposed to Rambert to make an appointment two days later, at eight in the morning, under the porch of the cathedral. "Two more days," said Rambert. - It's not easy, said Raoul. We have to find people. The horse praised once more and Rambert approved without passion. The rest of the lunch was spent searching for a topic of conversation. But everything became very easy when Rambert discovered that the horse was a football player. He himself had practiced this sport a lot. We therefore talked about the French championship, the value of the English professional teams and the tactics in W. At the end of lunch, the horse was quite animated, and he was close to Rambert to persuade him that there was had no better place in a team than that of the center half. "You understand," he said, "the center half is the one who distributes the game. And distributing the game is football. Rambert agreed, although he had always played center-forward. The discussion was only interrupted by a radio, which, after having muted sentimental melodies, announced that, the day before, the plague had killed one hundred and thirty-seven victims. No one reacts in the audience. The horse-faced man shrugged and stood up. Raoul and Rambert followed suit. As he left, the half-center shook Rambert's hand with energy: - My name is Gonzales, he said. These two days seemed endless to Rambert. He went to Rieux's house and told him about his procedures in detail. Then he accompanied the doctor on one of his visits. He said goodbye to her at the door of the house where a suspect was waiting for him. In the corridor, a noise of races and voices: the family was informed of the doctor's arrival. - I hope Tarrou won't delay, murmured Rieux. He looked tired. - Is the epidemic going too fast? asked Rambert. Rieux says it wasn't that, and even the statistics curve was slowing. There simply weren't enough ways to fight the plague. "We are running out of equipment," he said. In all the armies of the world, one generally replaces the lack of material by men. But we are short of men too. - He came from outside doctors and medical staff. - Yes, said Rieux. Ten doctors and a hundred men. It's a lot, apparently. It is barely enough for the present state of the disease. It will not be enough if the epidemic spreads. Rieux listened to the sounds of the interior, then smiled at Rambert. - Yes, he said, you should hurry to succeed. A shadow passed over Rambert's face: "You know," he said in a low voice, "that is not what made me leave. Rieux replied that he knew it, but Rambert continued: - I think I'm not a coward, at least most of the time. I had the opportunity to experience it. Only, there are ideas that I cannot bear. The doctor looked him in the face. "You will find her," he said. - Maybe, but I can't bear the idea that this will last and that she will age all this time. At thirty, you start to age, and you have to take advantage of everything. I don't know if you can understand. Rieux murmured that he thought he understood when Tarrou arrived, very animated. - I just asked Paneloux to join us. - Well? asked the doctor. - He thought about it and said yes. - I'm happy with that, said the doctor. I am glad to know it better than his preaching. - Everyone is like that, said Tarrou. You just have to give them an opportunity. He smiled and winked at Rieux. - It's my job in life to provide opportunities. "Forgive me," said Rambert, "but I must go." On the Thursday of the meeting, Rambert went to the cathedral porch, five minutes before eight o'clock. The air was still pretty cool. In the sky progressed small white and round clouds which, just now, the rise of heat would suddenly swallow. A faint smell of humidity still rose from the parched yet dry lawns. The sun, behind the houses in the east, only warmed the helmet of the Joan of Arc, entirely gilded, which adorned the square. A clock struck the eight shots. Rambert took a few steps under the deserted porch. Vague chants came from inside with old cellar and incense scents. Suddenly the songs fell silent. A dozen small black shapes came out of the church and began to trot towards the city. Rambert began to get impatient. Other black forms ascended the large stairs and headed for the porch. He lit a cigarette, then realized that perhaps the place did not allow it. At 8:15 a.m., the cathedral organs began to play muted. Rambert entered under the dark arch. After a while, he could see the black shadows that had passed in front of him in the nave. They were all gathered in a corner, in front of a sort of improvised altar where they had just installed a Saint Roch, hastily executed in one of the workshops of our city. Kneeling, they seemed to have curled up again, lost in the greyness like pieces of coagulated shadow, barely thicker, here and there, than the coagulated shade, barely thicker, here and there, than the mist in which they floated. Above them the organs made endless variations. When Rambert came out, Gonzalès was already coming down the stairs and headed for the city. "I thought you were gone," he said to the reporter. It was normal. He explained that he had waited for his friends at another date that he had given them nearby, at ten minutes past eight. But he had waited twenty minutes, in vain. - There's an obstacle, that's for sure. We are not always comfortable in the work we do. He proposed another meeting the next day, at the same time, in front of the war memorial. Rambert sighed and threw his felt back. - It's nothing, concludes Gonzales laughing. Think about all the combinations, downhills and assists you need to make before scoring a goal. "Of course," said Rambert again. But the game only lasts an hour and a half. The monument to the dead of Oran is in the only place from where you can see the sea, a kind of promenade along, for a fairly short distance, the cliffs overlooking the port. The next day, Rambert, the first to meet, carefully read the list of those killed on the field of honor. A few minutes later, two men approached, looked at him with indifference, then went to lean on the parapet of the promenade and seemed completely absorbed by the contemplation of the empty and deserted quays. They were both the same size, both wearing blue pants and short-sleeved navy knitwear. The reporter walked away a bit, then sat on a bench and could watch them at leisure. He then realized that they were probably no more than twenty years old. At that moment, he saw Gonzales walking towards him, apologizing. "Here are our friends," he said, and took him to the two young men whom he introduced under the names of Marcel and Louis. From the front they looked very much alike and Rambert believed they were brothers. - Here, said Gonzales. Now the knowledge is made. We will have to fix the matter itself. Marcel or Louis then said that their guard tour started in two days, lasted a week and that the most convenient day should be identified. There were four of them guarding the west gate and the other two were regulars. There was no question of putting them in the business. They weren't sure and, moreover, it would increase the cost. However, it sometimes happened that the two colleagues went to spend part of the night in the back room of a bar they knew. Marcel or Louis thus proposed to Rambert to come and settle in their home, near the doors, and to wait for someone to come and get him. The passage then would be quite easy. But we had to hurry because there was talk recently of installing double posts outside the city. Rambert approved and offered some of his last cigarettes. The one of the two who had not yet spoken asked Gonzalès if the question of costs was settled and if we could receive advances. - No, said Gonzales, it's not worth it, he's a friend. Fees will be paid on departure. A new meeting was agreed. Gonzales offered dinner at the Spanish restaurant two days later. From there, we could go to the guards' house. - For the first night, he said to Rambert, I will keep you company. The next day, Rambert, going up to his room, met Tarrou on the stairs of the hotel. - I'm going to join Rieux, said the latter, do you want to come? "I'm never sure I won't disturb him," said Rambert after a hesitation. - I don't think he told me much about you. The journalist thought: - Listen, he said. If you have a moment after dinner, even late, come to the hotel bar both. "It depends on him and the plague," said Tarrou. At eleven o'clock in the evening, however, Rieux and Tarrou entered the bar, small and narrow. Thirty people went there elbowed and spoke aloud. Coming from the silence of the foul city, the two arrivals stopped, a little dizzy. They understood this agitation when they saw that alcohol was still being served. Rambert was at one end of the counter and gestured to them from the top of his stool. They surrounded him, Tarrou quietly pushing away a noisy neighbor. - Doesn't alcohol scare you? - No, said Tarrou, on the contrary. Rieux sniffed the smell of bitter herbs from his glass. It was difficult to speak in this uproar, but Rambert seemed mostly busy drinking. The doctor could not yet judge if he was drunk. At one of the two tables which occupied the rest of the narrow room where they stood, a naval officer, a woman on each arm, told a large congested interlocutor of an epidemic of typhus in Cairo: "Camps," he said. , we had made camps for the natives, with tents for the sick and, all around, a cordon of sentries who fired on the family when they tried to smuggle remedies for good women. It was hard, but it was fair. At the other table, occupied by elegant young people, the conversation was incomprehensible and was lost in the measures of Saint James Infirmary, spilled by a high-pitched pickup truck. - Are you happy? said Rieux, raising his voice. - It's approaching, said Rambert. Maybe in the week. "Too bad," cried Tarrou. - Why? Tarrou looked at Rieux. - Oh! said this one, Tarrou said that because he thinks you could have been useful to us here. But I understand your desire to leave too well. Tarrou offered another tour. Rambert got down from his stool and looked him in the face for the first time: - How would I be useful to you? - Well, said Tarrou, reaching for his glass without hurrying, in our health facilities. Rambert resumed the air of stubborn reflection that was usual for him and climbed back onto his stool. – Don't these training courses seem useful to you? said Tarrou, who had just drunk and looked at Rambert attentively. - Very useful, said the journalist, and he drank. Rieux noticed that his hand was shaking. He thought that decidedly, yes, he was quite drunk. The next day, when Rambert entered the Spanish restaurant for the second time, he passed in the middle of a small group of men who had taken chairs out of the entrance and were enjoying a green and gold evening when the heat was only beginning to s collapse. They were smoking a pungent-smelling tobacco. Inside, the restaurant was almost deserted. Rambert went to sit at the back table where he had met Gonzales the first time. He tells the waitress that he will wait. It was half past seven. Little by little, the men entered the dining room and settled down. They began to serve them, and the lowered vault filled with noises of cutlery and deaf conversations. At eight o'clock, Rambert was still waiting. We gave light. New customers settled at his table. He ordered his dinner. At 8:30 p.m., he had finished without seeing Gonzalès or the two young men. He smoked cigarettes. The room was slowly emptying. Outside, night fell very quickly. A warm breath coming from the sea gently lifted the curtains of the French windows. When it was nine o'clock, Rambert noticed that the room was empty, and that the waitress was looking at him in amazement. He paid and went out. Opposite the restaurant, a cafe was open. Rambert sat at the counter and watched the entrance to the restaurant. At 9:30 p.m., he headed for his hotel, trying in vain to reach Gonzales, whose address he did not have, his heart distraught at the idea of all the steps that should be taken. It was at this point, in the night crossed by fleeting ambulances, that he realized, as he had to tell Doctor Rieux, that during all this time he had somehow forgotten his wife, to apply himself all in search of an opening in the walls that separated him from her. But it was also at this moment that, all the tracks once again blocked, he found her again at the center of his desire, and with such a sudden burst of pain that he started to run towards his hotel, to to flee from this atrocious burn which he nevertheless carried with him and which ate his temples. Very early the next day, however, he came to see Rieux, to ask him how to find Cottard: - All that remains for me to do, he said, is to follow the sector again. - Come tomorrow night, said Rieux, Tarrou asked me to invite Cottard, I don't know why. He must come at ten o'clock. Arrive at half past ten. When Cottard arrived at the doctor the next day, Tarrou and Rieux were talking about an unexpected healing that had taken place in the doctor's service. - One out of ten. He was lucky, said Tarrou. - Ah! well, said Cottard, it wasn't the plague. It was assured that it was indeed this disease. - It is not possible since he is cured. You know as well as I do that the plague cannot be forgiven. "In general, no," said Rieux. But with a little stubbornness, we have surprises. Cottard laughed. - It doesn't appear. Have you heard the numbers tonight? Tarrou, who looked kindly on the annuitant, said that he knew the numbers, that the situation was serious, but what did that prove? It showed that even more exceptional measures were needed– Hey! You have already taken them. - Yes, but everyone must take them for their own account. Cottard looked at Tarrou without understanding. He said that too many men remained inactive, that the epidemic was everyone's business and that everyone had to do their duty. Voluntary training was open to everyone. - It's an idea, said Cottard, but it won't do any good. The plague is too strong. "We will know," said Tarrou patiently, "when we have tried everything." Meanwhile, Rieux at his desk was copying cards. Tarrou was still looking at the rentier who was waving in his chair. - Why don't you come with us, Mr. Cottard? The other stood up in an offended look, took his round hat in his hand: - It's not my job. Then, in a tone of bravado: - Besides, I feel good there, me, in the plague, and I don't see why I should get involved in making it stop. Tarrou struck his forehead, as if illuminated by a sudden truth: - Ah! that's right, I forgot, you would be arrested without it. Cottard gasped and grabbed the chair as if it were going to fall. Rieux had stopped writing and looked at him with a serious and interested air. - Who told you that? cried the annuitant. Tarrou looked surprised and said: - But you. Or at least that's what the doctor and I thought I understood. And as Cottard, suddenly overcome with a rage too strong for him, mumbled incomprehensible words: "Don't get angry," added Tarrou. It's not the doctor or me who will report you. Your story is none of our business. Besides, the police, we never liked that. Come on, sit down. The annuitant looked at his chair and sat down, after hesitation. After a while, he sighed. - It's an old story, he admitted, that they came out. I thought it was forgotten. But there was one who spoke. They called me and told me to be available until the end of the investigation. I understood that they would end up arresting me. – Is It serious? asked Tarrou. - It depends on what you mean. It's not murder anyway. - Prison or forced labor? Cottard looked very dejected. - Prison, if I'm lucky ... But after a moment, he resumed vehemently: - This is a mistake. Everybody makes mistakes. And I can't bear the idea of being kidnapped for that, of being separated from my house, from my habits, from everyone I know. - Ah! asked Tarrou, is that why you invented yourself to hang yourself? - Yes, stupidity, of course. Rieux spoke for the first time and told Cottard that he understood his concern, but maybe everything would be fine. - Oh! for the moment, I know I have nothing to fear. - I see, said Tarrou, you will not enter our training. The other, who turned his hat between his hands, looked up at Tarrou with an uncertain look: - You mustn't blame me. - Surely not. But at least try, said Tarrou with a smile, not to deliberately spread the germ. Cottard protested that he hadn't wanted the plague, that it had happened like that, and that it wasn't her fault that she was arranging her affairs for the time being. And when Rambert arrived at the door, the annuitant added, with great energy in his voice: - Besides, my idea is that you will get nowhere. Rambert learned that Cottard did not know Gonzales' address but that one could always return to the little cafe. We made an appointment for the next day. And as Rieux expressed the desire to be informed, Rambert invited him with Tarrou for the end of the week at any time of the night, in his room. In the morning, Cottard and Rambert went to the little cafe and left Garcia an appointment for the evening, or the next day if he was unable to attend. In the evening they waited for him in vain. The next day Garcia was there. He listened in silence to Rambert's story. He was not aware of it, but he knew that entire neighborhoods had been logged for twenty-four hours in order to conduct home checks. It was possible that Gonzalès and the two young people could not get through the roadblocks. But all he could do was put them in touch with Raoul again. Of course, it wouldn't be until two days later. - I see, said Rambert, we have to start all over again. Two days later, at the corner of a street, Raoul confirmed Garcia's hypothesis; the low quarters had been consigned. We had to get back in touch with Gonzales. Two days later, Rambert had lunch with the football player. - This is stupid, said the latter. We should have agreed on a way to find each other. This was also Rambert's opinion. - Tomorrow morning, we will go to the little ones, we will try to arrange everything. The next day, the little ones were not at home. We left them an appointment for the next noon at Place du Lycée. And Rambert returned home with an expression that struck Tarrou when he met him in the afternoon. - Are you okay? asked Tarrou. - It is by force to start again, said Rambert. And he renewed his invitation: - Come this evening. In the evening, when the two men entered Rambert's room, he was stretched out. He got up, filled the glasses he had prepared. Rieux, taking his, asked him if it was on the right track. The journalist said that he had made a full tour again, that he had arrived at the same point and that he would soon have his last appointment. He drank and added: - Naturally, they will not come. "It should not be made a principle," said Tarrou. "You haven't understood yet," replied Rambert, shrugging. - What? - Plague. - Ah! said Rieux. - No, you did not understand that it is to start again. Rambert went to a corner of his room and opened a small phonograph. - What is this record? asked Tarrou. I know him. Rambert replied that it was Saint James Infirmary. In the middle of the disc, two shots were heard clicking in the distance. "A dog or an escape," said Tarrou. A moment later, the disc ended and the call from an ambulance became more precise, grew, went under the windows of the hotel room, diminished, then finally died out. - This record is not funny, said Rambert. And then it's been ten times that I've heard it today. - Do you like it that much? - No, but I only have that one. And after a moment: - I tell you that it consists in starting again. He asked Rieux how the formations worked. There were five teams at work. We were hoping to train others. The journalist sat on his bed and seemed concerned about his nails. Rieux was examining his short, powerful figure, gathered on the edge of the bed. He suddenly noticed that Rambert was looking at him. - You know, doctor, he said, I thought a lot about your organization. If I'm not with you, it's because I have my reasons. For the rest, I think I would still be able to pay personally, I fought in the Spanish War. - Which side? asked Tarrou. - On the side of the vanquished. But since then, I've been thinking about it a bit. - To what? said Tarrou. - Courage. Now I know that man is capable of great actions. But if he is not capable of a great feeling, he does not interest me. - It looks like he's capable of anything, said Tarrou. - But no, he is unable to suffer or be happy for a long time. He is therefore incapable of anything worthwhile. He looked at them, and then: - Come, Tarrou, are you able to die for love? - I don't know, but I don't think so now. - Here. And you are able to die for an idea, it is visible to the naked eye. Well, I've had enough of people dying for an idea. I do not believe in heroism; I know it is easy and I learned that it was murderous. What interests me is that we live and die of what we love. Rieux listened carefully to the journalist. Without stopping to look at him, he said gently: - Man is not an idea, Rambert. The other jumped out of bed, his face on fire. - It's an idea, and a short idea, from the moment he turns away from love. And precisely, we are no longer capable of love. Resign ourselves, doctor. Let's wait to become one and if it's really not possible, wait for general deliverance without playing the hero. I don't go any further. Rieux rose, with an air of sudden weariness. - You are right, Rambert, absolutely right, and for nothing in the world I would not want to divert you from what you are going to do, which seems fair and good to me. But I must tell you, though, that this is not heroism in all of this. It's about honesty. It's an idea that can make people laugh, but the only way to fight the plague is to be honest. - What is honesty? said Rambert, suddenly serious. - I don't know what it is in general. But in my case, I know it is about doing my job. - Ah! said Rambert, with rage, I don't know what my job is. Perhaps I am in the wrong in choosing love. Rieux faced him: - No, he said forcefully, you are not in the wrong. Rambert looked at them thoughtfully. - You two, I guess you have nothing to lose in all of this. It's easier to be on the right side. Rieux emptied his glass. - Come on, he said, we have to do. - Come on, he said, we have to do. He went. Tarrou followed him, but seemed to change his mind as he left, turned to the journalist, and said: - Do you know that Rieux's wife is in a nursing home a few hundred kilometers from here? Rambert made a gesture of surprise, but Tarrou was already gone. At the first hour the next day, Rambert telephoned the doctor: - Would you accept that I work with you until I found the way to leave the city? There was a silence on the phone, and then: - Yes, Rambert. Thank you. III Thus, all week long, the prisoners of the plague struggled as they could. And some of them, like Rambert, even imagined, as we can see, that they were still acting as free men, that they could still choose. But, in fact, you could then, in the middle of August, say that the plague had covered everything. There were no longer individual destinies, but a collective history which was the plague and feelings shared by all. The greatest was separation and exile, with all that entailed fear and revolt. This is why the narrator believes that it is appropriate, at this peak of heat and illness, to describe the general situation and, by way of example, the violence of our living fellow citizens, the burials of the deceased and the suffering of lovers. separated. It was in the middle of that year that the wind picked up and blew for several days over the foul city. The wind is particularly feared by the inhabitants of Oran because it does not encounter any natural obstacle on the plateau where it is built, and it thus rushes into the streets with all its violence. After those long months when not a drop of water had refreshed the city, it was covered with a gray coating which peeled off under the wind. The latter thus raised waves of dust and papers which beat the legs of strollers who became rarer. They were seen hurrying through the streets, bent forward, a handkerchief or hand over their mouths. In the evening, instead of the gatherings where we tried to prolong these days as much as possible, each of which could be the last, we met with small groups of people eager to return home or to cafes, so that for a few days, at the twilight which arrived much more quickly at this time, the streets were deserted and the wind alone pushed continuous complaints. From the rising sea, still invisible, rose a smell of seaweed and salt. This deserted city, white with dust, saturated with sea odors, all sound of the cries of the wind, then groaned like an unhappy island. So far, the plague had claimed many more victims in the outer districts, which were more populated and less comfortable, than in the center of the city. But all of a sudden, she seemed to be getting closer and also settling in the business districts. Residents accused the wind of carrying germs of infection. "He's muddying the waters," said the hotel manager. But whatever it was, the central districts knew that their turn had come when they heard vibrating very close to them, in the night, and more and more frequently, the timbre of the ambulances which made resound under their windows the dreary and passionless call of the plague. Even inside the city, the idea was to isolate certain particularly hard-hit neighborhoods and to allow them to leave only men whose services were essential. Those who had lived there until then could not help but consider this measure as bullying specially directed against them, and in any case, they thought of residents of other neighborhoods in contrast as free men. The latter, on the other hand, in their difficult moments, found consolation in imagining that others were even less free than them. "There is always more prisoner than me" was the sentence which then summed up the only hope possible. Around this time, there was also an increase in fires, especially in the pleasure districts, at the western gates of the city. It was inquired that they were people who had returned from quarantine and who, mourned by mourning and misfortune, set fire to their house in the illusion that they were killing the plague there. It was very difficult to fight these companies whose frequency subjected whole districts to a perpetual danger because of the strong wind. After having shown in vain that the disinfection of houses carried out by the authorities was sufficient to exclude any risk of contamination, it was necessary to issue very severe penalties against these innocent arsonists. And undoubtedly, it was not the idea of the prison which made then push back these unfortunate people, but the certainty common to all the inhabitants that a prison sentence was equivalent to a death sentence because of the excessive mortality that 'we were in the municipal jail. Of course, this belief was not without foundation. For obvious reasons, it seemed that the plague was particularly hard on all those who had become accustomed to living in groups, soldiers, religious or prisoners. Despite the isolation of some detainees, a prison is a community, and what proves it is that in our municipal prison the guards, as much as the prisoners, paid their price for the disease. From the superior point of view of the plague, everyone, from the warden to the last detainee, was convicted and, perhaps for the first time, absolute justice prevailed in the prison. The authorities tried in vain to introduce hierarchy into this leveling, by conceiving the idea of decorating prison guards who died in the exercise of their functions. As the state of siege was decreed and that, from a certain angle, we could consider that the prison guards were mobilized, they were given the military medal posthumously. But if the detainees did not allow any protests to be heard, the military did not take it well and rightly pointed out that unfortunate confusion could arise in the minds of the public.

Their request was granted, and the easiest thought was to award the guards who died in the epidemic medal. But for the first, the damage was done, one could not think of taking away their decoration, and the military circles continued to maintain their point of view. On the other hand, with regard to the medal of epidemics, it had the disadvantage of not producing the moral effect that one had obtained by the attribution of a military decoration, since in time of epidemic it it was commonplace to get such a decoration. Everyone was unhappy. In addition, the prison administration could not operate like religious and, to a lesser extent, military authorities. The monks of the only two convents in the city had, in fact, been dispersed and temporarily housed in pious families. Likewise, whenever possible, small companies had been detached from barracks and garrisoned in schools or public buildings. Thus, the disease which, apparently, had forced the inhabitants to a solidarity of besieged, broke at the same time the traditional associations and returned the individuals to their loneliness. It was distressing. One might think that all these circumstances, added to the wind, also brought fire to certain minds. The city gates were attacked again during the night, and repeatedly, but this time by small armed groups. There were exchanges of gunfire, the wounded, and some escapes. The guard posts were reinforced, and these attempts ceased fairly quickly. They were enough, however, to raise in the city a breath of revolution which provoked some scenes of violence. Houses, burnt down or closed for health reasons, were looted. Indeed, it is difficult to assume that these acts were premeditated. Most of the time, a sudden occasion brought people, hitherto honorable, to reprehensible actions which were imitated immediately. He thus found himself mad to rush into a house still in flames, in the presence of the owner himself, dazed by pain. In front of his indifference, the example of the first ones was followed by many spectators and, in this dark street, by the light of the fire, we saw fleeing from all sides shadows distorted by dying flames and by objects or the furniture they carried on their shoulders. It was these incidents that forced the authorities to assimilate the state of the plague to the state of siege and to apply the resulting laws. Two thieves were shot, but it is doubtful whether it would make an impression on the others, because in the midst of so many deaths, these two executions went unnoticed: it was a drop in the sea. And, in truth, similar scenes were repeated quite often without the authorities pretending to intervene. The only measure which seemed to impress all the inhabitants was the institution of the curfew. From eleven o'clock, plunged into complete night, the city was of stone. Under the moon's skies, it aligned its whitish walls and straight streets, never stained by the black mass of a tree, never disturbed by the footsteps of a walker or the cry of a dog. The great silent city was then no more than an assembly of massive and inert cubes, between which the silent effigies of forgotten benefactors or former great men forever suffocated in bronze tried themselves alone, with their false stone faces or iron, to evoke a degraded image of what had been the man. These mediocre idols were enthroned under a thick sky, in the lifeless, insensitive brutes crossroads which represented fairly well the immobile reign into which we had entered or at least its ultimate order, that of a necropolis where the plague, stone and night would have finally silences all voices. But the night was also in all hearts and truths like the legends that were reported on the subject of burials were not made to reassure our fellow citizens. Because we have to talk about funerals and the narrator apologizes. He feels very well the reproach that could be made against him in this regard, but his only justification is that there were burials during all this time and that in a certain way, we forced him, as we forced everyone his fellow citizens to worry about funerals. It is not, in any case, that he had a taste for these kinds of ceremonies, preferring on the contrary the society of the living and, to give an example, sea bathing. But, in short, sea bathing had been suppressed and the society of the living feared all day long of being forced to give way to the society of the dead. This was the obvious. Of course, you could always try not to see it, to plug your eyes and refuse it, but the evidence has a terrible force that always ends up taking everything. The way, for example, to refuse burials, the day when those you love need burials? Well, what characterized our ceremonies at the start was speed! All the formalities had been simplified and, in general, the funeral home had been eliminated. The sick died far from their families and ritual evenings were forbidden, so that the one who died in the evening spent his night alone and the one who died during the day was buried without delay. We notified the family, of course, but within the deadline. The family was notified, of course, but in most cases the family could not move, being in quarantine if they had lived with the patient. In the event that the family did not live with the deceased, they arrived at the time indicated, which was that of their departure for the cemetery, the body having been washed and put in beer. Suppose that this formality took place at the auxiliary hospital under the care of Dr. Rieux. The school had an exit behind the main building. A large storage room overlooking the hallway contained coffins. In the corridor itself, the family found a single coffin already closed. Immediately, we went to the most important thing, that is to say that the head of the family signed papers. We then loaded the body into a motor car which was either a real van or a large ambulance. The parents got into one of the taxis still authorized and, at full speed, the cars reached the cemetery by outside streets. At the door, gendarmes stopped the convoy, stamped on the official pass, without which it was impossible to have what our fellow citizens call a last home, faded, and the cars were going to stand near of a square where many pits were waiting to be filled. A priest welcomed the body because the funeral services had been cut at the church. We took out the beer under prayers, we corded it, it was dragged, it slipped, stumbled against the bottom, the priest waved his bottle brush and already the first earth bounced on the lid. The ambulance had left a short time before to undergo a disinfectant spray and, while the shovels of clay resounded more and more quietly, the family rushed into the taxi. A quarter of an hour later, she had returned to her home. So, everything really happened with maximum speed and minimum risk. And no doubt, at least at the beginning, it is evident that the natural feeling of families was crumpled. But in times of plague, these are considerations that cannot be considered: we had sacrificed everything for efficiency. Moreover, if, at the beginning, the morale of the population had suffered from these practices, because the desire to be decently buried is more widespread than we believe, a little later, luckily, the problem of supplies became delicate and the interest of the inhabitants was diverted towards more immediate concerns. Absorbed by the queues to be made, the procedures to be completed and the formalities to be completed if they wanted to eat, people did not have time to think about how they died around them and how they would die one day. Thus, these material difficulties which must have been an evil turned out to be a benefit thereafter. And everything would have been for the best, if the epidemic had not spread, as we have already seen. Because the coffins became rarer, the canvas was missing for the shrouds and the place in the cemetery. We had to advise. The simplest, and always for reasons of efficiency, appeared to group the ceremonies and, when necessary, to multiply the trips between the hospital and the cemetery. As for Rieux's service, the hospital had five coffins at the time. When full, the ambulance charged them. In the cemetery, the boxes were emptied, the iron-colored bodies were loaded on the stretchers and waited in a hangar, fitted out for this purpose. The beers were sprayed with an antiseptic solution, brought back to the hospital, and the operation was repeated as many times as necessary. The organization was therefore very good, and the prefect was satisfied with it. He even told Rieux that it was better in the end than the carts of the dead driven by negroes, as found in the chronicles of the ancient plagues. - Yes, said Rieux, it's the same funeral, but we make cards. Progress is indisputable. Despite the administration's successes, the unpleasantness of the formalities now forced the prefecture to dismiss the parents from the ceremony. We only tolerated that they came to the door of the cemetery and, again, it was not official. Because, with regard to the last ceremony, things had changed a little. At the end of the cemetery, in a bare space covered with mastic trees, we had dug two huge pits. There was the men's and women's graves. From this point of view, the administration respected the conveniences and it was only much later that, by necessity, this last modesty disappeared and that we buried pell-mell, one on top of the other, men and women, without concern for decency. Fortunately, this ultimate confusion only marked the last moments of the plague. In the period which occupies us, the separation of the pits existed, and the prefecture held there very much. At the bottom of each, a thick layer of quicklime smoked and boiled. At the edges of the hole, a brisk smoked and bubbled. On the edges of the hole, a mound of the same lime let its bubbles burst in the open air. When the ambulance trips were over, the stretchers were brought in procession, the bodies were stripped to the bottom, roughly next to each other, the bare and slightly twisted bodies and, at that time, they were covered with lime lively, then of earth, but only up to a certain height, in order to spare the place of future guests. The next day, the parents were asked to sign on a register, which marked the difference that there could be between men and, for example, dogs: control was always possible. For all these operations, personnel was needed, and we were always on the verge of being short of them. Many of these nurses and gravediggers, first official, then improvised, died of the plague. Whatever precaution we took, the contagion would one day happen. But to think about it, the most surprising thing was that there was never a shortage of men to do this job during the entire period of the epidemic. The critical period took place shortly before the plague had reached its peak, and Dr. Rieux's concerns were then well founded. Neither for the executives nor for what he called the big jobs, the manpower was not sufficient. But, from the moment when the plague had really taken hold of the whole city, then its very excess had very convenient consequences, because it disorganized all economic life and thus aroused a considerable number of unemployed. In most cases, they did not provide recruitment for executives, - but as for the low works, they were made easier. From that moment, in fact, one always saw misery appear to be stronger than fear, especially as the work was paid in proportion to the risks. The health services were able to have a list of canvassers and, as soon as a vacancy had just occurred, the first to be notified of the list who, unless in the meantime they had also gone on vacation, did not fail to present oneself. This is how the prefect, who had hesitated for a long time to use the condemned, time or life, for this kind of work, could avoid reaching this end. As long as there were unemployed people, he was of the opinion that we could wait. Somehow, and until the end of August, our fellow citizens could therefore be taken to their last home, if not decently, at least in sufficient order for the administration to remain aware that it was performing its duty. But it is necessary to anticipate a little on the continuation of the events to report the last processes to which it was necessary to have recourse. On the landing where the plague continued in effect from August, the accumulation of victims far surpassed the possibilities that our little cemetery could offer. No matter how much they tore down sections of wall, opening an escape to the dead on the surrounding grounds, something else had to be found very quickly. It was decided at first to bury the night, which suddenly dispensed with taking certain considerations. More and more bodies could be crammed into the ambulances. And the few backward strollers who, against all rules, were still in the outer quarters after the curfew (or those whose profession brought them there) sometimes encountered long white ambulances which sped at full speed, making their tones ring out without the hollow streets of the night shine. The bodies were hurriedly thrown into the pits. They had not finished tipping over as the shovels of lime were crushed on their faces and the earth covered them anonymously, in holes that were dug deeper and deeper. A little later, however, we were forced to look elsewhere and take off. A prefectoral decree expropriated the occupants of the concessions in perpetuity and all the exhumed remains were transported to the crematorium. Soon the plague dead themselves had to be brought to the cremation. But then we had to use the old incineration oven which was in the east of the city, outside the gates. The stake was postponed further, and an employee of the town hall greatly facilitated the task of the authorities by advising to use the trams which, in the past, served the maritime ledge, and who were unemployed. To this end, the interior of the portable lamps and motor cars was fitted out by removing the seats, and the track was diverted to the height of the oven, which thus became the head of the line. And throughout the end of summer, as in the middle of the autumn rains, we could see along the ledge, in the heart of each night, passing strange convoys of trams without travelers, jiggling over the sea. The inhabitants had come to know what it was. And despite the patrols that prohibited access to the ledge, groups were often able to slip into the rocks overlooking the waves and throw flowers in the portable lights, as the trams pass. We could then hear the vehicles bumping again in the summer night, with their load of flowers and dead. Towards morning, in any case, the first days, a thick and smelly vapor hung over the eastern districts of the city. In the opinion of all doctors, these exhalations, although unpleasant, could not harm anyone. But the inhabitants of these districts immediately threatened to desert them, persuaded that the plague was thus falling on them from the sky, so that they were forced to divert the fumes by a system of complicated pipes and the inhabitants calmed down. On windy days only, a faint smell from the east reminded them that they were settled in a new order, and that the flames of the plague devoured their tribute every evening. These were the extreme consequences of the epidemic. But it is fortunate that it did not increase thereafter, because one might think that the ingenuity of our offices, the provisions of the prefecture and even the absorption capacity of the oven may have been exceeded. Rieux knew that desperate solutions, such as the dumping of corpses into the sea, had been planned then, and he could easily imagine their monstrous foam on the blue water. He also knew that if the statistics kept going up, no organization, however excellent, would resist it, that the men would come to die in the heap, to rot in the street, despite the prefecture, and that the city would see, in public places, the and that the city would see, in public places, the dying cling to the living with a mixture of legitimate hatred and stupid hope. It was this kind of evidence or apprehension, in any case, that kept our fellow citizens feeling of their exile and separation. In this regard, the narrator knows perfectly well how unfortunate it is not to be able to report anything here that is truly spectacular, like for example some comforting hero or some brilliant action, like those found in old tales. Nothing is less spectacular than a plague and, by their very duration, great misfortunes are monotonous. In the memory of those who have lived through them, the terrible days of the plague did not appear as large sumptuous and cruel flames, but rather as an endless trampling which crushed everything in its path. No, the plague had nothing to do with the big, uplifting images that chased Dr. Rieux at the start of the epidemic. It was first of all a prudent and impeccable administration, in good working order. It is thus, be it said in parentheses, that in order not to betray anything and especially not to betray himself, the narrator has tended to objectivity. He hardly wanted to change anything with the effects of art, except for the basic needs of a roughly consistent relationship. And it is objectivity itself which commands him to say now that if the great suffering of this era, the most general as well as the most profound, was separation, if it is essential in conscience to give a new one description at this stage of the plague, it is not the less true that this suffering itself then lost its pathos. Did our fellow citizens, those at least who had suffered the most from this separation, get used to the situation? It would not be entirely fair to say so. It would be more accurate to say that in moral as in physical, they suffered from emaciation. At the beginning of the plague they remembered very well the being they had lost, and they regretted it. But if they clearly remembered the beloved face, his laughter, such a day which they recognized afterwards that he had been happy, they hardly imagined what the other could do at the very moment when they evoked it and in places now so far away. In short, at that time, they had memory, but insufficient imagination. At the second stage of the plague, they also lost their memory. Not that they had forgotten that face, but what amounts to the same thing, he had lost his flesh, they no longer saw him inside themselves. And while they tended to complain in the first weeks that they were no longer dealing with shadows in the things of their love, they later realized that these shadows could become even more emaciated, losing even the smallest colors that they remembered. At the end of this long period of separation, they no longer imagined that intimacy which had been theirs, nor how a living being could have lived close to them on which, at any time, they could lay their hands. From this point of view, they had entered the order of the plague, the more effective it was more mediocre. No one here had more great feelings. But everyone had monotonous feelings. "It is time for this to end," said our fellow citizens, because in times of plague, it is normal to wish for an end to collective suffering, and because in fact, they wanted it to end. But all this was said without the flame or the sour feeling of the beginning, and only with the few reasons that we still remained clear, and which were poor. The fierce outburst of the first weeks had been followed by an abatement which one would have been wrong to take for resignation, but which was nonetheless a kind of provisional consent. Our fellow citizens had stepped in, they had adapted, as they say, because there was no way to do otherwise. They still had, of course, the attitude of unhappiness and suffering, but they no longer felt the tip of it. Besides, Doctor Rieux, for example, considered that it was misfortune, precisely, and that the habit of despair is worse than despair itself. Before, the separated were not really unhappy, there was in their suffering an illumination which had just died out. Now you could see them on the street corners, in cafes or at their friends' places, placid and distracted, and their eyes so bored that, thanks to them, the whole city looked like a waiting room. For those who had a trade, they did it at the very pace of the plague, meticulously and without brilliance. Everyone was modest. For the first time, the separated had no reluctance to speak of the absent, to speak the language of all, to examine their separation from the same angle as the statistics of the epidemic. Whereas until then they had fiercely withdrawn their suffering from collective misfortune, they now accepted the confusion. Without memory and without hope, they settled in the present. In truth, everything became present to them. It must be said, the plague had taken away from everyone the power of love and even friendship. Because love requires a little future, and there were only moments left for us. Of course, none of this was absolute. Because if it is true that all the separated came to this state, it is right to add that they did not all arrive there at the same time and that as well, once installed in this new attitude, flashes , sudden returns of lucidity reduced the patients to a younger and more painful sensitivity. There had to be those moments of distraction when they formed some plan which implied that the plague had stopped. They had to feel unexpectedly, and by some grace, the bite of an objectless jealousy. Others also found sudden rebirths, went out of their torpor certain days of the week, Sunday naturally and Saturday afternoon, because these days were devoted to certain rites, from the time of the absent. Or even, a certain melancholy which took them at the end of the days gave them the warning, not always confirmed besides, that the memory was going to return to them. This evening hour, which for believers is that of the examination of conscience, this hour is hard for the prisoner or the exile who have only to examine emptiness. She kept them hanging for a while, then they returned to sluggishness, they locked themselves in the plague. We have already understood that this consisted in giving up what was most personal. Whereas in the early days of the plague, they were struck by the sum of little things that mattered a lot to them, without having any existence for others, and so they experienced professional life, now, on the contrary, they were only interested in what interested others, they had only general ideas and their very love had taken on the most abstract form for them. They were so abandoned to the plague that they sometimes hoped for nothing more than they were asleep and were surprised to think: "The buboes, and we are done with it!" But the truth was that they were already asleep, and it was only a long sleep. The city was populated by awake sleepers who really escaped their fate only those rare times when, during the night, their the apparently closed wound suddenly reopened. And awakened with a start, they felt then, with a sort of distraction, their irritated lips, rediscovering in a flash their suffering, suddenly rejuvenated, and, with it, the upset face of their love. In the morning, they returned to the plague, that is to say to the routine. But what, it will be said, did these separated seem? Well, that's simple, they looked nothing. Or, if you prefer, they looked like everyone else, quite general. They shared the placidity and the childish agitations of the city. They lost the appearance of critical thinking, while gaining the appearance of composure. We could see, for example, the most intelligent among them pretend to look like everyone else in the newspapers, or indeed in radio broadcasts, for reasons to believe in a rapid end of the plague, and apparently conceive hopes chimerical, or experiencing baseless fears, reading considerations that a journalist had written a little at random, yawning with boredom. For the rest, they drank their beer or cared for their sick, lazed or burned out, filed cards, or played records without distinguishing themselves from each other. In other words, they no longer chose anything. The plague had suppressed value judgments. And it shows in the way no one cares more about the quality of the clothes or the food we buy. We accepted everything as a block. Finally, we can say that the separated no longer had this curious privilege that preserved them at the start. They had lost the selfishness of love, and the benefit they derived from it. At least now the situation was clear, the scourge affected everyone. All of us in the midst of the bangs slamming at the gates of the city, the stamping of our life or our deaths, in the midst of fires and cards, terror and formalities, promised an ignominious but recorded death, among the appalling fumes and the quiet tones of the ambulances, we fed on the same bread of exile, waiting without knowing it for the same meeting and the same overwhelming peace. Our love was undoubtedly still there, but, simply, it was unusable, heavy to carry, inert in us, sterile like crime or condemnation. It was nothing more than a patience without future and a stubborn expectation. And from this point of view, the attitude of some of our fellow citizens made one think of these long lines in the four corners of the city, in front of food shops. It was the same resignation and the same long-suffering, both unlimited and without illusions. It would only be necessary to elevate this feeling to a thousand times greater scale with regard to separation, because it was then another hunger that could devour everything. In any case, supposing that we want to have a fair idea of the state of mind in which the people separated from our city were, it would again be necessary to evoke these eternal golden and dusty evenings, which fell on the city without trees , while men and women poured into all the streets. Because, strangely, what then went up to the still sunny terraces, in the absence of the noises of vehicles and machines which ordinarily make all the language of cities, it was only a huge rumor of steps and voices deaf, the painful sliding of thousands of soles punctuated by the whistling of the scourge in the heavy sky, an endless and suffocating trampling, which gradually filled the whole city and which, night after evening, gave its most faithful voice and the more dismal to the blind obstinacy which, in our hearts, replaced love.

IV

During the months of September and October, the plague kept the city withdrawn beneath it. Since these were trampling, several hundred thousand men still trampled for weeks on endless weeks. Mist, heat, and rain followed one another in the sky. Silent bands of starlings and thrushes, coming from the south, passed very high, but went around the city, as if the scourge of Paneloux, the strange piece of wood which whistled over the houses, was holding them. 'difference. In early October, heavy showers swept the streets. And during all this time, nothing more important happened than this enormous trampling. Rieux and his friends then discovered how tired they were. In fact, the men in the health facilities could no longer digest this fatigue. Doctor Rieux noticed this when he watched his friends and himself watch the progress of curious indifference. For example, these men who, until now, had shown such keen interest in all the news that concerned the plague didn't care about it anymore. Rambert, who had been temporarily assigned to run one of the quarantine houses recently installed in his hotel, was well aware of the number of those he had under observation. He was aware of the smallest details of the immediate evacuation system he had organized for those who suddenly showed signs of the disease. The statistics of the effects of serum on quarantines were engraved in his memory. But he was unable to say the weekly number of victims of the plague, he really did not know if it was ahead or back. And he, despite everything, still hoped for an upcoming escape. The others, absorbed in their workday and night, neither read the newspapers nor hear the radio. And if they were told a result, they pretended to be interested in it, but they actually welcomed it with the distracted indifference that one imagines to the combatants of the great wars, exhausted from work, applied only to not fail in their daily duty and no longer hoping for either the decisive operation or the day of the armistice. Grand, who continued to carry out the calculations necessary for the plague, would certainly have been unable to indicate the general results. Unlike Tarrou, Rambert and Rieux, visibly hard with fatigue, his health had never been good. However, he combined his duties as assistant to the town hall, his secretariat at Rieux and his night work. We could thus see him in a continual state of exhaustion, supported by two or three fixed ideas, like that of offering a complete vacation after the plague, for at least a week, and then working positively, "hat down ", to what he was having. He was also subject to sudden tenderness and, on these occasions, he willingly spoke of Jeanne to Rieux, wondered where she could be at the same time, and if, reading the newspapers, she thought of him. It was with him that Rieux found himself one day speaking of his own wife in the most mundane tone, which he had never done before. Uncertain of the credit to be attached to his wife's always reassuring telegrams, he had decided to wire the chief medical officer of the establishment where she was being treated. In return, he had received the announcement of a worsening in the patient's condition and the assurance that everything would be done to halt the progress of the disease. He had kept the news to himself and he couldn't explain, except from fatigue, how he could have told it to Grand. The employee, after talking to him about Jeanne, asked him about his wife and Rieux replied. "You know," said Grand, "it heals very well now." And Rieux nodded, simply saying that the separation was starting to take a long time and that perhaps his wife would have helped him overcome his illness, when today she must have felt completely alone. Then he was silent and only answered Grand questions evasively. The rest were in the same condition. Tarrou resisted better, but his notebooks show that if his curiosity had not diminished in depth, it had lost its diversity. During this entire period, in fact, he was apparently only interested in Cottard. In the evening, at Rieux's, where he had ended up settling since the hotel had been transformed into a quarantine house, he was barely listening to Grand or the doctor announcing the results. He immediately brought the conversation back to the little details of Oran life that usually occupied him. As for Castel, the day he came to tell the doctor that the serum was ready, and after they had decided to make the first test on the little boy of Mr. Othon who had just been brought to the hospital and whose case seemed desperate to Rieux, he was communicating to his old friend the latest statistics, when he realized that his interlocutor had fallen asleep deep in the hollow of his chair. And before this face where, usually, an air of sweetness and irony put a perpetual youth and which, suddenly abandoned, a trickle of saliva joining the parted lips, let see its wear and its age, Rieux felt his throat tighten. It was by such weaknesses that Rieux could judge his fatigue. His sensitivity escaped him. Knotted most of the time, hardened and withered, it punctured from time to time and abandoned it to emotions over which it was no longer in control. His only defense was to take refuge in this hardening and to tighten the knot that had formed in him. He knew it was the right way to continue. For the rest, he didn't have many illusions and his tiredness took away those he still had. Because he knew that, for a period of which he did not see the end, his role was no longer to heal. Its role was to diagnose. Discover, see, describe, record, then condemn, it was his task. Wives took her by the wrist and yelled, "Doctor, give him life!" But he was not there to give life, he was there to order isolation. What was the hatred he saw on his faces for? "You have no heart," she was told one day. But yes, he did. It served him to endure the twenty hours a day when he saw men who were made to live die. He used to start over every day. Now he had just enough heart for it. How would this heart have been enough to give life? No, it was not relief supplies that he distributed all day long, but information. It couldn't be called a man's profession, of course. But, after all, to whom, among this terrorized and decimated crowd, had they left the leisure to exercise their profession of man? It was still happy that there was fatigue. If Rieux had been fresher, this smell of death everywhere spread could have made him sentimental. But when you've only had four hours of sleep, you're not sentimental. We see things as they are, that is to say that we see them according to justice, the hideous and derisory justice. And the others, the condemned, felt it too. Before the plague, we received him as a savior. He was going to fix everything with three pills and a syringe, and he was squeezed by the arm as he led him down the halls. It was flattering, but dangerous. Now, on the contrary, he was showing up with soldiers, and it took shots with the butt so that the family decided to open. They wanted to drag him and bring all of humanity with them into death. Ah! it was very true that men could not do without men, that he was as destitute as these unfortunates and that he deserved the same trembling of pity that he allowed to grow in him when he had left them. It was at least, during those interminable weeks, the thoughts that Doctor Rieux was agitating with those concerning his state of separation. And it was also the ones whose reflections he read on the faces of his friends. But the most dangerous effect of the exhaustion which gradually won over all those who continued this fight against the scourge was not in this indifference to external events and the emotions of others, but in the neglect in which they let themselves go . Because they tended then to avoid all the gestures which were not absolutely essential, and which always appeared to them beyond their strength. This is how these men came to neglect more and more often the rules of hygiene which they had codified, to forget some of the many disinfections which they had to practice on themselves, to run sometimes, without to be protected against the contagion, near the patients affected by pulmonary plague, because, warned at the last moment that it was necessary to go to the infected houses, it had seemed to them in advance exhausting to return to some place to make the instillations required. There was the real danger, because it was the fight itself against the plague which then made them most vulnerable to the plague, they bet in short on chance and chance is nobody's. There was, however, a man in the city who seemed neither exhausted nor discouraged, and who remained the living image of satisfaction. It was Cottard. He continued to stay away, while maintaining his relationships with others. But he had chosen to see Tarrou as often as his work permitted, on the one hand, because Tarrou was well informed about his case and, on the other hand, because he knew how to welcome the small rentier with an unalterable cordiality. It was a perpetual miracle, but Tarrou, despite the hard work he provided, was always kind and attentive. Even when tiredness crushed him on certain evenings, he found new energy the next day. "With that one," Cottard said to Rambert, "we can chat, because he's a man. We are always understood. That's why Tarrou's notes, at that time, gradually converged on the character of Cottard. Tarrou tried to give a picture of Cottard's reactions and reflections, as they were given to him by him or as he interpreted them. Under the heading "Cottard and plague reports", this table occupies a few pages of the notebook and the narrator thinks useful to give an overview here. Tarrou's general opinion on the small annuitant was summed up in this judgment: "He is a character who is growing up. Apparently, moreover, he grew up in a good mood. He was not unhappy with the turn of events. He sometimes expressed the depth of his thought, before Tarrou, by remarks like this: "Of course, it's not getting better. But at least everyone is in the bath. "Of course," added Tarrou, "he is threatened like the others, but rightly so, he is with the others." And then he doesn't seriously think, I'm sure, that he can be affected by the plague. He seems to live on this idea, not so stupid by the way, that a man in the grip of a great illness, or a deep anguish, is dispensed at the same time from all other illnesses or anxieties. "Have you noticed," he said, that we cannot accumulate diseases? Suppose you have a serious or incurable disease, serious cancer, or good tuberculosis, you will never get plague or typhus, it is impossible. Besides, it goes even further, because you've never seen a cancer patient die from an automobile accident." True or false, this idea puts Cottard in a good mood. The only thing he doesn't want is to be separated from the others. He prefers to be besieged with all than a prisoner on his own. With the plague, there is no longer any question of secret investigations, files, files, mysterious instructions, and imminent arrest. Strictly speaking, there are no more police, no more old or new crimes, no more culprits, there are only convicts awaiting the most arbitrary pardons, and, among them, the police themselves. "Thus Cottard, and always according to Tarrou's interpretation, was justified in considering the symptoms of anxiety and dismay that our fellow citizens presented with this indulgent and understanding satisfaction which could be expressed by a:" Always speak, I have had before you. "No matter how much I told him that the only way to not be separated from others was after all to have a good conscience, he looked at me badly and he said to me:" So, at no one is ever with anyone. " And then: "You can go, I'm telling you. The only way to put people together is to send them the plague again. So, look around." And the truth is, I understand what he means and how comfortable life today should seem to him. How would he not recognize in passing the reactions that were his; everyone's attempt to have everyone with them; the kindness that one deploys to sometimes inform a lost passerby and the bad mood that is shown to him at other times; people's rush to luxury restaurants, their satisfaction at being there and lingering there; the disorderly crowd that lines up every day at the cinema, which fills all the theaters and the dance halls themselves, which spreads like a raging tide in all public places; the retreat from all contact, the appetite for human warmth which nevertheless pushes men towards each other, elbows towards elbows and the sexes towards the sexes? Cottard has known all of this before them, obviously. Except women, because with his head ... And I guess when he felt close to going to girls, he refused, so as not to give himself a bad gender which, later, could have served him. "In short, the plague succeeds. Of a lonely man who didn't want to be, she makes an accomplice. Because obviously it is an accomplice and an accomplice who revel. He is an accomplice of everything he sees, superstitions, illegitimate fears, the susceptibilities of these alert souls; of their obsession with wanting to talk as little as possible about the plague and not ceasing to talk about it; from their panic and pallor to the slightest headache since they knew the disease started with headache; and their irritated, susceptible, unstable sensitivity which turns into an oversight of offense and which grieves at the loss of a panty button. Tarrou often went out with Cottard in the evening. He then told, in his notebooks, how they plunged into the dark crowd of twilight or night, shoulder to shoulder, immersing themselves in a white and black mass where, from time to time, a lamp put out rare flashes, and accompanying the human herd towards the warm pleasures which defended it against the cold of the plague. What Cottard, a few months earlier, was looking for in public places, luxury, and ample living, what he dreamed of without being able to satisfy himself, that is to say unrestrained enjoyment, an entire people was going there now. When the price of all things went up irresistibly, we had never wasted so much money, and when most were lacking, we had never dissipated the superfluous better. We saw an increasing number of games of idleness which was, however, only unemployment. Tarrou and Cottard sometimes followed, for long minutes, one of these couples who previously applied themselves to hiding what linked them and who, now, huddled together, stubbornly walked through the city, without seeing the crowd that surrounded them, with the somewhat fixed distraction of great passions. Cottard was touched: "Ah! the fellows! " he said. And he spoke loudly, flourished amidst the collective fever, the royal tips that rang around them and the intrigue that knotted before their eyes. However, Tarrou felt that there was little wickedness in Cottard's attitude. His "I knew it before them" was more of a misfortune than a triumph. "I believe," said Tarrou, "that he begins to love these men imprisoned between the sky and the walls of their city. For example, he would gladly explain to them, if he could, it's not that bad: "You hear them, he told me: after the plague I will do this, after the plague I will do this… They poison themselves existence instead of being quiet. And they don't even realize their benefits. Could I say, myself: after my arrest, I will do this? Arrest is a beginning, not an end. While the plague ... You want my opinion?

They are unhappy because they do not let go. And I know what I'm saying." "He knows what he is saying," added Tarrou. He judges at their true price the contradictions of the inhabitants of Oran who, at the same time where they deeply feel the need for warmth which brings them together, cannot however abandon themselves to it because of the distrust which distances them from each other . We know all too well that you cannot trust your neighbor, that he is able to give you the plague without your knowledge and to take advantage of your abandonment to infect you. When you have spent your time, like Cottard, seeing possible indicators in all those for whom, however, you sought company, you can understand this feeling. We sympathize very well with people who live with the idea that the plague can, overnight, put their hand on their shoulder and that it may be preparing to do so, when we rejoices to be still unharmed. As much as possible, he is comfortable in terror. But because he has felt all of this before them, I believe he cannot quite experience the cruelty of this uncertainty with them. In short, with us, we who have not yet died of the plague, he feels that his freedom and his life are every day on the verge of being destroyed. But since he himself lived in terror; he finds it normal for others to know it in turn. More exactly, terror then seems to him less heavy to bear than if he were there alone. That's why he's wrong and more difficult to understand than others. But, after all, that's why he deserves more than others that we try to understand him. Finally, Tarrou's pages end with a story which illustrates this singular conscience which came at the same time to Cottard and the plague victims. This narrative roughly captures the difficult atmosphere of that era and that is why the narrator attaches importance to it. They had gone to the Municipal Opera where they played Orpheus and Eurydice. Cottard had invited Tarrou. It was about a troop which had come, in the spring of the plague, to give representations in our city. Blocked by illness, this troop was forced, after agreement with our Opera, to replay their show once a week. For months now, every Friday, our municipal theater has been ringing melodious complaints from Orpheus and helpless calls from Eurydice. However, this show continued to enjoy the public's favor and always made big receipts. Installed in the most expensive places, Cottard and Tarrou dominated a bed swollen to the brim with the most elegant of our fellow citizens. Those who arrived obviously applied themselves not to miss their entry. Under the dazzling light of the front curtain, while the musicians discreetly tuned their instruments, the silhouettes stood out precisely, went from one row to the other, bowed gracefully. In the slight hubbub of a bona fide conversation, the men regained the confidence they lacked a few hours earlier, among the black streets of the city. The coat hunted the plague. Throughout the first act, Orpheus complained with ease, a few women in tunics gracefully commented on her misfortune, and love was sung in wings. The room reacts with discreet warmth. It was scarcely noticed that Orpheus introduced tremors which did not appear in his air of the second act and asked the master of the Underworld with a slight excess of pathos to be touched by his tears. Certain jerky gestures which escaped him appeared to the most discerning as a stylization effect which added to the singer's interpretation. It took the great duo of Orpheus and Eurydice in the third act (it was the moment when Eurydice escaped her lover) for a certain surprise to run in the room. And as if the singer had only waited for this movement from the audience, or, more certainly still, as if the rumor from the floor confirmed it in what he felt, he chooses this moment to advance towards the ramp of a grotesque way, arms and legs spread in his antique costume, and to collapse in the middle of the sheepfolds of the decor which had never ceased to be anachronistic but which, in the eyes of the spectators, became it for the first time, and in a terrible way. Because, at the same time, the orchestra was silent, the people in the floor rose and slowly started to evacuate the room, first in silence as one leaves a church, the service finished, or a mortuary room after a visit, the women gathering their skirts and leaving head down, the men guiding their companions by the elbow and preventing them from colliding with the folding seats. But, little by little, the movement rushed, the whisper became exclamation and the crowd flocked to the exits and hurried there, to end up jostling there screaming. Cottard and Tarrou, who had only risen, remained alone in front of one of the images of what was their life then: the plague on the stage under the appearance of a disjointed thespian and, in the room, all a luxury become useless in the form of forgotten fans and lace dragging on the red of the armchairs. Rambert, during the first days of September, had seriously worked alongside Rieux. He had simply asked for a day off on the day when he was to meet Gonzalès and the two young men outside the boys' school. That day, at noon, Gonzalès and the journalist saw the two laughing little ones arrive. They said we had no luck the other time, but that was to be expected. In any case, it was no longer their week on call. We had to wait until next week. We would start again. Rambert says that was the word. Gonzalès therefore proposed an appointment for the following Monday. But this time, we would install Rambert at Marcel and Louis' home. "We will make an appointment, you and me. If I'm not there, you will go directly to them. We'll explain to you where they live. But Marcel, or Louis, said at that moment that the simplest thing was to lead the comrade right away. If it was not difficult, there was food for the four of them. And that way, he would realize. Gonzales said it was a very good idea and they went down to the port. Marcel and Louis lived at the end of the Marine district, near the doors that opened onto the ledge. It was a small Spanish house, thick with walls, with painted wooden shutters, bare and shady rooms. There was rice that the mother of the young men served, an old Spanish woman smiling and full of wrinkles. Gonzales was surprised because rice was already lacking in town. "We are working on the doors," says Marcel. Rambert ate and drank, and Gonzales said he was a real boyfriend, while the reporter only thought about the week he had to spend. In fact, he had two weeks to wait, because the watchtowers were extended to fifteen days, to reduce the number of teams. And, during those fifteen days, Rambert worked without sparing himself, uninterruptedly, his eyes closed, so to speak, from dawn until night. Late at night, he went to bed and slept in a heavy sleep. The sudden shift from idleness to this exhausting toil left him almost dreamless and without strength. He said little about his upcoming escape. Only one notable fact: after a week, he told the doctor that for the first time, the night before, he got drunk. Leaving the bar, he suddenly had the impression that his groins were getting bigger and that his arms were difficult to move around the armpit. He thought it was the plague. And the only reaction he could have then and which he agreed with Rieux that it was not reasonable, was to run up the city, and there, from a small place, from where one still did not discover the sea, but from where we could see a little more sky, he called his wife with a loud cry, over the city walls. Returning home and finding no signs of infection on his body, he was not very proud of this sudden attack. Rieux said that he understood very well that we could do this: "In any case," he said, "it may happen that we want to." "Mr. Othon told me about you this morning," said Rieux suddenly, as Rambert left him. He asked me if I knew you, "Advise him, then," he said, "not to go into smuggling circles." He stood out there. " - What does that mean? - It means you have to hurry. - Thank you, said Rambert, shaking the doctor's hand. Suddenly he turned on the door. Rieux noticed that for the first time since the start of the plague, he was smiling. - So why don't you stop me from leaving? You have the means. Rieux shook his head with his usual movement, and said that it was Rambert's business, that he had chosen happiness and that he, Rieux, had no arguments to oppose. He felt unable to judge what was right or wrong in this matter. - Why tell me to act quickly, under these conditions? Rieux smiles in turn. - It may be that I, too, want to do something for happiness. The next day, they no longer talked about anything, but worked together. The following week, Rambert was finally installed in the small Spanish house. He had been made a bed in the common room. As the young men did not come home for the meal, and as he was asked to go out as little as possible, he lived there alone, most of the time, or conversed with the old mother. She was dry and active, dressed in black, brown, and wrinkled face, under very clean white hair. Silent, she only smiled with all her eyes when she looked at Rambert. Other times, she asked him if he was not afraid to bring the plague to his wife. He thought it was a chance to run, but in short it was minimal, while staying in the city, they risked being separated forever. - She's nice? said the old woman, smiling. - Very nice. - Pretty one? - I believe. - Ah! she said, that's why. Rambert was thinking. It was probably for that, but it was impossible that it was only for that. - You don't believe in the good Lord? said the old woman who went to mass every morning. Rambert recognized that it was not, and the old woman said it was for that. - You have to join her, you're right. If not, what would you have left? The rest of the time, Rambert went round in circles around the bare, plastered walls, caressing the fans nailed to the walls, or else counted the balls of wool that fringed the table carpet. In the evening, the young people returned. They didn't talk much, except to say that it wasn't time yet. After dinner, Marcel played the guitar and they drank an aniseed liqueur. Rambert seemed to be thinking. On Wednesday, Marcel returned saying, "It's for tomorrow night, at midnight. Get ready. Of the two men who held the post with them, one had plague and the other, who usually shared the first room, was under observation. Thus, for two or three days, Marcel and Louis would be alone. During the night, they were going to work out the last details. The next day, it would be possible. Rambert thanked. " You are happy? Asked the old woman. He says yes, but he was thinking of something else. The next day, under a heavy sky, the heat was humid and stifling. The news of the plague was bad. The old Spanish woman, however, kept her serenity. "There is sin in the world," she said. So, necessarily! Like Marcel and Louis, Rambert was shirtless. But whatever he did, sweat ran down his shoulders and across his chest. In the half-light of the house with closed shutters, it made them brown and varnished torsos. Rambert was going around in circles without speaking. Suddenly, at four o'clock in the afternoon, he got dressed and announced that he was going out. - Watch out, said Marcel, it's midnight. Everything is in place. Rambert went to the doctor. Rieux's mother told Rambert he would find him at the hospital in the upper town. In front of the guardhouse, the same crowd was still spinning around. "Move on!" Said a sergeant with protruding eyes. The others were traveling, but in circles. "There is nothing to expect," said the sergeant, whose sweat pierced the jacket. It was also the opinion of the others, but they still stayed, despite the deadly heat. Rambert showed his pass to the sergeant who pointed to Tarrou's office. The door opened onto the courtyard. He crossed Father Paneloux, who was leaving the office. In a dirty little white room that smelled like a pharmacy and a damp sheet, Tarrou, seated behind a black wooden desk, his shirt sleeves rolled up, dabbed the sweat running down his blood from his arm with a tissue. - Still there? he says. - Yes, I would like to speak to Rieux. - He's in the room. But if it can be arranged without him, it would be better. - Why? - He's overworked. I avoid him what I can. Rambert looked at Tarrou. This one had lost weight. Fatigue blurred his eyes and features. His strong shoulders were gathered in a ball. There was a knock on the door, and a nurse entered, masked in white. He placed a bundle of cards on Tarrou's desk and, in a voice that the linen was stifling, said only: "Six", then left. Tarrou looked at the journalist and showed him the cards which he spread out like a fan. - Nice cards, huh? Well, no, they are the dead of the night. His forehead had widened. He folded the pack of cards. - The only thing we have left is accounting. Tarrou stood up, taking support on the table. - Are you going to leave soon? - Tonight, at midnight. Tarrou says that it pleased him and that Rambert had to watch over him. - Are you saying that sincerely? Tarrou shrugged: - At my age, one is necessarily sincere. Lying is too tiring. - Tarrou, said the journalist, I would like to see the doctor. Excuse me. - I know. He is more human than me. Let's go. - That's not it, said Rambert with difficulty. And he stopped. Tarrou looked at him and suddenly glowed. They followed a small corridor, the walls of which were painted light green and where an aquarium light was floating. Just before arriving at a double-glazed door, behind Just before arriving at a double-glazed door, behind which we saw a curious movement of shadows, Tarrou entered Rambert in a very small room, entirely lined with cupboards. He opened one of them, pulled two hydrophilic gauze masks from a sterilizer, handed one to Rambert and invited him to cover it. The journalist asked if it was useful for something and Tarrou answered that it was not, but that it gave confidence to the others. They pushed open the glass door. It was a huge room, with hermetically sealed windows, despite the season. At the top of the walls were purring air-freshening devices, and their curved propellers stirred the creamy, overheated air, above two rows of gray beds. From all sides rose deaf or high moans that made only a monotonous complaint. Men, dressed in white, moved slowly, in the cruel light that poured out from the tall bays lined with bars. Rambert felt uncomfortable in the terrible heat of this room and he found it difficult to recognize Rieux, leaning over a groaning form. The doctor incised the patient's groins, which two nurses, on each side of the bed, held quartered. When he got up, he dropped his instruments in the tray that an assistant was holding out to him and remained motionless for a moment, looking at the man we were dressing. - What's up? he said to Tarrou as he approached. - Paneloux agrees to replace Rambert at the quarantine house. He has already done a lot. It will remain the third prospecting team to regroup without Rambert. Rieux nodded. - Castel has completed its first preparations. He offers an essay. - Ah! said Rieux, that is good. - Finally, there is Rambert here. Rieux turned around. Over the mask, his eyes narrowed when he saw the reporter. - What are you doing here? he says. You should be somewhere else. Tarrou said it was for midnight tonight and Rambert added, "Basically. Each time one of them spoke, the gauze mask swelled and moistened in the area of the mouth. It made for a somewhat unreal conversation, like a dialogue of statues. "I would like to speak to you," said Rambert. - We will go out together if you don't mind. Wait for me in Tarrou's office. A moment later, Rambert and Rieux settled in the back of the doctor's car. Tarrou was driving. - No more gas, he said as he started. Tomorrow we will go on foot. - Doctor, said Rambert, I'm not leaving, and I want to stay with you. Tarrou did not flinch. He continued to drive. Rieux seemed unable to emerge from his fatigue. - And she? he said in a low voice. Rambert said that he had thought it over again, that he continued to believe what he believed, but that if he left, he would be ashamed. It would bother him to love the one he had left. But Rieux straightened up and said firmly that it was stupid and that there was no shame in preferring happiness. - Yes, said Rambert, but there can be shame in being happy alone. Tarrou, who had kept silent until then, without turning his head towards them, pointed out that if Rambert wanted to share the misfortune of men, he would never have time for happiness again. You had to choose. - That's not it, said Rambert. I always thought that I was a stranger to this city and that I had nothing to do with you. But now that I've seen what I've seen, I know I'm here, whether I like it or not. This story concerns us all. No one answered and Rambert seemed to get impatient. - You know that! Or what else would you do in this hospital? Have you therefore chosen yourself and renounced happiness? Neither Tarrou nor Rieux replied yet. The silence lasted a long time, until we approached the doctor's house. And Rambert again asked his last question, even more forcefully. And, alone, Rieux turned to him. He raised himself with effort: turned towards him. He raised himself with effort: "Pardon me, Rambert," he said, "but I don't know." Stay with us as you wish. A swerve from the car silenced him. Then he went on, looking in front of him: - Nothing in the world is worth turning away from what you like. And yet I turn away from it, too, without being able to know why. He dropped back onto his cushion. - It's a fact, that's all, he said wearily. Let's record it and draw the consequences. - What consequences? asked Rambert. - Ah! said Rieux, you cannot heal and know at the same time. So, let's heal as quickly as possible. This is the most urgent. At midnight, Tarrou and Rieux were making Rambert the map of the neighborhood he was responsible for prospecting, when Tarrou looked at his watch. Raising his head, he met Rambert's gaze. - Have you warned? The journalist looked away: "I had sent a word," he said with effort, before going to see you. It was in the last days of October that Castel's serum was tried. In practice, he was Rieux's last hope. In the event of a new failure, the doctor was confident that the city would be left to the whims of the disease, either that the epidemic would last for many more months, or that it would stop without reason. The day before Castel came to visit Rieux, Mr. Othon's son had fallen ill and the whole family must have been in their forties. The mother, who had left shortly before, therefore found herself isolated for the second time. Respecting the instructions given, the judge had called Doctor Rieux as soon as he recognized the signs of the disease on the child's body. When Rieux arrived, the father and mother were standing at the foot of the bed. The little girl had been removed. The child was in the abatement period and allowed himself to be examined without complaining. When the doctor looked up, he met the gaze of the judge and, behind him, the pale face of the mother who had put a handkerchief over her mouth and was following the doctor's gestures with wide eyes. - That's it, isn't it? said the judge in a cold voice. "Yes," replied Rieux, looking at the child again. The mother's eyes widened, but she still didn't speak. The judge was also silent, then said in a lower tone: - Well, doctor, we must do what is prescribed. Rieux avoided looking at the mother who still held her handkerchief over her mouth. "It will be done quickly," he said hesitantly, "if I can call. Mr. Othon says he was going to drive it. But the doctor turned to the woman: - I'm sorry. You should prepare some business. You know what it is. Mrs. Othon seemed banned. She was looking down. - Yes, she said, nodding, that's what I'm going to do. Before leaving them, Rieux couldn't help but ask them if they needed anything. The woman was still watching him in silence. But the judge looked away this time. - No, he said, then he swallowed, but save my child. The quarantine, which at the beginning was only a simple formality, had been organized by Rieux and Rambert, very strictly. In particular, they demanded that members of the same family should always be isolated members of the same family should always be isolated from each other. If one of the family members had been infected without knowing it, the chances of the disease should not be increased. Rieux explained these reasons to the judge who found them to be good. However, his wife and him looked at him in such a way that the doctor felt how distraught this separation left them. Mrs. Othon and her granddaughter were accommodated in the quarantine hotel run by Rambert. But for the examining magistrate, there was no more room, except in the isolation camp that the prefecture was organizing, on the municipal stadium, using tents loaned by the service of roads. Rieux apologized, but Mr. Othon said that there was only one rule for all and that it was right to obey. As for the child, he was transported to the auxiliary hospital, in an old classroom where ten beds had been installed. After twenty hours, Rieux considered his case hopeless. The little body let itself be devoured by the infection, without a reaction. Very small, painful, but barely formed buboes blocked the joints of its slender limbs. He was defeated in advance. This is why Rieux had the idea of trying Castel's serum on him. That evening, after dinner, they practiced the long inoculation, without getting a single reaction from the child. At dawn the next day, everyone went to the little boy to judge this decisive experience. The child, out of his torpor, turned convulsively in the sheets. The doctor, Castel and Tarrou, had been standing near him for four hours, following step by step the progress or the halts of the disease. At the head of the bed, Tarrou's massive body was a little hunched. At the foot of the bed, seated near Rieux standing, Castel was reading, with all the appearances of tranquility, an old work. Gradually, as the day widened in the old school hall, the others arrived. Paneloux first, who placed himself on the other side of the bed, in relation to Tarrou, and leaned against the wall. A pained expression could be seen on his face, and the tiredness of all those days when he had paid for himself had drawn lines on his congested forehead. In turn, Joseph Grand arrived. It was seven o'clock and the employee apologized for being short of breath. He was only going to stay for a while, maybe we already knew something specific. Without saying a word, Rieux showed him the child who, his eyes closed in a decomposed face, his teeth clenched at the limit of his strength, his body motionless, turned and turned his head from right to left, on the bolster without a sheet. When it was day enough, at last, so that at the back of the room, on the blackboard that had remained in place, one could make out the traces of old formulas of equation, Rambert arrived. He leaned against the foot of the next bed and took out a pack of cigarettes. But after looking at the child, he put the package back in his pocket. Castel, still seated, looked at Rieux over his glasses: - Have you heard from the father? - No, said Rieux, he's in the isolation camp. The doctor squeezed the bar of the bed where the child was moaning. He did not take his eyes off the little patient who stiffened suddenly and, teeth clenched again, widened a little at the waist, slowly spreading his arms and legs. From the small body, naked under the military blanket, rose a smell of wool and sour sweat. The child gradually relaxed, brought his arms and legs back to the center of the bed and, still blind and dumb, seemed to breathe faster. Rieux met the look of Tarrou who looked away. They had already seen children die since terror had not chosen for months, but they had never followed their suffering minute by minute, as they had done since morning. And, of course, the pain inflicted on these innocent people never ceased to seem to them what it really was, that is to say a scandal. But until then at least, they were scandalized abstractly, in a way, because they had never looked in the face, so long, the agony of an innocent. The child, as if bitten in the stomach, was bending again, with a small groan. He stayed like this for long seconds, shaken by shivers and convulsive tremors, as if his frail carcass was bending under the furious wind of the plague and creaking under the repeated breaths of fever. The flurry past, he relaxed a little, the fever seemed to recede and abandon him, gasping, on a wet and poisonous strike where rest was already like death. When the hot stream reached it again for the third time and lifted it a little, the child curled up, recoiled at the bottom of the bed in the terror of the flame which was burning him and waved his head madly, throwing off his blanket . Large tears, gushing under the inflamed eyelids, began to flow on his leaded face, and, at the end of the crisis, exhausted, tensing his bony legs and his arms whose flesh had melted in forty-eight hours, the child took a grotesque crucified pose in the devastated bed. Tarrou leaned over and with his heavy hand wiped the little face soaked in tears and sweat. For some time, Castel had closed his book and was looking at the patient. He started a sentence, but was forced to cough to be able to finish it, because his voice abruptly detonated: - There was no morning remission, was there, Rieux? Rieux says not, but that the child resisted longer than he was normal. Paneloux, who seemed a little slumped against the wall, said dully: - If he has to die, he will have suffered longer. Rieux turned suddenly to him and opened his mouth to speak, but he fell silent, made a visible effort to dominate himself and returned his gaze to the child. Light swelled in the room. On the other five beds, shapes moved and moaned, but with a discretion that seemed concerted. The only one crying at the other end of the room uttered small exclamations at regular intervals which seemed to express more astonishment than pain. It seemed that, even for the sick, it was not the dread of the beginning. There was, now, a kind of consent in their way of taking the disease. Alone, the child was struggling with all his might. Rieux who, from time to time, took his pulse, needlessly elsewhere and rather to get out of the impotent stillness he was in, felt, closing his eyes, this agitation mixed with the tumult of his own blood. He then became confused with the tortured child and tried to support him with all his strength, still intact. But one minute together, the pulsations of their two hearts went out of tune, the child escaped him, and his effort sank into a void. He then let go of the thin wrist and returned to his place. Light went from pink to yellow along the whitewashed walls. Behind the glass, a morning of heat began to crackle. Barely did we hear Grand leave saying he would come back. All were waiting. The child, eyes still closed, seemed to calm down a bit. The hands, now like claws, gently plowed the sides of the bed. They went back up, scratched the blanket near their knees, and suddenly the child folded his legs, brought his thighs close to his stomach and came to a stop. He then opened his eyes for the first time and looked at Rieux who was in front of him. In the hollow of his face now frozen in gray clay, his mouth opened and, almost immediately, he issued a single continuous cry, hardly breathed in, which suddenly filled the room with a monotonous protest, discord, and so inhuman that it seemed to come from all men at once. Rieux clenched his teeth and Tarrou turned away. Rambert approached the bed near Castel, who closed the book, which remained open on his lap. Paneloux looked at that childish mouth, soiled by illness, full of that cry of all ages. And he dropped to his knees and everyone found it natural to hear him say in a slightly muffled voice, but separate behind the anonymous complaint that didn't stop, "My God, save this child. But the child continued to cry and, all around him, the sick became agitated. The man whose exclamations had not stopped, at the other end of the room, hastened the rhythm of his complaint to make it, too, a real cry, while the others moaned louder and louder. A tide of sobs surged through the room, covering the prayer of Paneloux, and Rieux, clinging to his bed-bar, closed his eyes, drunk with fatigue and disgust. When he opened them again, he found Tarrou near him. - I have to go, said Rieux. I can't take it anymore. But suddenly the other patients fell silent. The doctor then recognized that the child's cry had weakened, that it was still weakening and that he had just stopped. Around him, the complaints resumed, but quietly, and as a distant echo of this struggle which had just ended. Because it was over. Castel had gone to the other side of the bed and said it was over. With his mouth open, but mute, the child lay in the hollow of the messy blankets, suddenly shrunk, with the remains of tears on his face. Paneloux approached the bed and gestured for the blessing. Then he picked up his dresses and went out through the central aisle. - Will we have to start all over again? asked Tarrou of Castel. The old doctor was shaking his head. - Maybe, he said with a tight smile. After all, he resisted for a long time. But Rieux was already leaving the room, with such hasty steps, and with such an air that, when he passed Paneloux, he stretched out his arm to hold him back. "Come on, doctor," he said. In the same carried away movement, Rieux turned and threw him violently: - Ah! that one, at least, was innocent, you know that! Then he turned away and, crossing the doors of the room before Paneloux, he reached the back of the schoolyard. He sat down on a bench between the small powdery trees and wiped the sweat that was already running down his eyes. He wanted to shout again to finally untie the violent knot that was crushing his heart. The heat fell slowly between the branches of the ficus trees. The blue morning sky was quickly covered with a whitish pillowcase which made the air stuffier. Rieux let himself go on his bench. He looked at the branches, at the sky, slowly regaining his breath, gradually reducing his fatigue. - Why did you speak to me with that anger? said a voice behind him. For me too, this spectacle was unbearable. Rieux turned to Paneloux: - It's true, he said. Excuse me. But fatigue is madness. And there are hours in this city where I only feel my revolt. "I understand," murmured Paneloux. This is revolting because it passes our measure. But perhaps we must love what we cannot understand. Rieux straightened up suddenly. He looked at Paneloux, with all the strength and passion of which he was capable and shook his head. - No, father, he said. I have another idea of love. And I will refuse until death to love this creation where children are tortured. On Paneloux's face, an upset shadow passed. - Ah! doctor, "he said sadly," I just understood what is called grace. But Rieux had let himself go back to his bench. From the depths of his comeback fatigue, he replied with more gentleness: - That's what I don't have, I know it. But I don't want to discuss this with you. We are working together for something that unites us beyond blasphemy and prayer. That alone is important. Paneloux sat near Rieux. He looked moved. - Yes, he said, yes, you too work for the salvation of man. Rieux was trying to smile. - Human salvation is too big a word for me. I don't go that far. It's his health that interests me, his health first. Paneloux hesitated. - Doctor, he said. But he stopped. On his forehead, too, sweat began to trickle. He whispered, "Goodbye," and his eyes were bright when he got up. He was about to leave when Rieux, who was thinking, also got up and took a step towards him. "Forgive me again," he said. This radiance will never be renewed. Paneloux stretched out his hand and said with sadness: - And yet I have not convinced you! - What does it do? said Rieux. What I hate is death and evil, you know that. And whether you like it or not, we are together to suffer and fight them. Rieux was holding Paneloux's hand. - You see, he said, avoiding looking at him, God himself cannot separate us now. Since entering the health facilities, Paneloux had not left the hospitals and the places where the plague was encountered. Among the rescuers, he had placed himself in the rank which seemed to him to be his, that is to say the first. He had not missed the spectacle of death. And although in principle he was protected by serum, the concern for his own death was not foreign to him either. Apparently, he had always kept calm. But from that day when he had long watched a child die, he seemed changed. Growing tension could be seen on his face. And the day he said to Rieux, smiling, that he was currently preparing a short treatise on the subject: "Can a priest consult a doctor? ", The doctor got the impression that it was something more serious than Paneloux seemed to say. As the doctor expressed the desire to take cognizance of this work, Paneloux announced to him that he had to preach at the mass of men, and that on this occasion he would expose some, at least, of his points of view: - I would like you to come, doctor, the subject will interest you. The father delivered his second preaching on a windy day. Indeed, the ranks of the audience were sparser than during the first preaching. It's that this kind of spectacle no longer had the attraction of novelty for our fellow citizens. In the difficult circumstances that the city was going through, the very word "novelty" had lost its meaning. Besides, most people, when they had not completely deserted their religious duties, or when they did not coincide with a deeply immoral personal life, had replaced ordinary practices with unreasonable superstitions. They were more willing to wear protective medals or St. Roch amulets than they went to mass. We can give as an example the immoderate use that our fellow citizens made of prophecies. In the spring, in fact, we had waited, from one moment to the next, for the end of the disease, and no one dared ask others for details on the duration of the epidemic, since everyone was persuaded that she would not have one. But as the days went by, it became feared that this misfortune was truly endless and, at the same time, the cessation of the epidemic became the object of all hopes. We passed, from hand to hand, various prophecies from magi or saints of the Catholic Church. Printers in the city quickly saw the advantage they could draw from this craze and distributed the texts that circulated in numerous copies. Realizing that the curiosity of the public was insatiable, they caused research, in the municipal libraries, on all the testimonies of this kind that the little history could provide, and they spread them in the city. When history itself ran out of prophecies, it was ordered from journalists who, on this point at least, were as competent as their models of past centuries. Some of these prophecies even appeared in the soap opera in the newspapers and were not read with less avidity than the sentimental stories which one could find there, at the time of health. Some of these forecasts were based on bizarre calculations involving the vintage of the year, the number of dead and the count of months already spent under the plague. Others made comparisons with the great plagues in history, drew out their similarities (which the prophecies called constant) and, by means of no less bizarre calculations, claimed to draw lessons relating to the present test. But the most appreciated by the public were undoubtedly those which, in an apocalyptic language, announced a series of events each of which could be the one that experienced the city and whose complexity allowed all interpretations. Nostradamus and Saint Odile were thus consulted daily, and always with fruit. What remained common to all the prophecies was that they were ultimately reassuring. Alone, the plague was not. These superstitions therefore took the place of religion for our fellow citizens and that is why the preaching of Paneloux took place in a church which was only three-quarters full. On the evening of the preaching, when Rieux arrived, the wind, which was seeping in air streams through the swinging doors of the entrance, was circulating freely among the listeners. And it was in a cold and silent church, in the midst of an audience exclusively composed of men, that he took his place and saw the father go up in the pulpit. The latter spoke in a softer and more reflective tone than the first time and, on several occasions, the assistants noticed a certain hesitation in his flow. Interestingly enough, he no longer said "you", but "we". However, his voice gradually grew stronger. He began by recalling that, for many months, the plague was among us and that now that we know it better for having seen it so many times sit at our table or at the bedside of those we love, walk near us and wait for our arrival at the workplace, now therefore, perhaps we could better receive what she told us relentlessly and that, in the first surprise, it was possible that we had not listened well. What Father Paneloux had already preached in the same place remained true - or at least it was his conviction. But, perhaps still, as it happened to all of us, and he hit his chest, he had thought it and said without charity. What remained true, however, was that there was always something to remember. The cruelest test was still beneficial for the Christian. And, precisely, what the Christian in this case had to look for was his benefit, and what the benefit was made of, and how one could find it. At that time, around Rieux, people seemed to square themselves between the armrests of their bench and settle down as square between the armrests of their bench and settle down as comfortably as they could. One of the padded doors at the entrance beat gently. Someone went out of their way to maintain it. And Rieux, distracted by this agitation, barely heard Paneloux resuming his preaching. He said roughly that one should not try to explain the spectacle of the plague but try to learn what one could learn from it. Rieux confusedly understood that, according to the father, there was nothing to explain. His interest became fixed when Paneloux strongly said that there were things that could be explained in the eyes of God and others that we could not. There was certainly good and evil, and, in general, it was easy to explain what separated them. But inside the evil, the difficulty began. There was, for example, the apparently necessary evil and the apparently unnecessary evil. There was don Juan plunged into Hell and the death of a child. Because if it is right that the libertine is struck down, one does not understand the suffering of the child. And, in truth, there was nothing on earth more important than the suffering of a child and the horror that suffering carries with it and the reasons to be found for it. In the rest of life, God made everything easier for us and, until then, religion was without merit. Here, on the contrary, he put us at the foot of the wall. We were thus under the walls of the plague and it is in their mortal shadow that we had to find our benefit. Father Paneloux even refused to give himself easy advantages which enabled him to climb the wall. It would have been easy for him to say that the eternity of the delights awaiting the child could compensate for his suffering, but, in truth, he knew nothing about it. Who could indeed say that the eternity of a joy could compensate for a moment of human pain? It would not be a Christian, of course, whose Master experienced the pain in his limbs and in his soul. No, the father would remain at the foot of the wall, faithful to this quartering of which the cross is the symbol, face to face with the suffering of a child. And he would fearlessly say to those who listened to him that day, "My brothers, the moment has come. You have to believe everything or deny everything. And who among you would dare to deny everything? Rieux barely had time to think that the father was rubbing shoulders with the heresy that the other was already taking up with force, to affirm that this injunction, this pure requirement, was the benefit of the Christian. It was also his virtue. The father knew that there was excess in the virtue he was going to talk about that would shock many minds, accustomed to a more lenient and classic morality. But the religion of the time of plague could not be the religion of every day and if God could admit, and even desire, that the soul rests and rejoices in times of happiness, he wanted it excessive in the excesses of misfortune. God was doing his creatures today the favor of putting them in a misfortune such that they had to find and assume the greatest virtue which is that of All or Nothing. A secular author, in the last century, had claimed to reveal the secret of the Church by claiming that there was no Purgatory. By this he meant that there were no half measures, that there was only Heaven and Hell and that one could only be saved or damned, depending on what one had chosen. It was, to believe Paneloux, a heresy like it could only be born within a libertine soul. Because there was a Purgatory. But there were undoubtedly times when this Purgatory should not be too much hoped for, there were times when one could not speak of venial sin. All sin was mortal and all criminal indifference. It was all or it was nothing. Paneloux stopped, and Rieux heard better at that moment, under the doors, the complaints of the wind which seemed to redouble outside. The father said at the same time that the virtue of total acceptance of which he spoke could not be understood in the restricted sense that it was usually given, that it was not trivial resignation, nor even the difficult humility. It was a humiliation, but a humiliation where the humiliated was consenting. Certainly, a child's suffering was humiliating for the mind and the heart. But that's why you had to enter it. But that's why, and Paneloux assured his audience that what he was going to say was not easy to say, he had to want it because God wanted it. Thus, only the Christian would spare nothing and, all closed issues, would go to the bottom of the essential choice. He would choose to believe everything so as not to be reduced to denying everything. And like the brave women who, in the churches at the moment, having learned that the buboes which formed were the natural way by which the body rejected its infection, said: "My God, give him buboes", the Christian would know surrender to the divine will, even incomprehensible. You couldn't say, "I understand that; but this is unacceptable ", we had to jump to the heart of this unacceptable that was offered to us, precisely so that we could make our choice. The suffering of children was our bitter bread, but without this bread, our soul would perish of its spiritual hunger. Here the muffled commotion which generally accompanied Father Paneloux's breaks began to be heard when, unexpectedly, the preacher resumed forcefully, pretending to ask instead of his listeners what was, in short, the course of action. He suspected it, we were going to pronounce the frightening word of fatalism. Well, he wouldn't back down from the term if he was only allowed to join the adjective "active." Certainly, and again, we should not imitate the Abyssinian Christians he spoke of. One should not even think of joining these Persian plague victims who threw their clothes on the Christian sanitary pickets by invoking the sky aloud to beg him to give the plague to these infidels who wanted to fight the evil sent by God. But conversely, one should not imitate either the monks of Cairo who, in the epidemics of the past century, gave communion by taking the host with tweezers to avoid contact with these humid and warm mouths where the infection could sleep. Persian plague victims and monks also sinned. For the former, the suffering of a child did not count and, for the latter, on the contrary, the very human fear of pain had invaded everything. In both cases, the problem was avoided. All remained deaf to the voice of God. But there were other examples that Paneloux wanted to point out. If we were to believe the chronicler of the great plague of Marseilles, of the eighty-one religious of the Convent of Mercy, only four survived the fever. And of these four, three fled. Thus, spoke the chroniclers and it was not their job to say more. But in reading this, all of Father Paneloux's thought went to the one who had remained alone, despite seventy-seven corpses, and especially above all the example of his three brothers. And the father, striking his fist on the edge of the pulpit, exclaimed: "My brothers, you must be the one who stays! It was not a question of refusing the precautions, the intelligent order that a society introduced in the disorder of a plague. We should not listen to these moralists who said that we should kneel and abandon everything. You just had to start walking forward, in darkness, a little blindly, and try to do good. But for the rest, it was necessary to remain, and to accept to rely on God, even for the death of the children, and without seeking personal recourse. Here, Father Paneloux spoke of the high figure of Bishop Belzunce during the Marseilles plague. He recalled that, towards the end of the epidemic, the bishop, having done all that he had to do, believing that there was no longer any remedy, locked himself up with provisions in his house which he made to wall ; that the inhabitants of which he was the idol, by a return of feeling such as one finds in the excess of the pains, became angry with him, surrounded his house with corpses to infect him and even threw bodies over it the walls, to make it perish more surely. Thus, the bishop, in a last weakness, had thought to isolate himself in the world of death and the dead fell to him from the sky on the head. So again, of us, who had to persuade ourselves that there is no island in the plague. No, there was no middle. We had to admit the scandal because we had to choose to hate God or to love him. And who would dare to choose hatred of God? "My brothers," said Paneloux at last, announcing that he was concluding, "the love of God is a difficult love. It presupposes total self-abandonment and self-disdain. But he alone can erase the suffering and death of children, he alone in any case make it necessary, because it is impossible to understand it and one can only want it. This is the difficult lesson I wanted to share with you. Here is faith, cruel in the eyes of men, decisive in the eyes of God, which must be approached. With this terrible image, we must equalize ourselves. On this summit, everything will merge and equalize, the truth will spring from the apparent injustice. Thus, in many churches in the South of France, plague victims sleep for centuries under the slabs of the choir, and priests speak above their tombs, and the spirit they propagate springs from this ashes where children have nevertheless put their share. When Rieux came out, a strong wind blew through the half-open door and assaulted the faithful in the face. He brought a smell of rain into the church, a scent of wet sidewalk that let them guess the look of the city before they got out. In front of Doctor Rieux, an old priest and a young deacon who were going out at the time had trouble retaining their hairstyles. The older boy couldn't stop holding their hairstyle. The older did not stop commenting on the preaching. He paid tribute to the eloquence of Paneloux, but he was worried about the boldness of thought that the father had shown. He believed that this preach showed more concern than strength, and, at the age of Paneloux, a priest had no right to be worried. The young deacon, his head bowed to protect himself from the wind, assured him that he frequented the father a lot, that he was aware of his development and that his treaty would be much bolder still and probably would not have the imprimatur . - So, what is his idea? said the old priest. They had arrived on the forecourt and the wind surrounded them, howling, cutting off the youngest. When he was able to speak, he said only: - If a priest consults a doctor, there is a contradiction. To Rieux, who reported the words of Paneloux to him, Tarrou said that he knew a priest who had lost his faith during the war when he discovered the face of a young man with sunken eyes. "Paneloux is right," said Tarrou. When innocence has its eyes cut, a Christian must either lose faith or accept having his eyes cut. Paneloux does not want to lose faith, he will go to the end. That's what he meant. Does this observation of Tarrou shed some light on the unfortunate events that followed and where the conduct of Paneloux seemed incomprehensible to those around him? We will judge. A few days after the preaching, Paneloux, in fact, took care of moving. It was the time when the evolution of the disease caused constant moves in the city. And, just as Tarrou had to leave his hotel to stay with Rieux, so the father had to leave the apartment where his order had placed him, to come and stay with an old person, used to churches and still free from the plague . During the move, the father had felt his fatigue and anxiety growing. And that's how he lost the esteem of his landlady. For the latter having warmly praised the merits of the prophecy of Saint Odile, the priest had shown him a very slight impatience, no doubt due to his weariness. Whatever effort he then made to obtain at least a benevolent neutrality from the old lady, he did not succeed. He had made a bad impression. And, every evening, before returning to his room filled with waves of crocheted lace, he had to contemplate the back of his hostess, seated in his living room, at the same time as he carried away the memory of "Good evening, my father" that she addressed to him dryly and without turning around. It was on such an evening that when he went to bed, his head beating, he felt free from his wrists and temples the raging waves of fever that had been running for several days. What followed was then known only by the stories of his hostess. In the morning she got up early, as usual. After a while, astonished not to see the father come out of his room, she decided, with a lot of hesitation, to knock on his door. She had found him still in bed after a sleepless night. He suffered from oppression and appeared more congested than usual. In her own words, she had courteously offered to call a doctor, but her proposal had been rejected with a violence which she considered regrettable. She could only have pulled out. A little later, the father rang the bell and made him ask. He apologized for his moodiness and told him that there could be no question of the plague, that he had none of the symptoms and that it was transient fatigue. The old lady had replied with dignity that her proposal was not born out of a concern of this order, that she did not have in mind her own safety which was in the hands of God, but that she had only thought to the father's health, for which she considered herself partly responsible. But as he didn't add anything, his hostess, eager to de all his duty had again offered to call her doctor. The father, again, had refused, but adding explanations that the old lady had deemed very confused. She only thought she understood, and it just seemed incomprehensible to him that the father refused this consultation because it was not in accordance with his principles. She concluded that the fever disturbed her tenant's ideas, and she only brought him some herbal tea. Always determined to fulfill exactly the obligations that the situation created for her, she had regularly visited the patient every two hours. What struck her most was the constant agitation in which the father spent the day. He threw the sheets back and brought them back to him, running his hand over his sweaty forehead, and straightening up often to try to cough with a choking, raspy, wet cough like a tear. He then seemed unable to extract cotton swabs from the back of his throat that would have suffocated him. At the end of these crises, he dropped back, with all the signs of exhaustion. Finally, he half straightened up again and, for a short moment, looked ahead, with a more vehement steadfastness than all the previous agitation. But the old lady was still hesitant to call a doctor and upset her patient. It could be a simple bout of fever, as spectacular as it seemed. In the afternoon, however, she tried to speak to the priest and received only a few confused words in response. She renewed her proposal. But then the father got up and half choking, he replied distinctly that he did not want a doctor. At that time, the hostess decided that she would wait until the next morning and that, if the father's condition was not improved, she would telephone the number that the Ransdoc agency repeated ten times daily to the radio. Always attentive to her homework, she thought of visiting her tenant during the night and watching over him. But in the evening, after giving her fresh herbal tea, she wanted to lie down a bit and did not wake up until the next day at dawn. She ran to the bedroom. The father was stretched out, without a movement. The extreme congestion of the previous day had been succeeded by a kind of lividity, which was all the more noticeable since the facial forms were still full. The father stared at the small chandelier of multicolored pearls which hung above the bed. As the old lady entered, he turned his head towards her. According to his hostess, he appeared to have been beaten all night and had lost all strength to react. She asked him how he was doing. And in a voice of which she noted the strangely indifferent sound, he said that he was ill, that he did not need a doctor and that it would be enough that he was transported to the hospital for everything to be in the rules. Terrified, the old lady ran to the phone. Rieux arrived at noon. To the hostess' account, he only replied that Paneloux was right and that it must have been too late. The father greeted him with the same indifferent air. Rieux examined her and was surprised to find none of the main symptoms of bubonic or pulmonary plague, except the engorgement and oppression of the lungs. Anyway, the pulse was so low and the general condition so alarming that there was little hope: - You have none of the main symptoms of the disease, he said to Paneloux. But, in reality, there is doubt, and I must isolate you. The father smiled oddly, as if politely, but fell silent. Rieux went out to telephone and returned. He was looking at the father. - I will stay near you, he said softly. The other appeared to revive and turned to the doctor's eyes where a kind of heat seemed to return. Then he articulated with difficulty, in such a way that it was impossible to articulate with difficulty, so that it was impossible to know whether he said it sadly or not: - Thank you, he said. But the religious do not have friends. They placed everything in God. He asked for the crucifix that was placed at the head of the bed and, when he had it, turned to look at it. At the hospital, Paneloux did not lose his teeth. He gave himself up as a thing to all the treatments imposed on him, but he never let go of the crucifix. However, the priest's case continued to be ambiguous. Doubt persisted in Rieux's mind. It was the plague and it was not her. For some time now, she had seemed to enjoy diverting the diagnoses. But in the case of Paneloux, what followed was to show that this uncertainty was unimportant. The fever went up. The cough became more and more hoarse and tortured the patient all day. Finally, in the evening, the father expectorated this cotton wool that was suffocating him. It was red. In the midst of the tumult of fever, Paneloux kept his eyes indifferent and when, the next morning, he was found dead, half poured out of the bed, his eyes expressed nothing. They wrote on his card: "Doubtful cases. " All Saints' Day that year was not what it used to be. Of course, time was of the moment. It had suddenly changed, and the late heat had suddenly given way to the coolness. Like in other years, a cold wind was now blowing continuously. Large clouds ran from one horizon to the other, covering with shade the houses on which fell, after their passage, the cold and golden light of the November sky. The first raincoats had appeared. But there was a surprising number of rubberized and shiny fabrics. The newspapers had in fact reported that, two hundred years earlier, during the great plagues of the South, the doctors dressed in oiled cloths for their own preservation. The stores had taken advantage of this to sell a stock of old-fashioned clothes with which everyone hoped for immunity. But all these signs of the season could not make us forget that the cemeteries were deserted. In other years, the trams were full of the stale odor of chrysanthemums and theories of women went to the places where their loved ones were buried, in order to flower their graves. It was the day when attempts were made to compensate the deceased for the isolation and forgetfulness in which he had been held for many months. But that year, no one wanted to think about the dead anymore. We were already thinking too much about it, precisely. And it was no longer a question of coming back to them with a little regret and a lot of melancholy. They were no longer the neglected people who come to justify themselves one day a year. They were the intruders we want to forget. This is why the Festival of the Dead, that year, was somewhat hidden. According to Cottard, to whom Tarrou recognized an increasingly ironic language, it was the Day of the Dead every day. And really, the plague bonfires burned with ever greater joy in the crematorium. From one day to the next, the number of deaths, it is true, did not increase. But it seemed that the plague had settled comfortably in its paroxysm and that it brought to its daily murders the precision and regularity of a good civil servant. In principle, and in the opinion of the competent personalities, this was a good sign. The graph of the plague's progress, with its incessant rise, then the long plateau which followed it, seemed quite comforting to Doctor Richard, for example. "It's a good one, it's a great graphic," he said. He believed that the disease had reached what he called a plateau. From now on, it could only decrease. He attributed the credit to the new Castel serum, which had just had some unexpected successes. The old Castel did not contradict it, but believed that in fact, nothing could be foreseen, the history of epidemics involving unforeseen twists. The prefecture which, for a long time, wished to bring an appeasement to the public spirit, and to whom the plague did not give the means, proposed to gather the doctors to ask them for a report on this subject, when doctor Richard was kidnapped by the plague, too, and precisely on the level of the disease. The administration, faced with this example, no doubt impressive, but which, after all, proved nothing, returned to pessimism with as much inconsistency as it had initially welcomed optimism. Castel, on the other hand, only prepared his serum as carefully as he could. There was no longer, in any case, a single public place which was not transformed into a hospital or a lazaretto, and if one still respected the prefecture, it was because one had to keep a place to gather. But, in general, and due to the relative stability of the plague at that time, the organization planned by Rieux was by no means exceeded. The doctors and aides, who were making an exhausting effort, did not have to imagine even greater efforts. They only had to continue with this regularity, so to speak, this superhuman work. The pulmonary forms of the infection that had already appeared were now multiplying all over the city, as if the wind was igniting and activating fires in the breasts. In the midst of vomiting blood, the patients were removed much more quickly. Contagiousness was now likely to be greater, with this new form of the epidemic. In reality, the opinions of specialists had always been contradictory on this point. To be on the safe side, however, health personnel continued to breathe under masks of disinfected gauze. At first glance, in any case, the disease should have spread. But, as the cases of bubonic plague decreased, the balance was in balance. There were other concerns, however, due to the increasing supply difficulties. Speculation had gotten into it, and basic necessities that were lacking on the mainstream market were being offered at fabulous prices. Poor families were thus in a very distressing situation, while wealthy families lacked almost nothing. While the plague, by the effective impartiality which it brought in its ministry, should have reinforced equality among our fellow citizens, by the normal play of selfishness, on the contrary, it made the feeling of injustice. There remained, of course, the blameless equality of death, but nobody wanted that. The hungry poor people thought even more nostalgically of the neighboring towns and countryside, where life was free, and bread was inexpensive. Since they could not be fed enough, they felt, moreover unreasonable, that they should have been allowed to leave. So much so that a slogan ended up running, which was sometimes read on the walls, or which was shouted, at other times, on the prefect's passage: "Bread or air." This ironic phrase signaled certain protests that were quickly put down, but whose seriousness was not lost on anyone. Newspapers, of course, obeyed the optimism they received at all costs. On reading them, what characterized the situation was "the moving example of calm and composure" given by the population. But in a city closed in on itself, where nothing could remain secret, nobody was mistaken on the "example" given by the community. And to get a fair idea of the calm and composure in question, it was enough to enter a place of quarantine or one of the isolation camps which had been organized by the administration. It turns out that the narrator, called elsewhere, did not know them. And that's why he can only quote Tarrou's testimony here. Tarrou reports, in fact, in his notebooks, the account of a visit he made with Rambert to the camp installed on the municipal stadium. The stadium is located almost at the gates of the city, on one side overlooking the street where the trams pass, on the other on vacant lots that extend to the edge of the plateau where the city is built. It is usually surrounded by high cement walls and it had been sufficient to have sentries at the four front doors to make the escape difficult. Likewise, the walls kept outsiders from pestering the unfortunate who were in quarantine. On the other hand, the latter, all day long, heard, without seeing them, the trams that were passing by, and guessed, to the rumor that they were hanging out with them, the hours of entry and exit from the offices. They thus knew that the life from which they were excluded continued a few meters from them, and that the walls of cement separated two more foreign universes from each other than if they had been in different planets. It was a Sunday afternoon that Tarrou and Rambert chose to head for the stadium. They were accompanied by Gonzalès, the football player, whom Rambert had found and who had finally agreed to take turns monitoring the stadium. Rambert was to present it to the camp administrator. Gonzalès had told the two men, when they met, that it was the time when, before the plague, he was getting dressed to start his match. Now that the stadiums were requisitioned it was no longer possible and Gonzalès felt, and looked, completely idle. This was one of the reasons why he had accepted this surveillance, provided that he only had to exercise it on weekends. The sky was half covered and Gonzalès, his nose raised, noted with regret that this weather, neither rainy nor hot, was the most favorable for a good part. He evoked as best he could the smell of embarrassment in the locker rooms, the crumbling grandstands, the brightly colored jerseys on the tawny ground, the lemons of the half-time or the lemonade which stings the throats of a thousand refreshing needles. Tarrou also notes that, throughout the journey, through the battered streets of the suburb, the player kept kicking the stones he encountered. He was trying to send them right down the drain, and when he succeeded, "one to zero," he said. When he had finished his cigarette, he spat his cigarette butt in front of him and tried, on the fly, to catch him with his foot. Near the stadium, children who were playing sent a ball towards the passing group and Gonzalès went out of his way to return it to them with precision. They finally entered the stadium. The stands were full of people. But the ground was covered by several hundred red tents, inside of which we could see from a distance bedding and bundles. We had kept the stands so that the internees could take shelter in hot or rainy weather. Simply, they had to return to the tents at sunset. Under the stands were the showers that had been fitted out and the old players' locker rooms that had been converted into offices and infirmaries. Most of the internees filled the stands. Others wandered over the keys. Some were squatting at the entrance of their tent and looking around at everything. Many in the stands were sprawled and seemed to be waiting. - What do they do during the day? asked Tarrou of Rambert. - Nothing. Almost all, in fact, had swinging arms and empty hands. This huge assembly of men was curiously silent. - The first days, we didn't get along here, said Rambert. But as the days went by, they talked less and less. If his notes are to be believed, Tarrou understood them, and he saw them at first, crammed into their tents, busy listening to flies or scratching, howling their anger or fear when they found a complacent ear. But from the time the camp was overcrowded, there had been less and less complacent ears. All that remained was to remain silent and to be wary. There was indeed a kind of mistrust which fell from the gray sky, and yet luminous, on the red camp. Yes, they all looked suspicious. Since they had been separated from the others, it was not without reason, and they showed the faces of those who seek their reasons, and who fear. Each of those whom Tarrou was looking at had an unoccupied eye, all of them seemed to suffer from a very general separation from what made their life. And since they couldn't always think of death, they didn't think of anything. They were on vacation. "But the worst part," wrote Tarrou, "is that they are forgotten and that they know it." Those who knew them forgot them because they are thinking of something else and that is understandable. As for those who love them, they have also forgotten them because they must exhaust themselves in procedures and projects to get them out. By dint of thinking about this exit, they no longer think of those it is a question of bringing out. This too is normal. And at the end of it all, we realize that no one is really able to think of anyone, even in the worst of misfortunes. Because to really think of someone is to think about it minute by minute, without being distracted by anything, neither the care of the household, nor the flying fly, nor the meals, nor an itch. But there are still flies and itching. This is why life is difficult to live. And they know it well. The administrator, who was returning to them, told them that a Mr. Othon was asking to see them. He led Gonzales to his office, then led them to a corner of the galleries where Mr. Othon, who had been seated at a distance, rose to receive them. He was always dressed the same way and wore the same hard collar. Tarrou only noticed that his tufts on the temples were much spikier and that one of his laces was untied. The judge looked tired, and not once did he look his interlocutors in the face. He said that he was happy to see them and that he asked them to thank Doctor Rieux for what he had done. The others were silent. - I hope, said the judge after a while, that Philippe did not suffer too much. It was the first time Tarrou had heard him say his son's name and he realized that something had changed. The sun was lowering on the horizon and, between two clouds, its rays entered laterally in the stands, gilding their three faces. - No, said Tarrou, no, he really didn't suffer. When they withdrew, the judge continued to look where the sun came from. They went to say goodbye to Gonzalès, who was studying a watch table by rotation. The player laughs, shaking their hands. - I found the locker room at least, he said, that's still it. Shortly thereafter, the administrator was escorting Tarrou and Rambert, when an enormous crackling noise was heard in the stands. Then the loudspeakers which, in better times, were used to announce the results of the matches or to present the teams, declared by nasalizing that the internees had to return to their tents so that the evening meal could be distributed. Slowly, the men left the stands and made their way to the tents. When they were all installed, two small electric cars, as seen in stations, passed between the tents, carrying large pots. The men stretched out their arms, two ladles plunged into two pots and came out to land in two bowls. The car was restarting. We started again at the next tent. - It's scientific, said Tarrou to the administrator. - Yes, said the latter with satisfaction, shaking their hand is scientific. The twilight was there, and the sky was uncovered. A soft and fresh light bathed the camp. In the evening peace, sounds of spoons and plates rose from all sides. Bats hovered over the tents and suddenly disappeared. A streetcar was screaming on a switch on the other side of the walls. "Poor judge," murmured Tarrou, walking through the doors. Something should be done for him. But how do you help a judge? There were thus, in the city, several other camps of which the narrator, by scruples and by lack of direct information, cannot say more. But what he can say is that the existence of these camps, the smell of men coming from them, the enormous voices of the loudspeakers in the twilight, the mystery of the walls and the fear of these places disapproved, weighed heavily on the morale of our fellow citizens and added to the dismay and discomfort of all. Incidents and conflicts with the administration increased. By the end of

November, however, the mornings became very cold. Rains of deluge washed the pavement with great water, cleaned the sky and left it pure of clouds above the glistening streets. A weak sun shone on the city every morning, a sparkling and icy light. Towards evening, on the contrary, the air became warm again. It was the moment that Tarrou chose to discover himself a little with Doctor Rieux. One day, around ten o'clock, after a long and exhausting day, Tarrou accompanied Rieux, who was going to pay the old asthmatic his evening visit. The sky glowed softly over the houses of the old quarter. A light wind blew noiselessly through the dark crossroads. Coming from the quiet streets, the two men fell on the old man's chatter. The latter taught them that there were some who did not agree, that the butter plate was always for the same, that so much goes the jug with water that in the end it breaks and that probably, and there he rubbed his hands, there would be mayhem. The doctor treated him without stopping to comment on the events. They could hear walking above them. The old woman, noticing Tarrou's interested air, explained to them that neighbors were standing on the terrace. They learned at the same time that we had a beautiful view from up there, and that the terraces of houses often joining on one side, it was possible for women in the neighborhood to visit each other without leaving their homes. - Yes, said the old man, come on up. Up there is fresh air. They found the terrace empty and furnished with three chairs. On the one hand, as far as the view could extend, we only saw terraces which ended up leaning against a dark and stony mass where they recognized the first hill. On the other side, over a few streets and the invisible harbor, the gaze plunged on a horizon where the sky and the sea mingled in an indistinct palpitation. Beyond what they knew to be the cliffs, a gleam of which they did not perceive the source reappeared regularly: the lighthouse of the pass, since the spring, continued to turn for ships which diverted towards other ports. In the sky swept and shiny by the wind, pure stars shone, and the distant glow of the lighthouse mingled there, from moment to moment, a fleeting ash. The breeze smelled of spices and stone. The silence was absolute. - It's nice, said Rieux, sitting down. It's as if the plague never went up there. Tarrou turned his back to him and looked at the sea. - Yes, he said after a moment, the weather was good. He came to sit with the doctor and looked at him carefully. Three times the glow appeared in the sky. The sound of shocked dishes went up to them from the depths of the street. A door slammed into the house. - Rieux, said Tarrou in a very natural tone, you never tried to find out who I was? Do you have friendship with me? - Yes, replied the doctor, I have friendship for you. But so far we have run out of time. - Well, that reassures me. Do you want this time to be one of friendship? In response, Rieux glows. - Well, here ... A few streets away, a car seemed to slide for a long time on the wet pavement. She walked away and, after her, confused exclamations from far away broke the silence again. Then he fell back on the two men with all his weight of sky and stars. Tarrou had risen to perch on the parapet of the terrace, facing Rieux, still huddled in the palm of his chair. We saw only a massive shape, cut out in the sky. He spoke for a long time and here is roughly his reconstituted speech: - Let's put it for simplicity, Rieux, that I already suffered from the plague long before I knew this city and this epidemic. It is enough to say that I am like everyone else. But there are people who do not know it, or who are well in this state and people who know it and who would like to get out of it. I always wanted to get out. "When I was young, I lived with the idea of my innocence, that is to say with no idea at all. I am not the type that is tormented, I started off the right way. Everything worked for me, I was at ease in intelligence, at best with women, and if I had some concerns, they would pass as they came. One day I started to think. Now ... "I must tell you that I was not poor like you. My father was an attorney general, which is a situation. However, he didn't look like that, being a natural fellow. My mother was simple and unobtrusive, I never stopped loving her, but I prefer not to talk about it. He cared for me with affection and I even think he was trying to understand me. He had adventures outside, I'm sure of it now, and, as well, I'm far from indignant. He behaved in all this as he had to wait for him to behave, without shocking anyone. To put it briefly, he was not very original and, today that he died, I realize that if he did not live as a saint, he was not a bad man either. He was in the middle, that's all, and he's the type of man for whom we feel a reasonable affection, the one who keeps us going. "However, he had a peculiarity: the great indicator Chaix was his bedside book. It was not that he was traveling, except on vacation, to Britain, where he had a small property. But he was able to tell you exactly the departure and arrival times of Paris-Berlin, the combinations of schedules that had to be made to go from Lyon to Warsaw, the exact mileage between the capitals of your choice. Can you tell how we are going from Briançon to Chamonix? Even a station master would get lost. My father was not lost in it. He practiced practically every evening to enrich his knowledge on this point, and he was rather proud of it. It amused me a lot, and I often questioned him, delighted to check his answers in Chaix and admit that he was not mistaken. These little exercises linked us a lot to each other, because I provided him with an audience whose goodwill he appreciated. As for me, I found that this superiority which related to the railways was worth another. "But I let myself go and I risk giving too much importance to this honest man. Because, in the end, it only had an indirect influence on my determination. At most, it provided me with an opportunity. When I was seventeen, my father invited me to go and listen to him. It was an important case, in the assize court, and, certainly, he had thought it would appear in its best light. I also believe that he was counting on this ceremony, capable of striking young imaginations, to push me to enter the career that he himself had chosen. I had accepted, because it pleased my father and because, as well, I was curious to see and hear him in a role other than the one he played among us. I didn't think of anything more. What was going on in court had always seemed to me as natural and inevitable as a July 14 review or a prize distribution. I had a very abstract idea that did not bother me. "However, I kept only one image from this day, that of the culprit. I believe he was guilty indeed; it doesn't matter what. But this poor red-haired little man, in his thirties, seemed so determined to recognize everything, so sincerely frightened by what he had done and what we were going to do to him, that after a few minutes I only had eyes for him. He looked like an owl startled by too bright a light. The bow of his tie did not exactly fit the angle of the collar. He bit his nails with one hand, the right ... Anyway, I do not insist, you understood that he was alive. "But I suddenly noticed this, whereas, until now, I had only thought of him through the convenient category of" accused ". I cannot say that I forgot my father then, but something was tightening my stomach which took away all my attention other than that which I paid to the accused. I hardly listened to anything, I felt that we wanted to kill this living man and a formidable instinct like a wave carried me by its side with formidable as a wave carried me by its side with a kind of stubborn blindness. I only really woke up with my father's indictment. "Transformed by his red dress, neither good-natured nor affectionate, his mouth was teeming with immense sentences, which kept coming out like snakes. And I understood that he was asking for the death of this man on behalf of society and that he was even asking to have his neck cut off. He said only, it is true: "This head must fall." But, in the end, the difference was not great. And it came back to the same, indeed, since he got that head. He just didn't do the work then. And I, who followed the affair then until its conclusion, exclusively, I had with this unfortunate man a much more dizzying intimacy than my father never had. The latter was, however, according to custom, to attend what was politely called the last moments and which must be called the most abject of assassinations. "From that day on, I could only look at the Chaix indicator with abominable disgust. From that day on, I became horrified in justice, to death sentences, to executions and I noticed with dizziness that my father must have attended the assassination several times and that these were the days when, precisely, he got up very early. Yes, he would wake up in these cases. I dared not tell my mother about it, but I watched her better then and I realized that there was nothing left between them and that she was leading a life of renunciation. It helped me to forgive him, as I said then. Later, I knew that there was nothing to forgive her, because she had been poor all her life until her marriage and that poverty had taught her to resign. "You are probably waiting for me to tell you that I left immediately. No, I stayed for several months, almost a year. But my heart was sick. One evening my father asked for his alarm clock because he had to get up early. I did not sleep all night. When he returned the next day, I was gone. Let's say right away that my father made me search, that I went to see him, that without explaining anything, I calmly told him that I would kill myself if he forced me to return. He ended up accepting, because he was naturally rather gentle, gave me a speech on the stupidity that there was in wanting to live his life (this is how he explained my gesture and I did not dissuade him) , a thousand recommendations, and suppressed the sincere tears that came to him. Subsequently, long enough afterwards, however, I returned regularly to see my mother and I met him then. These reports were enough for him, I believe. For me, I had no animosity against him, only a little sadness in the heart. When he died, I took my mother with me and she would still be there if she hadn't died too. "I insisted at length on this beginning because it was indeed at the beginning of everything. I will go faster now. I experienced poverty when I was eighteen, coming out of affluence. I did a thousand jobs to make a living. It hasn't been too bad for me. But what interested me was the death sentence. I wanted to settle an account with the red owl. As a result, I played politics as they say. I didn't want to be a plague victim, that's all. I believed that the society I lived in was based on the death penalty and that by fighting it, I would fight murder. I believed it, others told me, and finally it was largely true. So, I put myself with the others that I loved and that I did not stop loving. I stayed there a long time and there are no countries in Europe whose struggles I have not shared. Let's move on. "Of course, I knew that we, too, occasionally convicted. But I was told that these few deaths were necessary to bring about a world where no one would be killed. It was true in a way and, after all, maybe I am not able to keep myself in this kind of truth. What is certain is that I hesitated. But I was thinking about the owl and it could go on. Until the day I saw an execution (it was in Hungary) and the same dizziness that had grabbed the child I was had obscured my human eyes. "Have you never seen a man shot? No, of course, this is usually done by invitation and the audience is chosen in advance. The result is that you stayed with prints and books. A blindfold, a pole, and in the distance some soldiers. Well no! Do you know that the gunners' platoon is on the contrary one and a half meters from the condemned? Did you know that if the condemned man took two steps forward, he would strike the guns with his chest? Did you know that at this short distance, the gunners concentrate their shooting on the area of the heart and that with all of them, with their large bullets, they make a hole there where one could put the first? No, you don't know because these are details that we don't talk about. not because these are details, we don't talk about. Men's sleep is more sacred than life for plague victims. Good people should not be prevented from sleeping. It would have bad taste, and the taste is not to insist, everyone knows that. But I haven't slept well since that time. The bad taste stayed in my mouth and I did not stop insisting, that is to say, thinking about it. "I understood then that I, at least, had not ceased to be a plague victim during all these long years when, however, with all my soul, I thought I was fighting against the plague. I learned that I had indirectly subscribed to the death of thousands of men, that I had even caused this death by finding good the actions and the principles which had fatally led to it. The others didn't seem embarrassed by it, or at least they never spoke of it spontaneously. I had my throat tied. I was with them and yet I was alone. When I happened to express my scruples, they told me that I had to think about what was at stake and they gave me often impressive reasons, to make me swallow what I could not swallow. But I replied that the big plague victims, those who wear red dresses, also have excellent reasons in these cases, and that if I accepted the reasons of force majeure and the necessities invoked by the little plague victims, I could not reject those of the big ones. They pointed out to me that the right way to give reason to the red dresses was to leave them the exclusivity of the condemnation. But then I thought to myself that, if we gave in once, there was no reason to stop. It seems to me that history has proven me right, today it will kill the most. They are all in the fury of the murder, and they cannot do otherwise. "My business, in any case, was not the reasoning. It was the red owl, this dirty adventure where dirty stinky mouths announced to a man in chains that he was going to die and regulated all things so that he died, indeed, after nights and nights of agony during which he expected to be murdered with his eyes open. My business was the hole in the chest. And I thought to myself that in the meantime, and for my part at least, I would refuse to ever give a single reason, a single reason, you hear, to this disgusting butchery. Yes, I chose this obstinate blindness while waiting to see more clearly. "Since then, I haven't changed. I have been ashamed for a long time, ashamed to die of having been, even from afar, even in good will, a murderer in my turn. Over time, I simply saw that even those who were better than others could not help killing or letting them kill today because it was in the logic where they lived and that we could not make a gesture in this world without risking death. Yes, I continued to be ashamed, I learned this, that we were all in the plague, and I lost my peace. I'm still looking for it today, trying to understand them all and not be anyone's deadly enemy. I only know that it is necessary to do what it takes to no longer be a plague victim and that this is what can, alone, make us hope for peace, or a good death in its absence. This is what can relieve men and, if not save them, at least do them the least harm possible and even sometimes a little good. And that's why I decided to refuse everything that, directly or indirectly, for good or bad reasons, kills or justifies that we kill. "This is why this epidemic still teaches me nothing, except that it must be combated by your side. I know from certain science (yes, Rieux, I know everything about life, you can see it) that everyone carries it in themselves, the plague, because nobody, no, nobody in the world is unscathed. And that you have to watch yourself all the time so that you don't have to breathe in someone else's face and stick the infection to him in a minute of distraction. What is natural is the germ. The rest, health, integrity, purity, if you will, it is an effect of the will and a will that must never stop. The honest man, the one who hardly infects anyone, is the least distracted. And it takes willpower and tension to never be distracted! Yes, Rieux, it's very tiring to be a plague victim. But it's even more tiring not to want to be. This is why everyone is tired since everyone today is a bit plagued. But this is why some, who want to stop being so, experience an extremity of fatigue from which nothing will deliver them more than death. "Until then, I know that I am no longer worth anything for this world itself and that from the moment I gave up killing, I condemned myself to a final exile. These are the ones to kill, I condemned myself to a permanent exile. Others will make history. I also know that I cannot apparently judge these others. There is a quality that I lack to make a reasonable murderer. So, it's not a superiority. But now I agree to be what I am, I learned modesty. I'm just saying that there are plagues and victims on this earth and that we must, as much as possible, refuse to be with the plague. It may seem a bit simple to you, and I don't know if it's simple, but I know it's true. I have heard so much reasoning which almost turned my head, and which turned enough other heads to make them consent to the assassination, that I understood that all the misfortune of men came from the fact that they did not have clear language. So, I decided to speak and act clearly, to put myself on the right path. Therefore, I say that there are the plagues and the victims, and nothing more. If, saying that, I become a plague myself, at least, I do not agree. I'm trying to be an innocent murderer. You see that it is not a big ambition. "There should, of course, be a third category, that of real doctors, but it is a fact that one does not meet many and that it must be difficult. This is why I decided to put myself on the side of the victims, on all occasions, to limit the damage. In the middle of them, I can at least find out how we get to the third category, that is to say peace. In closing, Tarrou swung his leg and stamped his foot gently against the terrace. After a silence, the doctor stood up a bit and asked if Tarrou had any idea of the path to take to reach peace. - Yes, sympathy. Two ambulance tones rang in the distance. The exclamations, just confused, gathered at the edge of town, near the stony hill. At the same time, we heard something that sounded like a detonation. Then silence returned. Rieux counted two beacons. The breeze seemed to gain more force, and at the same time, a breath coming from the sea brought a smell of salt. You could now hear distinctly the dull breath of the waves against the cliff. - In short, said Tarrou with simplicity, what interests me is how you become a saint. - But you don't believe in God. - Exactly. Can we be a godless saint, this is the only concrete problem I know today. Suddenly, a great light came from the side where the screams had come from and, going up the river from the wind, an obscure clamor reached the two men. The glow darkened immediately and far, at the edge of the terraces, there remained only a glow. In a wind outage, the cries of men were distinctly heard, then the sound of a landfill and the clamor of a crowd. Tarrou got up and was listening. We couldn't hear anything anymore. - We fought again at the doors. - It's over now said Rieux. Tarrou whispered that it was never over and that there would still be victims because it was in order. - Perhaps, replied the doctor, but you know, I feel more solidarity with the vanquished than with the saints. I have no taste, I believe, for heroism and holiness. What interests me is to be a man. - Yes, we are looking for the same thing, but I am less ambitious. Rieux thought Tarrou was joking and looked at him. But in the vague gleam which came from the sky, he saw a sad and serious face. The wind picked up again and Rieux felt he was warm on his skin. Tarrou shook himself: - Do you know, he said, what we should do for friendship? "What you want," said Rieux. - Take a sea bath. Even for a future saint it is a worthy pleasure. Rieux was smiling. - With our passes, we can go to the pier. In the end, it's too silly to live only in the plague. Of course, a man must fight for the victims. But if he stops loving nothing else, what is the point of fighting? - Yes, said Rieux, let's go. A moment later, the car stopped near the port gates. The moon had risen. A milky sky projected everywhere port. The moon had risen. A milky sky cast pale shadows everywhere. Behind them lay the city and there came a warm and sick breath which pushed them towards the sea. They showed their papers to a guard who examined them at some length. They passed and across the barrel-covered grounds, among the scents of wine and fish, they took the direction of the pier. Shortly before arriving there, the smell of iodine and algae announced the sea. Then they heard it. She hissed softly at the foot of the large blocks of the pier and, as they climbed them, she appeared to them, thick as velvet, flexible and smooth like an animal. They settled on the rocks facing the sea. The waters swelled and descended slowly. This calm breathing of the sea gave birth and disappeared oily reflections on the surface of the waters. Before them, the night was limitless. Rieux, who felt the hailstones of the rocks beneath his fingers, was full of strange happiness. Turned to Tarrou, he guessed, on the calm and serious face of his friend, that same happiness which forgot nothing, not even the assassination. They undressed. Rieux was the first to dive. Cold at first, the waters seemed lukewarm when he came back up. After a few fathoms, he knew that the sea that evening was lukewarm, the warmth of the autumn seas which take the earth's heat from the earth for many months. He swam regularly. The flapping of his feet left a foaming foam behind him, water flowing down his arms to stick to his legs. A heavy lapping told him that Tarrou had dived. Rieux lay on his back and stood motionless, facing the inverted sky, full of moon and stars. He took a deep breath. Then he heard more and more distinctly the sound of beaten water, strangely clear in the silence and solitude of the night. Tarrou was getting closer, we soon heard his breathing. Rieux turned around, got to his friend's level, and swam in the same rhythm. Tarrou advanced with more power than him and he had to rush his pace. For a few minutes, they advanced with the same cadence and the same vigor, lonely, far from the world, finally freed from the city and the plague. Rieux stopped first and they returned slowly, except at one point when they entered an icy current. Without saying anything, they both rushed their movement, whipped by this surprise from the sea. Dressed again, they left without having said a word. But they had the same heart and the memory of that night was sweet to them. When they saw the sentinel of the plague from afar, Rieux knew that Tarrou said to himself, like him, that the disease had just forgotten them, that it was good, and that it was now necessary to start again. Yes, we had to start again, and the plague never forgot anyone for too long. During the month of December, it blazed in the chests of our fellow citizens, it lit the oven, it populated the shadows camps with empty hands, it finally did not stop advancing with its patient and jerky pace. The authorities had counted on the cold days to stop this advance, and yet it passed through the first rigors of the season without stopping. We still had to wait. But we no longer wait by dint of waiting, and our entire city lived without a future. As for the doctor, the fleeting instant of peace and friendship that had been given to him had no tomorrow. Another hospital had been opened, and Rieux had no more head-to-head than with the sick. He noted, however, that at this stage of the epidemic, as the plague increasingly took on the pulmonary form, the patients seemed to be helping the doctor somehow. Instead of surrendering to the prostration or the follies from the start, they seemed to have a fairer idea of their interests and they claimed for themselves what could be most favorable to them. They kept asking for a drink, and everyone wanted heat. Although the fatigue was the same for the doctor, he nevertheless felt less alone on these occasions. Towards the end of December, Rieux received a letter from Mr. Othon, the investigating judge, who was still in his camp, saying that his quarantine time had passed, that the administration could not find the date of his entry. and that surely, he was still kept in the internment camp by mistake. His wife, who had been out for some time, had protested at the prefecture, where she had been badly received and where she had been told that there was never a mistake. Rieux brought in Rambert and a few days later saw M. Othon arrive. There had indeed been a mistake and Rieux was indignant a little. But Monsieur Othon, who had lost weight, raised a limp hand, and said, weighing his words, that everyone could be wrong. The doctor only thought there was something changed. - What are you going to do, judge? Your files are waiting for you, says Rieux. "Well, no," said the judge. I would like to take time off. - Indeed, you must rest. - That's not it, I would like to return to camp. Rieux was surprised: - But you're getting out! - I got it wrong. I was told that there are administration volunteers in this camp. The judge rolled his round eyes a bit and tried to flatten one of his tufts ... - You see, I would have a job. And then, it's stupid to say, I would feel less separated from my little boy. Rieux looked at him. It was not possible that in these hard and flat eyes a softness would suddenly settle. But they had become hazier, they had lost their purity of metal. - Of course, said Rieux, I'll take care of it, since you want it. The doctor took care of it, indeed, and the life of the foul city resumed its train, until Christmas. Tarrou continued to carry his effective tranquility everywhere. Rambert told the doctor that he had established, thanks to the two little guards, a system of secret correspondence with his wife. He received a letter from time to time. He offered Rieux to take advantage of his system and he accepted. He wrote for the first time in many months, but with the greatest difficulty. There was a language he had lost. The letter left. The answer was slow to come. For his part, Cottard prospered and his little speculations enriched him. As for Grand, the holiday season was not to be successful. Christmas that year was more of a feast of Hell than a feast of the Gospel. The empty shops and deprived of lights, the dummy chocolates or the empty boxes in the shop windows, the trams loaded with dark figures, nothing reminded of the past Christmas. In this party where everyone, rich or poor, once met, there was only room for a few celebrations. lonely and ashamed that privileged people obtained at high prices, at the bottom of a filthy back shop. The churches were filled with complaints rather than thanksgiving. In the dreary and frozen city, some children were running, still ignorant of what threatened them. But no one dared to announce to them the god of the past, laden with offerings, old like human grief, but new like young hope. There was no longer any place in everyone's heart except for a very old and dismal hope, the very one which prevents men from letting themselves go to death and which is only a simple obstinacy to live . The day before, Grand had missed his date. Rieux, worried, had gone to his house early in the morning without finding him. Everyone had been alerted. Around eleven o'clock, Rambert came to the hospital to warn the doctor that he had seen Grand from afar, wandering the streets, his face decomposed. Then he lost sight of him. The doctor and Tarrou drove to find him. At noon, freezing hour, Rieux, getting out of the car, was looking at Grand from afar, almost pressed against a window, full of toys roughly carved in wood. Tears ran down the face of the old official. And these tears upset Rieux because he understood them and he also felt them in the hollow of his throat. He also remembered the unhappy man's engagement, in front of a Christmas shop, and Jeanne knocked over to say that she was happy. From the depths of distant years, at the very heart of this madness, Jeanne's fresh voice returned to Grand, that was certain. Rieux knew what the crying old man was thinking at the moment, and he thought as he did, that this world without love was like a dead world and that there is always an hour when we get tired of prisons, work and work. courage to claim the face of a being and the heart amazed with tenderness. But the other saw him in the mirror. Without ceasing to cry, he turned and leaned against the window to watch it coming. - Ah! doctor ah! doctor, he said. Rieux nodded to approve, unable to speak. This distress was hers and what was writhing in his heart at the time was the immense anger that comes to man before the pain that all men share. - Yes, Grand, he said. - I wish I had time to write her a letter. So that she would know ... and so that she could be happy without remorse ... With a kind of violence, Rieux made Grand move forward. The other continued, almost letting himself be dragged, stammering bits of the sentence. - It's been too long. We want to let go, it's forced. Ah! doctor! I look calm, like that. But it always took a huge effort to be just normal. So now it's still too much. He stopped, trembling with all his limbs and his eyes He stopped, trembling with all his limbs and his eyes mad. Rieux took her hand. She was burning. - We must return. But Grand escaped him and ran a few steps, then he stopped, spread his arms, and began to swing back and forth. He turned on himself and fell on the icy sidewalk, his face soiled with tears which continued to flow. Passers-by watched from a distance, suddenly stopped, no longer daring to advance. Rieux had to take the old man in his arms. In his bed now, Grand was suffocating: the lungs were taken. Rieux was thinking. The employee had no family. What good is it to transport it? He would be alone, with Tarrou, to treat him ... Grand was sunk in the hollow of his pillow, his skin green and his eye out. He was staring at a meager fire that Tarrou lit in the fireplace with the debris from a crate. "It's bad," he said. And from the bottom of his flaming lungs came a strange crackling sound that accompanied everything he said. Rieux advised him to be quiet and said he would come back. A strange smile came to the patient and with him a sort of tenderness rose to his face. He blinked with effort. "If I go out, low hat, doctor!" But immediately afterwards he fell into prostration. A few hours later, Rieux and Tarrou found the patient, half upright in his bed, and Rieux was frightened to read on his face the progress of the disease that was burning him. But he seemed more lucid, and immediately, in a strangely hollow voice, he begged them to bring him the manuscript he had put in a drawer. Tarrou gave him the sheets which he hugged without looking at them, then handed them to the doctor, inviting him to read them. It was a short manuscript of about fifty pages. The doctor leafed through it and understood that all these sheets carried only the same sentence indefinitely copied, altered, enriched, or impoverished. Without stop, the month of May, the Amazon and the alleys of the Wood confronted and arranged in various ways. The book also included explanations, sometimes excessively long, and variants. But at the end of the last page, an applied hand had only written, in fresh ink: "My very dear Jeanne, today is Christmas ..." Above, carefully calligraphed, featured the last version of the sentence. "Read," said Grand. And Rieux read. "On a beautiful May morning, a slender Amazon, mounted on a sumptuous chestnut mare, roamed through the paths of the Woods among the flowers ..." - Is that it? said the old man in a feverish voice. Rieux did not look up at him. - Ah! said the other, waving, I know. Beautiful, beautiful is not the right word. Rieux took her hand on the blanket. - Leave, doctor. I won't have time ... His chest rose with difficulty and he suddenly shouted: - Burn him! The doctor hesitated, but Grand repeated his order with such a terrible accent and such pain in his voice that Rieux threw the leaves into the almost extinguished fire. The room quickly lit up and a brief warmth warmed it. When the doctor returned to the patient, his back was turned, and his face almost touched the wall. Tarrou was looking out the window, like a stranger to the scene. After injecting the serum, Rieux told his friend that Grand wouldn't stay overnight, and Tarrou volunteered to stay. The doctor agreed. All night long he was chased by the idea that Grand was going to die. But the next morning, Rieux found

Grand sitting on his bed, talking to Tarrou. The fever was gone. There were only signs of general exhaustion. - Ah! doctor, said the employee, I was wrong. But I will do it again. I remember everything, you will see. "Wait," said Rieux to Tarrou. But by noon nothing had changed. In the evening, Grand could be considered saved. Rieux understood nothing about this resurrection. At about the same time, however, a patient was brought to Rieux whose condition he considered desperate and whom he had isolated upon his arrival at the hospital. The girl was delirious and had all the symptoms of pneumonic plague. But the next morning the fever had gone down. The doctor thought he still recognized, as in Grand's case, the morning remission that experience accustomed him to regard as a bad sign. By noon, however, the fever had not gone up. In the evening it increased by only a few tenths and by the next morning it was gone. The girl, although weak, breathed freely in her bed. Rieux told Tarrou that she was saved from all the rules. But during the week, four similar cases presented themselves in the doctor's department. At the end of the same week, the old asthmatic greeted the doctor and Tarrou with all the signs of great agitation. - That's it, he said, they're still going out. - Who? - Well! rats! Since April, no dead rats have been discovered. - Will it start again? said Tarrou to Rieux. The old man was rubbing his hands. - You have to see them running! It's a pleasure. He had seen two live rats enter his house through the street door. Neighbors had told him that the animals had returned to their homes too. In some frames, we heard again the remodeling forgotten for months. Rieux awaited the publication of general statistics which took place at the beginning of each week. They revealed a decline in the disease.

V

Although this sudden retreat from illness was unexpected, our fellow citizens did not hasten to rejoice. The past few months, while increasing their desire for release, had taught them to be cautious and accustomed them to count less and less on an imminent end of the epidemic. However, this new development was on everyone's lips, and deep in their hearts was a great, unacknowledged hope. Everything else went into the background. The new victims of the plague weighed very little against this exorbitant fact: the statistics had dropped. One of the signs that the era of health, without being openly hoped for, was however awaited in secret, is that our fellow citizens readily spoke from this moment, albeit with the air of indifference, of how life goes would rearrange after the plague. Everyone agreed that the conveniences of the past would not be found all at once and that it was easier to destroy than to rebuild. We simply felt that the provisioning itself could be improved a little, and that in this way we would be rid of the most pressing concern. But, in fact, under these harmless remarks, an insane hope was unleashed at the same time and to the point that our fellow citizens sometimes became aware of it and then asserted, with haste, that in any event, deliverance was not for the next day. And, indeed, the plague did not stop the next day, but, on the surface, it was weakening faster than one could reasonably have hoped. During the first days of January, the cold settled with an unusual persistence and seemed to crystallize above the city. And yet, the sky had never been so blue. For days on end, its unchanging, icy splendor flooded our city with uninterrupted light. In this purified air, the plague, in three weeks and by successive falls, seemed to be exhausted in the fewer and fewer corpses that it lined up. In a short space of time, it lost almost all of the forces it had taken months to accumulate. To see her miss prey all designated, like Grand or the young girl of Rieux, to exacerbate in certain districts during two or three days whereas it disappeared completely from certain others, to multiply the victims on Monday and, on Wednesday, to let them escape almost all, to see her thus running out of steam or rushing forward, one would have said that she was disorganized by nervousness and weariness, that she was losing, at the same time as her dominion over herself, the mathematical efficiency and sovereign who had been his strength. All of a sudden, Castel's serum was experiencing streaks of success that had so far been denied. Each of the measures taken by the doctors, which had previously yielded no results, suddenly seemed to be working. It seemed that the plague in turn was being hunted down and that its sudden weakness made the strength of the blunt armies that had hitherto opposed it. From time to time only, the disease stiffened and, in a sort of blind start, took away three or four patients whose recovery was hoped for. They were the unlucky ones of the plague, the ones it killed in hope. This was the case of Judge Othon who had to be evacuated from the quarantine camp, and Tarrou said of him indeed that he had had no luck, without it being possible to know, however, whether he was thinking of death or to the life of the judge. But on the whole, the infection was receding all the way down and the prefecture's press releases, which had first given birth to a shy and secret hope, ended up confirming, in the minds of the public, the conviction that victory was acquired and that the disease abandoned its positions. In truth, it was difficult to decide that it was a victory. We were only obliged to note that the disease seemed to go away as it had come. The strategy against him had not changed, ineffective yesterday and, today, apparently happy. It just felt like the disease had run out on its own, or maybe it would go away after reaching all of its goals. In a way, his role was finished. It seemed, however, that nothing had changed in town. Always silent during the day, the streets were invaded in the evening by the same crowd where only the overcoats and scarves dominated. Cinemas and cafes did the same business. But, on closer inspection, you could notice that the faces were more relaxed and that they sometimes smiled. And it was the occasion to note that, until now, nobody smiled in the streets. In reality, in the opaque veil which, for months, had surrounded the city, a tear had just been made and, every Monday, everyone could note, by the news of the radio, that the tear was growing and that finally he was going to be allowed to breathe. It was still a very negative relief that did not take a frank expression. But whereas before we would not have learned without some disbelief that a train had left or a boat arrived, or that cars would again be allowed to circulate, the announcement of these events in mid-January on the contrary would have provoked no surprise. It was probably little. But this slight nuance reflected, in fact, the enormous progress made by our fellow citizens in the way of hope. It can be said, moreover, that from the moment the smallest hope became possible for the population, the effective reign of the plague was ended. The fact remains that, throughout the month of January, our fellow citizens reacted in a contradictory manner. Exactly, they went through alternations of excitement and depression. This was how new attempts to escape were recorded, even when the statistics were most favorable. This greatly surprised the authorities, and the guard posts themselves, since most of the escapes were successful. But, in reality, the people who escaped at these times obeyed natural feelings. In some, the plague had rooted a deep skepticism which they could not get rid of. Hope had no hold on them. Even as the time of the plague was over, they continued to live by its standards. They were behind the scenes. Among the others, on the contrary, and they were recruited especially from those who had lived until then separated from the beings they loved, after this long time of confinement and despondency, the wind of hope which rose had lit a fever and impatience that robbed them of all self-control. A kind of panic took them to the thought that they could, so close to the goal, die perhaps, that they would not see again the being that they cherished and that these long sufferings would not be paid to them. Whereas for months, with obscure tenacity, despite prison and exile, they had persisted in waiting, the first hope is enough to destroy what fear and despair could not have started. They rushed like crazy to get ahead of the plague, unable to follow its pace until the last moment. At the same time, moreover, spontaneous signs of optimism appeared. This is how we saw a significant drop in prices. From the point of view of the pure economy, this movement could not be explained. The difficulties remained the same, the quarantine formalities had been kept at the gates, and supplies were far from being improved. We were therefore witnessing a purely moral phenomenon, as if the decline in the plague had repercussions everywhere. At the same time, optimism won over those who had previously lived in groups and who had been forced to separate by illness. The two convents of the city began to be reconstituted and the common life could resume. It was the same for the soldiers, who were again assembled in the barracks which remained free: they resumed a normal life of garrison. These little facts were great signs. The population lived in this secret unrest until January 25. That week the statistics fell so low that after consultation with the medical committee, the prefecture announced that the epidemic could be considered to have been halted. The press release added, it is true, that, in a spirit of prudence which could not fail to be approved by the population, the city gates would remain closed for another two weeks and the prophylactic measures maintained for a month. During this period, at the slightest sign that the danger could resume, "the status quo should be maintained, and the measures renewed beyond". Everyone, however, agreed to consider these additions as clauses of style and, on the evening of January 25, a joyous agitation filled the city. To associate with the general joy, the prefect gave the order to restore the lighting of the time of health. In the illuminated streets, under a cold and pure sky, our fellow citizens poured out in noisy and laughing groups. Admittedly, in many houses, the shutters remained closed and families passed in silence this vigil which others filled with cries. However, for many of these bereaved beings, the relief was also profound, either that the fear of seeing other parents taken away was either that the fear of seeing other parents taken away was finally calmed, or that the feeling of their personal preservation was no longer on alert. But the families who were to remain the most foreign to general joy were, without a doubt, those who, at that very moment, had a patient struggling with the plague in a hospital and who, in quarantine houses or at home, were waiting that the scourge would really have ended with them, as it had ended with the others. These people certainly had hope, but they made a provision of them which they kept in reserve, and from which they refused to draw before they really had the right to do so. And this expectation, this silent vigil, halfway from agony and joy, seemed even more cruel to them, during general jubilation. But these exceptions did not detract from the satisfaction of others. No doubt the plague was not yet over, and she had to prove it. Yet, in everyone's minds already, weeks ahead of time, trains were whistling on endless tracks and ships were plying bright seas. The next day, the spirits would be calmer, and the doubts would be reborn. But for the moment, the whole city was shaking, leaving these closed, dark and motionless places, where it had thrown its stone roots, and finally setting off with its load of survivors. That evening, Tarrou and Rieux, Rambert and the others were walking in the middle of the crowd and also felt the ground missing under their feet. Long after leaving the boulevards, Tarrou and Rieux could still hear this joy chasing them, at the very time when, in deserted alleys, they were walking alongside shuttered windows. And because of their fatigue, they could not separate this suffering, which continued behind the shutters, from the joy that filled the streets a little further. The approaching deliverance had a face mixed with laughter and tears. At a time when the rumor became louder and more joyful, Tarrou stopped. On the dark pavement, a shape was running slightly. It was a cat, the first we had seen since the spring. He stopped for a moment in the middle of the road, hesitated, licked his paw, quickly ran it over his right ear, resumed its silent course and disappeared into the night. Tarrou smiles. The little old man would also be happy. But the moment the plague seemed to go away to regain the unknown den from where it had left in silence, there was at least someone in the city that this departure threw in dismay, and it was Cottard, if we believe Tarrou's notebooks Truth be told, these notebooks get pretty weird from the moment the statistics start to drop. Is it fatigue, but the writing becomes difficult to read and we move too often from one subject to another. In addition, and for the first time, these notebooks lack objectivity and give way to personal considerations. We thus find, in the middle of rather long passages concerning the case of Cottard, a small report on the old man with cats. According to Tarrou, the plague had never taken anything from his consideration for this character who interested him after the epidemic, as he had interested before and as, unfortunately, he could no longer interest him, although his own kindness, Tarrou, was not in question. Because he had tried to see him again. A few days after that evening on January 25, he posted himself at the corner of the small street. The cats were there, warming in the puddles of sun, faithful to the meeting. But at the usual time, the shutters remained stubbornly closed. During the following days, Tarrou never saw them open again. He had concluded curiously that the little old man was upset or dead, that if he was upset, it was because he thought he was right and that the plague had done him harm, but that if he was dead, he had to be ask about him, as for the old asthmatic, if he had been a saint. Tarrou did not think so but believed that there was an "indication" in the case of the old man. "Perhaps, observed the notebooks, one can only arrive at approximations of holiness. In this case, we should be content with a modest and charitable satanism. Always intertwined with observations concerning Cottard, we also find in the notebooks many remarks, often scattered, some of which concern Grand, now convalescent and who had gone back to work as if nothing had happened, and whose others evoke the mother of doctor Rieux. The few conversations that the cohabitation allowed between it and Tarrou, the attitudes of the old woman, her smile, her observations on the plague, are scrupulously noted. Tarrou insisted above all on the erasure of Mrs Rieux; on how she had to express everything in simple sentences; on the particular taste she showed for a certain window, overlooking the quiet street, and behind which she sat in the evening, a little straight, her hands calm and her gaze attentive until twilight had invaded the piece, making her a black shadow in the gray light which gradually darkened and then dissolved the motionless figure; the lightness with which she moved from one room to another; on the kindness of which she had never given precise proofs before Tarrou, but of which he recognized the gleam in all that she did or said; finally on the fact that, according to him, she knew everything without ever thinking, and that with so much silence and shadow, she could stay at the height of any light, even that of the plague. Here, by the way, Tarrou's writing gave bizarre signs of sagging. The lines that followed were difficult to read and, as if to give new proof of this decline, the last words were the first that were personal: "My mother was like that, I liked the same erasure in her and it was she that I always wanted to join. Eight years ago, I can't say she died. It just faded a little more than usual and when I turned around it was gone. But we must come to Cottard. Since the statistics were down, he had made several visits to Rieux, citing various pretexts. But in reality, each time, he asked Rieux for forecasts on the progress of the epidemic. "Do you think she can stop like this, suddenly, without warning? He was skeptical about it, or at least he said so. But the renewed questions he asked seemed to indicate a less firm conviction. In mid-January, Rieux responded fairly optimistically. And each time, these answers, instead of making Cottard happy, had drawn reactions from them, which varied from day to day, but which ranged from a bad mood to depression. Subsequently, the doctor had been led to tell him that, despite the favorable indications given by the statistics, it was better not yet to declare victory. - In other words, observed Cottard, we don't know anything, can it happen from one day to the next? - Yes, as it is also possible that the healing movement may accelerate. This uncertainty, worrying for everyone, had visibly relieved Cottard, and before Tarrou, he had engaged with the tradesmen of his district of the conversations where he tried to propagate the opinion of Rieux. He had no trouble doing it, it's true. Because after the fever of the first victories, in many minds a doubt had returned which had to survive the excitement caused by the prefectural declaration. Cottard reassured himself at the sight of this anxiety. Like other times too, he was discouraged. "Yes," he said to Tarrou, "we'll end up opening the doors." And you will see, they will all let me down! Until January 25, everyone noticed the instability of his character. For whole days, after having tried so long to reconcile his neighborhood and his relationships, he broke in visor with them. In appearance, at least, he then withdrew from the world and, overnight, began to live in savagery. We no longer saw him in the restaurant, the theater, or the cafes he liked. And yet he did not seem to regain the measured and obscure life he led before the epidemic. He lived completely secluded in his apartment and had meals brought up from a nearby restaurant. Only in the evening did he go on stealth trips, buy what he needed, leave the stores, and throw himself on lonely streets. If Tarrou met him then, he could only get monosyllables from him. Then, without transition, we found him sociable, speaking of the plague with abundance, soliciting everyone's opinion and plunging each evening with pleasure into the flood of the crowd. On the day of the prefectural declaration, Cottard disappeared completely from circulation. Two days later, Tarrou met him, wandering the streets. Cottard asked him to accompany him to the suburb. Tarrou, who felt particularly tired from his day, hesitated. But the other insisted. He looked very agitated, gesturing in a haphazard fashion, speaking quickly and loudly. He asked his companion if he thought that, really, the prefectural declaration put an end to the plague. Of course, Tarrou believed that an administrative declaration was not enough in itself to stop a plague, but it was reasonable to think that the epidemic, unless unforeseen, would end. - Yes, said Cottard, unless something unexpected happened. And there's always the unexpected. Tarrou pointed out to him that, moreover, the prefecture had foreseen in a way the unexpected, by the institution of a period of two weeks before the opening of the doors. "And she did well," said Cottard, still gloomy and agitated, "because the way things are going, she could have spoken for nothing." Tarrou believed it was possible but thought it best to consider opening the doors again and returning to normal life. - Admit, said Cottard, admit, but what do you call the return to normal life? - New films at the cinema, said Tarrou, smiling. But Cottard did not smile. He wanted to know if one could think that the plague would not change anything in the city and that everything would start all over again as before, that is to say as if nothing had happened. Tarrou thought that the plague would change and would not change the city, that, of course, the strongest desire of our fellow citizens was and would be to act as if nothing had changed and that, therefore, nothing in one sense would be changed, but that, in another sense, we cannot forget everything, even with the necessary will, and the plague would leave traces, at least in hearts. The little annuitant declared quite plainly that he was not interested in the heart and that even the heart was the last of his concerns. What interested him was whether the organization itself would not be transformed, if, for example, all services would function as in the past. And Tarrou had to admit that he didn't know. According to him, it had to be assumed that all these services, disrupted during the epidemic, would have a little trouble starting again. One might also think that a number of new problems would arise which would necessitate, at least, a reorganization of the old services. - Ah! said Cottard, it is possible, indeed, everyone will have to start all over again. The two walkers had arrived near Cottard's house. He was animated, striving for optimism. He imagined the city resuming living again, erasing its past to start from scratch. - Good, said Tarrou. After all, things may work out for you too. In a way, a new life is about to begin. They were at the door and shook hands. "You are right," said Cottard, more and more agitated, "to start from scratch would be a good thing." But, from the shadow of the corridor, two men had emerged. Tarrou barely had time to hear his companion ask what these birds might want. The birds, who had the air of dressed-up officials, asked Cottard if his name was Cottard and the latter, uttering a sort of deaf exclamation, turned on himself and was already sinking into the night without the others, not Tarrou, had time to make a gesture. Past surprise Tarrou asked the two men what they wanted. They looked reserved and polite to say it was intelligence and set off quietly in the direction Cottard had taken. When he got home, Tarrou reported this scene and immediately (the writing proved it enough) noted his fatigue He added that he still had a lot to do, but that was not a reason not to be ready, and wondered if, indeed, he was ready. He answered to finish, and it is here that Tarrou's notebooks end, that there was always an hour of the day and the night when a man was cowardly and that he was only afraid of that hour -the. The next day, a few days before the doors opened, Dr. Rieux returned home at noon, wondering if he was going to find the telegram he was waiting for. Although his days were as exhausting as at the height of the plague, waiting for final release had allayed his fatigue. He hoped now, and he rejoiced. You cannot always stretch your will and always stiffen, and it is a joy to finally untie, in the bestowal, this sheaf of braided forces for the fight. If the expected telegram was also favorable, Rieux could start again. And he believed that everyone would start again. He walked past the lodge. The new janitor, pressed against the window, smiled at him. Going back up the stairs, Rieux saw his face again, pale with fatigue and privation. Yes, he would start again when the abstraction was finished, and hopefully ... But he opened his door at the same time and his mother came to meet him to tell him that Mr. Tarrou was not fine. He got up in the morning but was unable to go out and had just gone back to bed. Mrs. Rieux was worried. - Maybe it's nothing serious, said her son. Tarrou was stretched out full length, his heavy head hollowed out the bolster, the strong chest was outlined beneath the thickness of the blankets. He had a fever; his head was making him suffer. He told Rieux that these were vague symptoms that could have been those of the plague as well. - No, nothing specific yet, said Rieux after examining him. But Tarrou was devoured by thirst. In the corridor, the doctor told his mother that it could be the beginning of the plague. - Oh! she said, it's not possible, not now! And immediately after: - Let's keep it, Bernard. Rieux reflected: - I have no right, he said. But the doors will open. I think this is the first right that I would take for myself if you were not there. - Bernard, she said, keep us both. You know that I have just been vaccinated again. The doctor said that Tarrou was too, but perhaps, out of fatigue, he must have missed the last injection of serum and forgotten some precautions. Rieux was already going to his office. When he returned to the bedroom, Tarrou saw that he was holding the huge vials of serum. - Ah! that's it, he says. - No, but it's a precaution. Tarrou reached out for an answer and he underwent the endless injection he had himself given to other patients. "We'll see tonight," said Rieux, and he looked Tarrou in the face. - What about isolation, Rieux? - It is not at all certain that you have the plague. Tarrou smiles with effort. - This is the first time I see injecting a serum without ordering isolation at the same time. Rieux turned away: - My mother and I will take care of you. You will be better here. Tarrou was silent and the doctor, who was storing the bulbs, waited for him to speak before turning around. At the end, he went to the bed. The patient looked at him. His face was tired, but his gray eyes were calm. Rieux glows. - Sleep if you can. I will come back later. When he got to the door, he heard Tarrou's voice calling him. He returned to him. But Tarrou seemed to be struggling against the very expression of what he had to say: - Rieux, he finally articulated, you will have to tell me everything, I need it. - I promise you. The other twisted his massive face a little with a smile. - Thank you. I don't want to die, and I will fight. But if the game is lost, I want to make a good end. Rieux stooped down and glistened on the shoulder. - No, he said. To become a saint, you have to live. Fight. During the day, the cold that had been intense decreased a little, but to make room, in the afternoon, for heavy showers of rain and hail. At dusk, the sky was exposed a little and the cold became more penetrating. Rieux returned home in the evening. Without leaving his overcoat, he entered his friend's room. His mother was knitting. Tarrou looked as if he hadn't moved, but his lips, whitened by fever, spoke of the fight he was fighting. - So? said the doctor. Tarrou shrugged a little, out of bed, his thick shoulders. - So, he said, I'm losing the game. The doctor leaned over him. Ganglia had been knotted under the burning skin; his chest seemed to resound from all the sounds of an underground forge. Tarrou curiously presented the two sets of symptoms. Rieux said as he stood up that the serum had not yet had time to give its full effect. But a flood of fever which came to roll in his throat drowned the few words which Tarrou tried to pronounce. After dinner, Rieux and his mother came to settle near the patient. The night was beginning for him in the fight and Rieux knew that this hard fight with the angel of the plague was to last until dawn. Tarrou's solid shoulders and large chest were not his best weapons, but rather the blood that Rieux had spouted out under his needle earlier, and, in this blood, which was more interior than the soul and that no science could update. And he only had to watch his friend fight. What he was going to do, the abscesses he had to promote, the tonics that he had to inoculate, several months of repeated failures had taught him to appreciate their effectiveness. His only task, in truth, was to provide opportunities for this chance which too often only happens when provoked. And chance had to bother. Because Rieux was in front of a face of the plague which disconcerted him. Once again, she set out to divert the strategies against her, she appeared in places where she was not expected to disappear from those where she seemed already installed. Once again, she set out to amaze. Tarrou was struggling, motionless. Not once during the night did, he oppose the agitation of the onslaught of evil, fighting only in all its thickness and silence. But not once did he speak, admitting in his own way that distraction was no longer possible for him. Rieux only followed the phases of the fight in the eyes of his friend, in turn open or closed, the eyelids tighter against the globe of the eye or, on the contrary, stretched, the gaze fixed on an object or brought back to the doctor and his mother. Each time the doctor met that look, Tarrou smiled, in great effort. At one point, we heard hurried steps on the street. They seemed to flee before a distant rumble which gradually approached and eventually filled the street with its runoff: the rain started again, soon mixed with hail banging on the sidewalks. Large draperies waved in front of the windows. In the shadow of the room, Rieux, distracted for a moment by the rain, looked again at Tarrou, lit by a bedside lamp. His mother was knitting, occasionally looking up to watch the patient closely. The doctor had now done everything there was to do. After the rain, the silence thickens in the room, full only of the silent tumult of an invisible war. Crammed by insomnia, the doctor imagined hearing, on the verge of silence, the soft and regular hiss that had accompanied him throughout the epidemic. He gestured to his mother to have her go to bed. She refused with her head, and her eyes brightened, then she carefully examined, with the end of her needles, a stitch of which she was not sure. Rieux got up to give the patient a drink and returned to sit down. Passers-by, taking advantage of the lull, walked quickly on the sidewalk. Their steps decreased and moved away. The doctor, for the first time, recognized that that night, full of late walkers and deprived of ambulance stamps, was similar to that of the past. ambulance stamps was similar to those of yesteryear. It was a night delivered from the plague. And it seemed that the disease, driven by the cold, the lights, and the crowd, had escaped from the dark depths of the city and taken refuge in this warm room to give its last assault to the inert body of Tarrou. The scourge no longer stirred the city sky. But he hissed softly in the heavy air of the room. He was the one Rieux had been hearing for hours. It was necessary to wait until there too it stopped, that there too the plague declared itself overcome. Shortly before dawn, Rieux leaned over to his mother: - You should go to bed so that you can take over at eight. Instill some before bed. Mrs. Rieux got up, put her knitting away and walked over to the bed. Tarrou, for some time now, had kept his eyes closed. Sweat curled his hair on the hard forehead. Mrs Rieux sighed and the patient opened his eyes. He saw the sweet face leaning towards him and, under the moving waves of fever, the stubborn smile reappeared again. But the eyes closed immediately. Left alone, Rieux settled into the chair that his mother had just left. The street was silent and silence now complete. The morning cold was starting to be felt in the room. The doctor dozed off, but the first car at dawn woke him from his drowsiness. He shivered and, looking at Tarrou, he understood that a break had taken place and that the patient was also sleeping. The wooden and iron wheels of the horse carriage still rolled away. The window was still dark at the window. When the doctor walked over to the bed, Tarrou was looking at him blankly, as if he was still on the sleep side. - You slept, right? asked Rieux. - Yes. - Do you breathe better? - A little. Does this mean anything? Rieux was silent and, after a while: - No, Tarrou, that doesn't mean anything. You know, like me, morning remission. Tarrou approved. - Thank you, he said. Always answer me exactly. Rieux sat at the foot of the bed. He felt the legs of the patient, long and hard like limbs lying on him. Tarrou was breathing more heavily. "The fever will start again, won't it, Rieux," he said in a breathless voice. - Yes, but at noon, we will be fixed. Tarrou closed his eyes, seeming to gather his strength. An expression of weariness could be seen on his features. He was waiting for the fever to rise, which was already moving somewhere inside him. When he opened his eyes, his gaze was tarnished. He only clears up when he sees Rieux leaning close to him. "Drink," said the latter. The other goal and dropped his head. - It's a long time, he said. Rieux took her arm, but Tarrou, looking away, no longer reacted. And suddenly, the fever visibly flowed back to her forehead as if she had punctured some inner dike. When Tarrou's gaze returned to the doctor, he was encouraged by his tense face. The smile that Tarrou still tried to form could not pass beyond the tight jaws and lips cemented by a whitish foam. But in the hardened face, eyes still shone with all the brilliance of courage. At seven o'clock, Mrs Rieux entered the room. The doctor returned to his office to telephone the hospital and arrange for his replacement. He also decided to postpone his consultations, lay down on the couch for a while, but got up almost immediately and returned to the bedroom. Tarrou's head was turned towards Mrs Rieux. He looked at the small shadow huddled close to him, on a chair, his hands clasped on his thighs. And he looked at her so intensely that Madame Rieux put a finger to her lips and got up to turn off the bedside lamp. But behind the curtains, the day was filtering quickly and, soon after, when the patient's features emerged from the darkness, Mrs Rieux could see that he was still looking at her. She leaned toward him, straightened her bolster, and, standing up, put her hand for a moment on the wet, twisted hair. Then she heard a muffled voice from afar say thank you and that now everything was fine. When she was seated again, Tarrou had closed her eyes and her exhausted face, despite the sealed mouth, seemed to smile again. At noon, the fever was at its peak. A sort of visceral cough shook the patient's body, which only began to spit blood. The nodes had stopped swelling. They were still there, hard as nuts, screwed into the hollow of the joints, and Rieux considered it impossible to open them. In the intervals of fever and cough, Tarrou from time to time still looked at his friends. But soon, his eyes opened less and less often, and the light which then came to illuminate his devastated face became paler each time. The storm which shook this body of convulsive jolts illuminated it with increasingly rare lightning and Tarrou was slowly drifting at the bottom of this storm. Rieux had only a mask now inert, where the smile had disappeared. This human form which had been so close to him, now pierced with spear blows, burned by a superhuman evil, twisted by all the hateful winds of the sky, immersed himself in his eyes in the waters of the plague and he could do nothing against this sinking. He had to stay on the shore, his hands empty and his heart twisted, unarmed and without recourse, once again, against this disaster. And in the end, it was the tears of helplessness that prevented Rieux from seeing Tarrou suddenly turn against the wall, and breathe out in a hollow complaint, as if somewhere in him, an essential cord had been broken. The night that followed was not that of the struggle, but that of silence. In this room entrenched from the world, above this now-dressed dead body, Rieux felt the surprising calm which, many nights before, on the terraces above the plague, had followed the attack on the doors. Already at that time he had thought of the silence rising from the beds where he had left men to die. It was the same break everywhere, the same solemn interval, always the same calm that followed the fights, it was the silence of defeat. But for the one who now enveloped his friend, he was so compact, he agreed so closely with the silence of the streets and of the city freed from the plague, that Rieux felt well that this was the final defeat, the one who ends wars and makes peace itself a suffering without healing. The doctor did not know if, in the end, Tarrou had found peace, but, at least at that moment, he thought he knew that there would never be more peace possible for himself, any more than he There is no armistice for the amputated mother of her son or for the man who buries his friend. Outside it was the same cold night, frozen stars in a clear, icy sky. In the semi-dark room, you could feel the cold weighing on the windows, the deep, pale breath of a polar night. Beside the bed, Madame Rieux was sitting, in her familiar attitude the right side lit by the bedside lamp. In the center of the room, far from the light, Rieux was waiting in his chair. The thought of his wife came to him, but he rejected her every time. By the start of the night, the heels of passersby had sounded clear in the cold night. - Did you take care of everything? said Madame Rieux. - Yes, I called. They then resumed their silent vigil. Madame Rieux looked at her son from time to time.

When he caught one of these looks, he smiled at her. The familiar sounds of the night had followed one another in the street. Although authorization had not yet been granted, many cars were running again. They quickly sucked on the pavement, disappeared, and then reappeared. Voices, calls, silence returned, the step of a horse, two tramps squeaking in a curve, vague rumors, and again the breath of the night. - Bernard? - Yes. - You're not tired? - No. He knew what his mother was thinking and what she loved, right now. But he also knew that it is not a big thing to love a being or at least that a love is never strong enough to find its own expression. So, he and his mother would always love each other in silence. And she too would die - or him - without their being able to go any further in admitting their tenderness. In the same way, he had lived next to Tarrou and he had died this evening, without their friendship having had time to be really lived. Tarrou had lost the game, as he said. But he, Rieux, what had he gained? He had only gained from knowing and remembering the plague, having known friendship, and remembering, knowing tenderness, and having to remember it one day. All that man could gain from the plague and life was knowledge and memory. Maybe that was what Tarrou called winning the game! Once again, a car went by and Mrs Rieux stirred a little in her chair. Rieux smiled at him. She said that she was not tired and immediately afterwards: - You will have to go and rest in the mountains, over there. - Of course, mom. Yes, he would rest there. Why not? It would also be a pretext for memory. But if that was it, winning the game, that it must be hard to live only with what you know and remember, and deprived of what you hope for. This was probably how Tarrou lived and he was aware of the sterile nature of a life without illusions. There is no peace without hope, and Tarrou who refused men the right to condemn anyone, who knew that no one can help but condemn and that even the victims happened to be sometimes executioners, Tarrou had lived in heartbreak and contradiction, he had never known hope. Was that why he wanted holiness and sought peace in the service of men? Truth be told, Rieux didn't know and it didn't matter. The only images of Tarrou that he would keep would be those of a man who was driving his car with both hands to drive it, or of that thick body, now stretched out without movement. A warmth of life and an image of death, that was knowledge. This is why, no doubt, Doctor Rieux, in the morning, calmly received the news of the death of his wife. He was in his office. Her mother had come almost running to bring her a telegram, then she had gone out to tip the porter. When she returned, her son was holding the open telegram in her hand. She looked at him, but he stubbornly gazed out the window at a magnificent morning that was rising over the harbor. - Bernard, said Mrs. Rieux. The doctor looked at him distractedly. - The telegram? she asked. - That's it, recognized the doctor. Eight days ago. Madame Rieux turned her head towards the window. The doctor was silent. Then he told his mother not to cry, that he expected it, but that it was still difficult. Simply, he knew, saying this, that his suffering was not surprising. For months and two days, it was the same pain that continued. The gates of the city finally opened, at the dawn of a beautiful February morning, greeted by the people, the newspapers, the radio, and the prefecture's press releases. It remains for the narrator to make himself the chronicler of the hours of joy that followed this opening of the doors, although he himself was one of those who did not have the freedom to mingle entirely. Great celebrations were organized for the day and for the night. At the same time, the trains started to smoke in the station while, coming from distant seas, ships were already heading for our port, marking in their own way that this day was, for all those who groaned to be separated, that of the big meeting. We can easily imagine here what could become of the feeling of separation that had inhabited so many of our fellow citizens. The trains which, during the day, entered our city were no less loaded than those who left it. Everyone had reserved their place for that day, during the two weeks of reprieve, worried that at the last moment the prefectural decision was canceled. Some of the travelers who approached the city were not completely rid of their apprehension, because if they generally knew the fate of those who touched them closely, they were ignorant of all others and the city it - even, to which they lent a formidable face. But this was only true for those whose passion had not burned during all this time. The enthusiasts, in fact, were delivered to their fixed idea. Only one thing had changed for them: this time that, during the months of their exile, they would have liked to push so that it was in a hurry, that they persisted in precipitating again, when they were already in sight of on the contrary, they wanted to slow it down and keep it suspended, as soon as the train started to brake before stopping. The feeling, both vague and acute in them, of all these months of life lost for their love, made them confusedly demand a sort of compensation by which the time of joy would have run half as fast as that of waiting. And those who waited for them in a room or on the quay, like Rambert, whose wife, who had been warned for weeks, had done what it took to arrive, were in the same impatience and dismay. Because this love or this tenderness that the months of plague had reduced to abstraction, Rambert waited, in a tremor, to confront them with the being of flesh which had been the support. He would have liked to become again the one who, at the start of the epidemic, wanted to run with a single dash out of the city and set off to meet the one he loved. But he knew it was no longer possible. He had changed, the plague had put in him a distraction which, with all his might, he was trying to deny, and which, however, continued in him like a dull anguish. In a sense, he felt that the plague had ended too suddenly, he didn't have his presence of mind. Happiness came at full speed; the event went faster than the wait. Rambert understood that everything would be returned to him at once and that joy is a burn that cannot be savored. All, moreover, more, or less consciously, were like him and it is of all that it is necessary to speak. On this station platform where they started their personal life again, they still felt their community by exchanging glances and smiles between them. But their feeling of exile, as soon as they saw the smoke of the train, suddenly died out in the downpour of confused and dizzying joy. When the train stopped, endless separations, which had often started on the same station platform, ended there, in a second, when arms closed with exultant greed on bodies whose shape, they had forgotten alive. Rambert did not have time to look at this form running towards him, that already, it fell on his chest. And holding her with full arms, clutching a head against him of which he only saw the familiar hair, he let his tears flow without knowing whether they came from his present happiness or from a pain that had been suppressed for too long, assured at least that they would prevent him from verifying whether this face buried in the hollow of his shoulder was the one he had dreamed of so much or, on the contrary, that of a stranger. He would know later if his suspicion was true. For the moment, he wanted to do like all those who seemed to believe, around him, that the plague can come and go without the hearts of men being changed. Pressed against each other, all then returned home, blind to the rest of the world, apparently triumphing over the plague, oblivious of all misery and of those who, also coming by the same train, had found no one and were disposing of to receive confirmation from them of the fears that a long silence had already aroused in their hearts. For the latter, who now had only their fresh pain for company, for others who vowed, at that moment, to the memory of a disappeared being, it was quite different, and the feeling of separation had reached its summit. For those, mothers, husbands, lovers who had lost all joy with being now lost in an anonymous pit or melted in a heap of ash, it was still the plague. But who thought of these solitudes? At noon the sun, triumphing over the cold breaths that had been wrestling in the air since morning, poured over the city the endless waves of still light. The day was stopped. The cannons of the forts, at the top of the hills, thundered continuously in the fixed sky. The whole city threw itself outside to celebrate this oppressed minute when the time of suffering was ending, and the time of oblivion had not yet begun. We danced in all the places. Overnight, traffic had increased considerably and cars, which had become more numerous, had difficulty circulating in the crowded streets. The city bells rang on the fly throughout the afternoon. They filled with their vibrations a blue and golden sky. In churches, in fact, thanksgiving was recited. But, at the same time, the places of celebration were bursting at the seams and the cafes, without worrying about the future, were distributing their last spirits. In front of their counters, crowded a crowd of similarly excited people, and among them, many entwined couples who were not afraid to perform. Everyone was screaming or laughing. The provision of life they had made during those months when everyone had put their soul on hold, they spent it on that day which was like the day of their survival. The next day would start life itself, with its precautions. For the moment, people of very different origins were elbowing and fraternizing. The equality that the presence of death had not in fact achieved, the joy of deliverance established, at least for a few hours. But this banal exuberance did not say everything and those who filled the streets at the end of the afternoon, alongside Rambert, often disguised, under a placid attitude, more delicate pleasures. Many couples and families, in fact, had no appearance other than that of peaceful strollers. Most made delicate pilgrimages to the places where they had suffered. The idea was to show newcomers the glaring or hidden signs of the plague, the vestiges of its history. In some cases, we were content to play the guide, the one who saw a lot, the contemporary of the plague, and we talked about the danger without mentioning fear. These pleasures were harmless. But in other cases, they were more thrilling routes where a lover, abandoned to the sweet anguish of memory, could say to his partner: "In this place, at that time, I desired you and you was not there. These passionate tourists could then recognize themselves: they formed islands of whispers and secrets during the tumult where they were walking. Better than the orchestras at the crossroads, they were the ones who announced real deliverance. Because these delighted couples, closely adjusted and stingy with words, affirmed during the tumult, with all the triumph and injustice of happiness, that the plague was over, and that the terror had had its day. They quietly denied, against all evidence, that we had ever known this insane world where the murder of a man was as daily as that of flies, this well-defined savagery, this calculated delirium, this imprisonment which brought with it an awful freedom to with regard to everything that was not present, this smell of death which amazed all those it did not kill, they finally deny that we were this stunned people of which every day a part, crammed in the mouth from one oven, evaporated into fatty smoke, while the other, laden with chains of helplessness and fear, waited for its turn. It was there, in any case, what burst in the eyes of Doctor Rieux who, seeking to reach the suburbs, walked alone, at the end of the afternoon, in the midst of the bells, cannon, music and deafening cries. His job continued, there is no leave for the sick. In the beautiful fine light that descended on the city, arose the old smells of grilled meat and aniseed alcohol. Around him hilarious faces spilled against the sky. Men and women clung to each other, their faces inflamed, with all the nervousness and the cry of desire. Yes, the plague was over, with terror, and those arms that knotted together said that it had been exile and separation, in the deepest sense of the word. For the first time, Rieux could give a name to this family resemblance which he had read for months on all the faces of passers-by. Now he just had to look around. Arrived at the end of the plague, with misery and privations, all these men had ended up taking the costume of the role which they already played for a long time, that of emigrants whose face first, the clothes now, said absence and distant homeland. From the moment the plague had closed the doors of the city, they had lived only in separation, they had been cut off from this human warmth that makes us forget everything. To varying degrees, in every corner of the city, these men and women had longed for a meeting that was not, for all, of the same nature, but which, for all, was equally impossible. Most of them had screamed with all their strength towards an absent person, the warmth of a body, tenderness, or habit. Some, often without knowing it, suffered from being placed outside the friendship of men, from being no longer able to reach them by the ordinary means of friendship which are letters, trains, and boats. Others, rarer, like Tarrou maybe, had desired the meeting with something they could not define, but which seemed to them the only desirable good. And for lack of another name, they sometimes called it peace. Rieux was still walking. As he advanced, the crowd grew around him, the din grew, and it seemed to him that the suburbs he wanted to reach were receding as much. Little by little, he melted into this great howling body of which he understood better and better the cry which, at least for part, was his cry. Yes, all had suffered together, as much in their flesh as in their soul, from a difficult vacancy, an exile without remedy and a thirst never satisfied. Among these heaps of deaths, the ambulance stamps, the warnings of what is known as fate, the obstinate trampling of fear and the terrible revolt of their hearts, a great rumor had not stopped running and to alert these frightened beings, telling them that they had to find their true homeland. For all of them, the true homeland lay beyond the walls of this stifled city. She was in those fragrant brushwood's on the hills, in the sea, in free countries and the weight of love. And it was towards her, it was towards happiness, that they wanted to return, turning away from the rest in disgust. As for the meaning that this exile and this desire for reunion could have, Rieux knew nothing about it. Always walking, pressed on all sides, challenged, he gradually arrived in less congested streets and thought that it is not important that these things make sense or not, but that we must see only what is answered to the hope of men. He now knew what was said and he saw it better in the first streets of the almost deserted suburbs. Those who, holding on to what little they were, only wanted to return to the house of their love, were sometimes rewarded. Certainly, some of them continued to walk in the city, lonely, deprived of the being they expected. Happy still those who had not been twice separated as some who, before the epidemic, could not build, at the first try, their love, and who had blindly pursued, for years, the difficult agreement which ends up seal enemy lovers to each other. These people had, like Rieux himself, the lightness of counting on time: they were separated for ever. But others, like Rambert, whom the doctor had left the same morning saying to him: "hang on, now is the time to be right," had unhesitatingly found the missing man who they thought was lost. For some time at least, they would be happy. They now knew that if there is one thing that one can always desire and sometimes get; it is human tenderness. For all those, on the contrary, who had addressed themselves above the man to something which they did not even imagine, there had been no answer. Tarrou had seemed to join this difficult peace of which he had spoken, but he had found it only in death, at a time when but he had only found it in death, at a time when it could not him serve nothing. If others, on the contrary, whom Rieux saw on the thresholds of the houses, in the waning light, entwined with all their strength and looking at each other with excitement, had obtained what they wanted, it is that they had asked for the only thing that depended on them. And Rieux, at the time of turning in the rue de Grand and de Cottard, thought that it was just that, from time to time at least, joy came to reward those who are enough of man and his poor and terrible love. This chronicle is coming to an end. It is time for Doctor Bernard Rieux to admit that he is the author. But before retracing the latest events, he would at least justify his intervention and make it clear that he wanted to take the tone of the objective witness. Throughout the duration of the plague, his trade enabled him to see most of his fellow citizens, and to collect their feelings. He was therefore in a good position to report what he had seen and heard. But he wanted to do it with desirable restraint. In general, he applied himself not to report more things than he could see, not to lend to his plague companions thoughts that in short they were not forced to train, and to use only the texts that chance or misfortune had put in his hands. Being called to testify, in connection with some sort of crime, he kept a certain reserve, as befits a goodwill witness. But at the same time, according to the law of an honest heart, he deliberately took the side of the victim and wanted to join men, his fellow citizens, in the only certainties that they have in common, and who are love , suffering and exile. This is how he is not one of the anxieties of his fellow citizens that he did not share, no situation that was also his own. To be a faithful witness, he had to report mainly acts, documents and rumors. But what, personally, he had to say, his expectations, his trials, he had to keep them quiet. If he used it, it was only to understand or make his fellow citizens understand and to give a form, as precise as possible, to what, most of the time, they felt confusedly. To tell the truth, this effort of reason hardly cost him. When he found himself tempted to mix his confidence directly with the thousand voices of the plague victims, he was stopped by the thought that there was not one of his sufferings which was not at the same time that of others and only in a world where pain is so often lonely, that was an advantage. Really, he had to speak for everyone. But he is at least one of our fellow citizens for whom Doctor Rieux could not speak. It is, in fact, the one about which Tarrou once said to Rieux: "His only true crime is to have approved in his heart what killed children and men. The rest, I understand, but this, I must forgive him. It is only fair that this column ends with him who had an ignorant, lonely, heart. When he got out of the noisy main streets of the party and when he turned into rue de Grand and de Cottard, Doctor Rieux was indeed arrested by a barrage of agents. He didn't expect it. The distant rumors of the party made the neighborhood seem silent and he imagined it as deserted as dumb. He pulled out his card. - Impossible, doctor, said the agent. There is a madman who shoots the crowd. But stay there, you can be useful. At that moment, Rieux saw Grand coming towards him. Grand didn't know anything either. He was stopped from passing and he learned that gunfire was coming from his house. From afar, you could see the facade, gilded by the last light of a sun without heat. Around it stood a large empty space that ran to the sidewalk opposite. In the middle of the road, we could clearly see a hat and a piece of dirty cloth. Rieux and Grand could see far away, on the other side of the street, a cordon of agents, parallel to that which prevented them from advancing, and behind which a few locals passed and passed quickly. Looking closely, they also saw agents, the revolver in their fist, carpet in the doors of the buildings that faced the house. All the shutters of it were closed. On the second, however, one of the shutters seemed to be half hung. There was complete silence in the street. You could only hear scraps of music coming from the center of town. At one point, from one of the buildings in front of the house, two revolver shots fired, and shards jumped from the dismantled shutter. Then there was silence again. From afar, and after the tumult of the day, it seemed a little unreal to Rieux. - This is Cottard's window, suddenly said Grand, very agitated. However, Cottard has disappeared. - Why are we shooting? Rieux asked the agent. - We're having fun. We are waiting for a bus with the necessary equipment because it shoots those who try to enter through the door of the building. There was a law enforcement officer. - Why did he shoot? - We do not know. People were having fun on the street. At the first shot, they didn't understand. On the second, there was a scream, one was injured, and everyone fled. What a madman! In the returned silence, the minutes seemed to drag on. Suddenly, on the other side of the street, they saw a dog come out, the first that Rieux had seen in a long time, a dirty spaniel that his masters had had to hide until then and trotting along the walls. When he got to the door, he hesitated, sat on his hindquarters, and rolled over to devour his fleas. Several whistles from the officers called him. He raised his head, then decided to cross the road slowly to sniff the hat. At the same time, a revolver shot came from the second and the dog turned like a pancake, waving its legs violently to finally overturn on its side, shaken by long jolts. In response, five or six detonations, coming from the doors opposite, crumbled the shutter again. Silence fell again. The sun had turned a bit and the shadow was beginning to approach Cottard's window. Brakes moaned softly in the street behind the doctor. - There they are, said the agent. - There they are, said the agent. Police came out behind them, carrying ropes, a ladder and two oblong packages wrapped in oiled canvas. They entered a street that went around the block, opposite Grand's building. A moment later, we guessed rather that we saw a certain agitation in the doors of these houses. Then we waited. The dog was no longer moving, but he was now bathing in a dark puddle. Suddenly, from the windows of the houses occupied by the agents, a machine-gun fire started. Throughout the shot, the shutter we were still aiming for literally leafed and left a black surface uncovered where Rieux and Grand, from their place, could not distinguish anything. When the shooting stopped, a second submachine gun crackled from another angle, a house further. The bullets probably entered the window square, as one of them blew up a piece of brick. At the same second, three officers ran across the road and rushed into the front door. Almost immediately, three others rushed in and the machine gun fire stopped. We still waited. Two distant detonations sounded in the building. Then a rumor spread, and we saw coming out of the house, carried rather than dragged, a little man in a shirt arm who was screaming non-stop. As if by a miracle, all the closed shutters of the street opened and the windows were filled with curious people, while a crowd of people came out of the houses and crowded behind the roadblocks. For a moment, we saw the little man in the middle of the road, his feet finally on the ground, his arms held back by the agents. He was shouting. An officer approached him and punched him twice, deliberately, deliberately, with some sort of application. - It's Cottard, Grand stammered. He became crazy. Cottard had fallen. We still saw the officer throwing his foot in the heap that lay on the ground. Then a confused group waved and walked over to the doctor and his old friend. - Move on! said the agent. Rieux looked away when the group walked past him. Grand and the doctor left in the late twilight. As if the event had shaken the torpor in which the neighborhood fell asleep, the side streets were again filled with the buzz of a cheering crowd. At the foot of the house, Grand said goodbye to the doctor. He was going to work. But when he got up, he told her that he had written to Jeanne and that now he was happy. And then he had started his sentence again: "I have deleted all the adjectives," he said. And with a clever smile, he took off his hat in a formal salute. But Rieux thought of Cottard and the thump of fists that crushed his face chased him as he headed for the old asthmatic's house. Perhaps it was harder to think of a guilty man than a dead man. When Rieux arrived at his old patient's house, the night had already devoured the whole sky. From the bedroom you could hear the distant rumor of freedom, and the old man continued, in an even mood, to pour out his peas. - They are right to have fun, he said, it takes everything to make a world. And your colleague, doctor, what has become of him? Detonations came to them, but they were peaceful: children sent out their firecrackers. "He is dead," said the doctor, examining the humming chest. - Ah! said the old man, a little disconcerted. "Plague," added Rieux. - Yes, admitted the old man after a while, the best are leaving. It's life. But he was a man who knew what he wanted. - Why do you say that? said the doctor who was putting away his stethoscope. - For nothing. He did not speak to say nothing. Finally, I liked him. But it's like that. The others say, "It's the plague, we had the plague. For a little bit, they would ask to be decorated. But what does that mean, the plague? This is life, and that's it. - Do your fumigations regularly. - Oh! fear nothing. I still have a long time and I will see them all die. I can live. Screams of joy answered him in the distance. The doctor stopped in the middle of the room. - Would you mind if I went on the terrace? - Oh no! You want to see them from up there, huh? To your pleasure. But they are always the same. Rieux went to the stairs. - Say, doctor, is it true that they're going to build a monument to the plague dead? - The newspaper says so. A stele or a plaque. - I was sure of it. And there will be speeches. The old man laughed with a strangled laugh. - I hear them from here: "Our dead ...", and they'll have a bite to eat. Rieux was already climbing the stairs. The great cold sky sparkled above the houses and, near the hills, the stars hardened like flint. That night was not that different from the one he and Tarrou had come to this terrace to forget about the plague. The sea was noisier than then, at the foot of the cliffs. The air was still and light, relieved of the salty breaths brought by the warm autumn wind. The rumor of the city, however, still beat the foot of the terraces with the sound of waves. But that night was that of deliverance, not of revolt. In the distance, a black glow indicated the location of the boulevards and the illuminated squares. In the now liberated night, desire became unhindered and it was his roar that reached Rieux. From the dark harbor the first rockets for official celebrations rose. The city greeted them with a long and muffled exclamation. Cottard, Tarrou, those whom Rieux had loved and lost, all, dead or guilty, were forgotten. The old man was right, the men were always the same. But it was their strength and innocence and it was here, above all pain, that Rieux felt he was joining them. In the midst of the cries which redoubled in strength and duration, which echoed for a long time until the foot of the terrace, as the multicolored sheaves rose more numerous in the sky, Doctor Rieux decided then to write the story that s end here, so as not to be silent, to testify in favor of these plague victims, to at least leave a memory of the injustice and violence which had been done to them, and to simply say what we learns in the midst of the plagues that there are more things to admire in men than things to despise. But he knew, however, that this chronicle could not be that of final victory. It could only be the testimony of what had to be accomplished and which, doubtless, should still accomplish, against terror and its tireless weapon, despite their personal heartbreak, all the men who, being unable to be saints and refusing to admit the plagues, strive however to be doctors. Listening, in fact, to the cries of joy rising from the city, Rieux remembered that this joy was always threatened. Because he knew what this joyful crowd ignored, and which one can read in the books, that the plague bacillus never dies or never disappears, that it can remain for decades asleep in the furniture and the linen, which he patiently awaits in bedrooms, cellars, trunks, handkerchiefs and paperwork, and that perhaps the day would come when, for the misfortune and the teaching of men, the plague would awaken his rats and would send them to die in a happy city.

-About this electronic edition Free text. Corrections, editing, computer conversion and publication by Ibrahima Diaby

Made in United States
North Haven, CT
20 January 2023

31344744R00054